"You're very courageous," Tyler told her.

"Or very stupid. My principles have often gotten me into trouble." Hannah smiled wryly.

"So Daycon's men left you for dead on the roadside? Why didn't they finish you off?"

"I figure they were supposed to bring me back. Without me, Daycon can't reproduce the formula," Hannah replied.

"Is Lionel Daycon capable of murder?" Tyler demanded.

"I think he's capable of hiring it to be done." Hannah shivered. "There's a lot of money at stake and he's a very greedy man. Do you see why time is running out? I'm sick, and getting sicker. And right now, I'm all alone."

"That's not true, Hannah."

Their gazes locked. She saw something in Tyler's eyes that gave her hope.

"You've got me."

Dear Reader,

We keep raising the bar here at Silhouette Intimate Moments, and our authors keep responding by writing books that excite, amaze and compel. If you don't believe me, just take a look RaeAnne Thayne's *Nothing To Lose,* the second of THE SEARCHERS, her ongoing miniseries about looking for family—and finding love.

Valerie Parv forces a new set of characters to live up to the CODE OF THE OUTBACK in her latest, which matches a sexy crocodile hunter with a journalist in danger and hopes they'll *Live To Tell*. Kylie Brant's contribution to FAMILY SECRETS: THE NEXT GENERATION puts her couple *In Sight of the Enemy*, a position that's made even scarier because her heroine is pregnant—with the hero's child! Suzanne McMinn's amnesiac hero had *Her Man To Remember*, and boy, does *he* remember *her*—because she's the wife he'd thought was dead! Lori Wilde's heroine is *Racing Against the Clock* when she shows up in Dr. Tyler Fresno's E.R., and now his heart is racing, too. Finally, cross your fingers that there will be a *Safe Passage* for the hero and heroine of Loreth Anne White's latest, in which an agent's "baby-sitting" assignment turns out to be unexpectedly dangerous—and passionate.

Enjoy them all, then come back next month for more of the most excitingly romantic reading around—only in Silhouette Intimate Moments.

Yours,

Leslie J. Wainger
Executive Editor

Please address questions and book requests to:
Silhouette Reader Service
U.S.: 3010 Walden Ave., P.O. Box 1325, Buffalo, NY 14269
Canadian: P.O. Box 609, Fort Erie, Ont. L2A 5X3

Racing Against the Clock

LORI WILDE

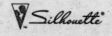

INTIMATE MOMENTS™

Published by Silhouette Books

America's Publisher of Contemporary Romance

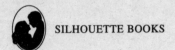 **SILHOUETTE BOOKS**

ISBN 0-373-27395-9

RACING AGAINST THE CLOCK

Copyright © 2004 by Laurie Blalock Vanzura

This edition published by arrangement with Harlequin Books S.A.

Visit Silhouette Books at www.eHarlequin.com

Printed in U.S.A.

LORI WILDE

realized from a very young age that she wanted to be a writer. Knowing it took many years of hard work to achieve that goal, she attended nursing school to have what her family called "a career to fall back on." As a registered nurse, she worked in a variety of clinical settings from house supervisor to dialysis to anesthesia recovery. Her years in nursing taught her the healing power of love, a subject she loves to visit in her stories. Lori retired from nursing in 1997 in order to write full-time. Although she loved helping people as a nurse, she feels she is truly blessed to be able to touch hearts through her love stories.

To Antonio—who never races against the clock.

Chapter 1

When Dr. Tyler Fresno stared down at the woman on the stretcher, he had the weirdest sensation that he had met his destiny and there was absolutely nothing he could do to alter his fate.

If someone had pressed him to elaborate on his feelings he would not have been able to put it into words, but there was no denying the rush of anxiety that clutched his stomach and held fast when he gazed upon her.

"Details," Tyler demanded of the eager young emergency room intern following at his heels.

"Jane Doe. MVA. Rollover. Found unconscious at the scene. BP seventy-two over forty-eight," the earnest physician-in-training reeled off. "X ray reveals hairline fracture of the right femur. Minor facial lacerations. Possible ruptured spleen. Neuro signs intact."

The woman's eyes were shuttered closed, her dark blond hair fanned across the pillowcase. Tyler placed her age somewhere between late twenties and early thirties. There was a superficial cut over one eyebrow and another along her jaw. Those wounds wouldn't even require stitches.

She was a beautiful woman with a proud aquiline nose that at the moment played host to green plastic oxygen tubing. Her lips were salmon-colored, her cheeks pale. Her face was slender, her complexion as flawless as a cosmetics model's.

Tyler snapped on a pair of rubber latex gloves, slipped a yellow barrier gown over his starched white lab jacket and tied a surgical mask over his clean-shaven face. He had just stepped from the shower after a twelve-hour workday when he had gotten the phone call. He'd been preparing for dinner out with friends, but as usual, the hospital had changed his plans at the last minute. Tyler couldn't say he minded too much. He was happiest when working and this case promised to be more intriguing than most.

And there was nothing he liked more than a complicated medical puzzle to solve.

"Go on," he prompted the intern, his eyes focused intently on the inert woman lying so still beneath the crisp green sheet.

A strange sensation slithered over him. Something he couldn't name. Not trepidation, but something similar. Apprehension?

But why should he feel apprehensive?

"She has what appears to be mild chemical burns scattered over her arms and legs."

"Chemical burns?" Tyler repeated, frowning.

The intern shrugged. "The paramedics found shattered glass vials throughout her car and an empty lockbox with a biohazard sticker on it. Apparently, she was transporting some volatile drug or chemical, and during the course of the accident the lockbox clasp was damaged and the vials tumbled out."

"Do we know what we're dealing with here?"

The intern shook his head. "The vials weren't labeled but the paramedics were able to retrieve a small sample."

"You're saying the paramedics were exposed?"

"Potentially."

Tyler swung his gaze to the younger man. "We could have toxic contamination."

The intern nodded.

"Dammit, where's the Hazardous Materials team?"

"On route."

"I want this side of the E.R. evacuated and this room sealed off. Immediately."

"Yes, sir."

"And anyone else who came in contact with this patient needs to be examined. Have those paramedics admitted for observation."

"Will do."

He could tell the intern thought he was going overboard, but the young pup was wet behind the ears. The man had no idea what lingering effects chemical substances could have on the human body, nor did he have a clue how serious this could be for the young woman. He hadn't seen the dark things Tyler had seen. Hadn't experienced the devastation of chemical warfare firsthand.

"Hop to it," Tyler commanded.

The intern spun on his heels and hurried out the door, pulling it tightly closed behind him.

"Well now, Jane," Tyler crooned, stepping up to the gurney. "Just what have you gotten yourself into?"

Jane Doe did not respond.

He studied the heart monitor attached by electrical wires leading to conductive gel pads on her chest. Normal sinus rhythm. A good sign. Apparently the mystery chemical hadn't affected her cardiac functioning.

Hang in there, Jane. He mentally willed her; determination a solid fist in his gut. *I'll take care of you.*

The emotional intensity of his thoughts startled him. He wanted to help all of his patients, but there was something special about this woman and he did not know what it was or why. He just knew that he felt committed to her case in a way he hadn't experienced in a very long time.

Peeling back the covers, he allowed his gaze to rove over her while his fingers investigated. A smattering of first-degree contact burns carpeted her arms and legs. Tyler sucked in his breath and shook his head.

Her chest rose and fell in a shallow rhythm. Her body was lithe, supple. Her firm musculature told him that she worked out often and her lack of a tan meant she was either conscientious about the use of sunscreen or spent most of her time indoors. Her breasts were high and firm. Her abdomen was flat.

Tyler registered these things and tried hard not to be moved by them. He was a professional. A doctor. He'd seen thousands of unclothed women and had never been aroused. He was a surgeon, and because of his stint in the first Gulf War, also something of an expert on chemical exposure. Apparently, that was why the intern had called him in to consult on the case.

Curiously enough, considering she'd been exposed to a potentially harmful chemical, her respirations were deep and unlabored. Color good. Her blood pressure was low but he could put that down to the internal bleeding from her spleen, not from the chemical.

Tyler made a mental note to get her lab analysis as soon as possible. Until he knew what he was up against he was not taking any unnecessary chances. She needed surgery but anesthesia at this juncture might be risky. He would not operate until he knew what he was dealing with or until her physical circumstances deteriorated, forcing his hand.

She moaned when he pressed the right-upper quadrant of her abdomen where her spleen was located. He glanced up and saw her eyelids flutter open.

Their gazes met.

The woman looked like a delicate doe startled in the woods by the sound of a hunter's gun.

Something stirred inside him. Her vulnerability reached out to him, strumming a chord that was far too familiar. In a flash, he saw a loneliness inside her that matched his own, a sense of desolation that ran as deep as the pain he had harbored for so long.

The connection was instantaneous and frightening in its power.

For God's sakes, Fresno, stop it.

She was his patient, he was her doctor and even if she weren't his patient, she deserved much more than a damaged man who'd lost his ability to love.

"Miss?" he said, purposefully denying the heavy *thump, thump, thump* of his heart. "Can you hear me?"

"Marcus," she mumbled.

"I'm Dr. Tyler Fresno, and you're in the emergency room at Saint Madeline's Hospital in Houston, Texas. You were involved in a motor vehicle accident." Tyler leaned closer and touched her shoulder. "Can you tell me your name?"

She shifted away.

"Are you in pain?"

She didn't answer or meet his gaze again.

Tyler pressed the button on the electronic blood pressure cuff—88/62. Her BP was up. Excellent news. Perhaps her spleen wasn't bleeding as profusely as he had feared.

"Can you tell me your name?" he repeated.

"Marcus."

"Your name is Marcus?"

"Marcus." Her lips puckered in a whisper. She stirred. "Where are you?"

Was Marcus her husband? Tyler glanced at her ring finger and saw that it was bare. A woman as beautiful as this one was no doubt married or engaged or at least had a significant other. Somewhere, somebody, probably this Marcus fellow, was worried about her.

A twist of pain stabbed through him as he imagined how frantic her husband must be. If she were his wife…

No. She wasn't his wife. She was a patient. She meant nothing to him beyond the healing of her injuries. That detached attitude had kept him sane and functioning for the last six years. It was the only attitude he could entertain.

"Miss," he said, "we need to take you to surgery. You've suffered internal injuries and your right leg has a hairline fracture."

Her eyes were closed again. She did not move.

Tyler shook her. "Is there someone we can call? A family member? Your boss?"

Her eyes flew open and he noticed they were as blue as the ocean outside his beach house on Galveston Island. "No," she snapped. "There's no one."

At least he had gotten a response. "What's your name?" he repeated.

Fear flitted across her face. She paused a moment before saying hesitantly, "I don't know."

He had the oddest notion that she was lying, but it wasn't that unusual for patients to suffer temporary amnesia following a major trauma such as a car accident. So maybe he was imagining things.

"Can you tell me what chemicals you were transporting? It's important."

"Chemicals?" Her voice went up an octave and she dropped her gaze. "I don't know what you're talking about. There were no chemicals in my car."

"The paramedics found broken glass vials and a damaged empty lockbox in your vehicle."

"I don't know what you're talking about," Jane Doe repeated, but she still refused to meet his gaze.

"It's important. Your life might depend upon this."

"I'm sorry," she insisted. "I don't remember anything about any chemical."

"Where were you going?"

She shook her head. "I can't recall. Are the paramedics okay? Did they come into contact with these chemicals?"

Something flickered in her eyes. Remorse? He knew now that she was lying but he had no idea why.

"Possibly." Two could play this withholding information game. A little guilt might loosen her tongue. "I've got to check your lab values, then I'll be right back with some papers for you to sign. Permission to do surgery. Since you don't know what your name is, you can sign with an *X*."

"All right," Jane Doe murmured, and he had the suspicion she was simply placating him.

He left the examining room and stepped into the empty work lane. He pulled the door closed behind him, sealing the woman inside. His mind whirled. What had just passed between the two of them? Why was his pulse thready, his breathing rapid?

The intern, obeying his command, had shut down one whole side of the E.R. The HAZMAT decontamination team had arrived garbed in gas masks and rubber suits. The three men carried instruments that looked something like Geiger counters. A band of curious nurses watched the proceedings from behind a glass partition. A representative from administration waited with them, safely out of harm's way, no doubt fretting over the cost involved.

"Doctor." One of the members of the decontamination unit moved to block his exit.

Tyler knew what to do without being told. He stopped, raised his arms level with his shoulders and allowed them to run their instruments over his body, searching for foreign material.

"You're clean," the man said at last. "But I recommend you decontaminate, just in case."

"Do you have any idea what the chemical is?" Tyler asked.

"No, sir." The man shook his head. "We just came from the accident site and we've impounded the car."

"Good."

Whatever the chemical was, it must have a short half-life if the HAZMAT crew had been unable to find anything. He would check with the lab, then visit the paramedics. Tyler stripped off the barrier gown, the rubber gloves and paper mask and tossed the items in a special biomedical-hazards bin located near the exit. After scouring his skin in the decontamination shower, he dressed in fresh hospital scrubs and combed his damp hair.

As he left the E.R. and headed for the lab, he was stopped in the corridor by a uniformed police officer.

"Dr. Fresno?"

"Yes?"

"I'm Officer Blankenship and I understand you examined the Jane Doe who was brought in this evening from the MVA on Interstate 45."

"That's correct."

"When can we interview her?"

Tyler shook his head. "I'm afraid she won't be much help. She's suffering from amnesia and I'll probably be taking her to surgery soon."

"We understand from several eyewitnesses that she was forced off the road by a white sedan. We need to confirm that."

"Come back in the morning, officer. You'll be able to talk to her then."

"Will do." The policeman thanked him and left.

Tyler continued on his way, his mind on his patient. Someone had intentionally run her off the road? If so, why? Did it have anything to do with those chemicals she was transporting? Or was it a random case of road rage? He worried his brow with his fingers and pushed through the door into the lab. There he found a wizened technician peering through a microscope.

"Any luck identifying the chemical that Jane Doe was transporting?" he asked the ruddy complexioned, sixty-year-old Irishman perched on the stool.

Danny O'Brien, of the twinkling blue eyes, infectious grin and short stature, abandoned the microscope. He greeted Tyler with a hearty slap on the shoulder. "I shoulda known you would be the one behind this mess. You've played havoc with my dinner hour."

"Hey, I didn't start it." Tyler grinned. "E.R. called me as a consult."

Danny sobered. "I think you better take a look at her blood work." He handed Tyler a computer printout with Jane Doe's name at the top and list of lab values beneath.

"Her white blood cell and reticulocyte counts are dangerously low." Tyler's heart plummeted.

Cancer.

The word ripped through his mind and he immediately thought of Yvette. Did Jane Doe have cancer? Had the woman taken matters into her own hands and concocted her own bizarre chemotherapy? She wouldn't have been the first to try such a daring and desperate experiment. It would explain her reluctance to admit to having the chemicals in her possession.

"Such a shame," he whispered and stroked a finger over the piece of paper as if stroking her in a gesture of comfort.

How tragic that a woman so young and beautiful could be in such dire trouble. He didn't want to feel the surge of sadness that rose inside him, but he did. He clenched his jaw, chasing away the softness in his heart. He plucked a prescription pad from the pocket of his lab jacket and scribbled something on it.

"Run these additional tests. And page me the minute you have a fix on that chemical."

"We don't have enough blood left to run all this," Danny said. "Could you get me another sample? The HAZMAT team is only letting essential personnel into her room."

"Will do." Tyler nodded. He felt sorry for her. She was in pain. All alone. Not even remembering her own name.

"She got to you, didn't she?"

"What?" Tyler stopped at the door and turned to stare at Danny.

"Jane Doe." Danny tapped the left side of his chest.

"No." Tyler denied Danny's perceptive observations.

How had he slipped? Usually, he maintained an impassive countenance. The stone wall he had erected over the years served him quite well. He lived his life on the surface, never delving too deeply into anything or anyone. Hadn't he prided himself on masking his feelings, on how well he kept out of his patients' personal lives? No cozy bedside manner for Tyler Fresno. He was all business. His colleagues admired his objectivity, his self-reliance. What would they say if they knew about the tender emotions Jane Doe had stirred in him?

He'd better watch himself. If Danny had picked up on his mind-set, others would too.

"You're full of romantic blarney, Danny O'Brien," Tyler said gruffly.

"Yes." Danny's eyes twinkled. "But without a little romantic drama where would a man be?"

Where indeed?

Then Tyler realized with alarming consternation the door he had slammed and locked shut six years ago had fallen off its hinges, revealing a gaping hole just aching to be filled.

Time was running out.

Dr. Hannah Zachary couldn't afford the luxury of a hospital stay. She had to find Marcus. It was imperative.

He was the only one who could help her now. The only one who could understand the gravity of the situation.

Lionel Daycon and his nefarious cronies would stop at nothing. She had learned that tragic lesson all too well and now she was paying a very high price for her naiveté.

Hannah bit down hard on her bottom lip, fighting back the swell of tears. She had no time for self-pity. Too much was at stake. Too many lives hung in the balance. It was up to her to stop Daycon before he unleashed *Virusall* on an unsuspecting world.

Virusall. The elixir that was supposed to have been a miracle cure that obliterated all viruses. A unique and stunning medication that anticipated a virus's ability to mutate and destroyed it completely.

Virusall. The drug she had invented. The drug that had once promised to revolutionize medicine.

Until three days ago when the results of the initial clinical trials had started coming in and her world had collapsed.

Hannah shuddered against the memory. The side effects were horrific. Everyone with type *O* blood who used *Virusall* experienced violent psychotic episodes three to four weeks after they'd ingested the drug. One test subject had committed suicide, another had beaten his family, yet another had randomly attacked a group of schoolchildren.

And she was the one responsible.

Hannah shuddered again.

Immediately after receiving the first disturbing report, she'd gone to see her boss Lionel Daycon. She'd never liked the unctuous man, but he'd had deep pockets and an amazing laboratory. He'd left her alone to work as she pleased, and Hannah had convinced herself that carrying out her deceased parents' groundbreaking experiments with the Ebola virus was far more important than trusting her boss. The virus had killed her parents. There was no better way to honor their deaths.

How she'd deluded herself!

On Monday afternoon, she'd walked into Daycon's office, but he wasn't there. Restless, agitated, she'd begun to pace and that's when the fax had come through. When the faxed paper floated to the floor, she'd picked it up. She hadn't meant to violate Daycon's privacy, but the word *Virusall* had caught her eye and compelled, she'd read on.

By the end of the letter, she was trembling with fear and fury.

What she learned from the fax was that Daycon had known for days about *Virusall*'s deadly side effects. Not only had he known about it, but he was capitalizing on it. He'd been corresponding with overseas terrorists, promising them tailor-made assassins for exorbitant sums of money. All they had to do was administer *Virusall* to anyone with type *O* blood, wait a few weeks and then put a weapon in their hands. Absolutely, carnage would result.

Most alarming of all, however, was that the fax had originated from inside the CIA. Someone high up in the government was not only sanctioning Daycon's exploits, but had actually instigated the contacts for him.

Armed with this knowledge, she knew she couldn't risk going to the authorities. Desperate to keep the drug out of the wrong hands, Hannah had taken an irrevocable step by obliterating every scrap of written data related to the drug. Except for an e-mail message she'd sent to Marcus that included an encrypted formula for *Virusall*.

She'd also had the presence of mind to reserve ten vials of the elixir in hopes that she and Marcus might create an antidote together in order to administer it to those unfortunate test subjects. She'd packed the vials carefully and secured them in a metal lockbox. After that, she'd set fire to the lab and fled without even retrieving her purse from the bottom drawer of her desk.

And then one cold, dreary November evening two desperate days later somewhere outside of Houston, on a stretch of rain-soaked highway, Daycon's henchmen had run her off the road. Only the presence of concerned motorists pulling over to help had saved her.

She recalled the sickening crunch of metal as her little Fiat had hydroplaned after being struck repeatedly by the henchmen's car. It had hit the median and rolled end over end. She cringed as she heard again the sound of her own screams, as the impact had wrenched open the lockbox sending the glass vials flying around the car. She'd felt the hot splash of *Virusall* burn her skin in numerous places and she remembered saying a prayer of thanks that she had type AB negative blood just before she'd lost consciousness.

Somewhere, Daycon's goons still lurked, waiting for the opportunity to finish the job they'd left undone.

She had to get out of here.

Now.

Five minutes after Dr. Be-Still-My-Beating-Heart Fresno had left her alone, Hannah sat up on the gurney, flung back the stiff green sheet that smelled of antiseptic and peered down at her right leg. Hadn't he claimed her femur was fractured?

Tentatively, she ran a hand along her thigh. Her leg seemed fine. Puzzled, Hannah looked around the room at the medical equipment stored on the shelves. A defibrillator and crash cart stood beside a suction machine and a heart monitor. She heard the steady *blip,* and saw that her heart rhythm was normal. Leaning over, Hannah flicked the Off button, silencing the machine.

The overhead lights beamed down hot and bright. She wore a flimsy hospital gown and nothing else. Not even her underwear. Where were her clothes?

Plucking the oxygen tubing from her nose and peeling the sticky monitor pads from her chest, she then carefully swung her legs over the edge of the gurney. Her head swam and she was forced to grip the railing for support. Once she had regained her equilibrium, Hannah eased her bare feet onto the tile floor and hissed in a breath against the shocking coldness.

She had to get out of here. Before Daycon's goons came back. Before the police showed up. Before Dr. Handsome returned and started demanding answers. She knew he hadn't believed her when she'd lied about not knowing her own name. She had seen the suspicion in his dark eyes, had heard the doubt echo in the richly resonant tones that matched his cautious demeanor. She lied to protect him, to keep him from getting any more involved with her than he already was.

And any minute he would be back, wanting to take her to surgery. Hannah couldn't allow that to happen. If she succumbed to anesthesia she would be too vulnerable.

What a predicament.

She had no money, no identification and no clothes. Plus, she had a movie-star handsome doctor who made her pulse race and wanted to slice her open. To top it all off, she was starving.

As if to illustrate the point, her stomach growled.

"Forget food. Get moving, Hannah," she whispered.

First things first. She had to focus, had to find where the hospital staff had stashed her clothes. She took a hesitant step toward the cabinet below the shiny stainless-steel sink in the corner. Her leg seemed to be working fine. Fractured indeed. Dr. Handsome had better learn how to read X rays. Thankfully for her, his diagnosis left a lot to be desired.

Reassured that everything was in proper working order, she stalked over to the sink and rummaged beneath it. Betadine wash. Antiseptic hand soap. Scrub brushes. Nothing that looked like her beige car coat, navy-blue jumper, black penny loafers and white-lace cotton blouse.

Hurry, you've got to get out of here before that studly doctor comes back.

She shut the cabinet door and closing the back of her immodest hospital gown with two fingers, moved across the floor to investigate the other side of the room.

There was a brown paper sack on the floor wedged behind a chair, beneath a heavy metal supply rack.

Aha. This looked promising.

Hannah bent over and touched the sack with her fingertips, but her arms were too short to reach it. The sack slid farther against the wall.

Shoot.

She settled herself onto her knees in the chair and leaned over the back, allowing the tail of her gown to flap as she strained to extend her arm. She was concentrating so hard on reaching her coveted prize that she didn't hear the door whisper open, but the next sound drew her attention.

A throat being cleared.

"What in the hell do you think you're doing?" Dr. Tyler Fresno demanded.

Chapter 2

Her head came up. Her eyes were wide and scared, but Tyler could not get the image of that round little fanny from his mind. When he had walked through the door and spotted the woman bending over the back of that chair, the thin cotton hospital gown draping loosely around her legs and revealing her naked backside, his initial response had been utterly masculine and not at all professional.

Physical passion, hot, hard and more powerful than anything Tyler had experienced in the past six years kicked him solidly in the gut. He had no business entertaining these thoughts. None whatsoever. Yet there they were.

Jane Doe scurried to her feet and spun around, a red stain coloring her cheeks. "I was just trying to find my things," she said, fumbling to close her gown and hide her nudity.

Immediately contrite, he was embarrassed at his overt sexual desire.

Then surprise ambushed him as he realized what she had been doing. The woman should not be able to stand on that leg, much less kneel in the seat of a chair. The pain would be too great.

"What are you doing out of bed?" he demanded, stalking toward her.

She backed up, her chest rising and falling so rapidly he couldn't stop himself from noticing the swell of her firm, unfettered breasts beneath that skimpy gown.

He shifted his stare to her right leg. The limb supported her without even trembling. Impossible! Confused, Tyler shook his head. The intern must have been wrong about the hairline fracture.

Jane Doe squared her shoulders, raised her head and took a stand. "I'm leaving the hospital against medical advice. Please, get me my clothes."

"No," he said.

"You can't hold me here against my will. I know my rights as a patient."

"The police are outside. They want to talk to you."

Her color paled and she looked stricken. "The police? Why would they want to speak to me?"

"About the accident. They're saying that someone tried to run you off the road."

"No." She forced a laugh. "Where did they get that idea?"

"Eyewitnesses." She was clearly afraid of the police. Why? Was she in some kind of trouble?

Tyler sank his hands on his hips and studied her face. The look of desperation in her eyes sliced him deep. He'd seen a similar expression before. In his own mirror. He remembered what it was like to feel utterly desperate and completely out of control.

After Yvette had died he'd gone off the deep end, drinking too much and isolating himself. Six weeks after her death, he'd taken off for Big Bend National Park and walked into the desert without any supplies, determined to stay there until he died. Three days later, dehydrated and malnourished, he'd become delusional and staggered into an illegal immigrant's camp. The man could have left him for dead. He'd taken a great risk, but he had stayed with Tyler and nursed him back to health. If a considerate stranger hadn't given him sanctuary during that grim time in his life, he would not have survived.

Did Jane Doe need that kind of help from him now?

Yeah, like you're capable of giving it. When was the last time you altruistically did anything for anyone? his cynical voice taunted.

After Yvette's death, he had become so accomplished at shutting off his own feelings that his concerns for his patients never extended beyond their surgical recovery time. What mattered to Tyler was that he performed their operations to the best of his ability. After that, it was out of his hands. He hadn't cared about their family life or spiritual well-being. He hadn't bothered with learning how they got around at home or if they had someone to cook and clean for them while they recovered. That was the job of social workers and nurses, not surgeons.

He was too rusty. His do-gooder instincts were flabby and out of shape. He should just get someone from social services to come consult on her case so he could wash his hands of everything but her medical condition.

Inside his head, he heard Yvette click her tongue that way she had when she was disappointed in him. He could almost feel her disapproving frown burning the back of his head.

Angrily, he shrugged off the sensation. Dammit! He had no reason to feel guilty. He hadn't asked for this assignment. He wasn't this woman's savior. Nor was she even asking him to be. He didn't want to get involved.

I'm my brother's keeper. Yvette's motto—his own old motto before he'd lost touch with his humanity—echoed in his ears.

Ah, hell.

"No one forced me off the road," Jane Doe denied. "The eyewitnesses are mistaken. It was wet and getting dark. I was driving too fast. My car hydroplaned and flipped."

"You can remember the accident but you can't remember your name?"

She shrugged.

He swept his gaze over her body, befuddled at the suddenness of her physical transformation. A short time ago she had been immobile, barely conscious. Her face had been lacerated and her blood pressure low. She had come into contact with an unknown chemical that was quite possibly toxic and she had acute upper-right quadrant pain. Now, she presented the picture of health. Her pasty color had been replaced by a lively pink sheen. Blond hair that had been damp and matted with blood now hung soft and luxuriant down her back. Plus, she was placing full weight on the bone that supposedly had a hairline fracture.

Something didn't jive. He had seen Olympic athletes that hadn't looked as good.

Then he remembered the results of the woman's blood work. The low white blood cell count, the elevated platelets, the numerous lymphocytes. She didn't look like an advanced cancer victim, either. Tyler narrowed his eyes and stroked his chin as he contemplated the evidence.

Maybe the chemicals she'd absorbed through her skin during the accident had altered her blood values, mutating her cells in some bizarre manner that resembled cancer. It was possible, although rare, to see such a change so quickly after exposure, but then again nothing about this woman seemed normal or predictable.

He had to get to the bottom of this anomaly. He had to find out how she could go from obtunded to robust in the span of half an hour.

What exactly had been in those vials?

"Get back on the gurney," Tyler commanded, pointing a finger at the stretcher.

Jane Doe raised her chin and glared at him defiantly. "No."

"I will not allow you to leave this hospital until I've examined you."

"You can't stop me." Her blue eyes flashed fire.

He folded his arms over his chest and moved to block the doorway. "Maybe not, but the police can. Shall I call them?"

"This is an outrage." She frowned. "It's blackmail."

"Sit," he commanded again and pointed at the bed. This time, she obeyed.

Jane Doe scooted herself up onto the gurney but instead of lying down, she stayed sitting on the edge, her feet dangling inches above the floor. She looked like a disgruntled kid forced to eat her broccoli before being allowed to have chocolate cake.

"Has it occurred to you that something isn't quite kosher here?" Tyler asked, stepping closer to the stretcher.

"What do you mean?"

"Your leg. It should be causing you terrible pain."

He could explain away her irregular lab values in the face of renewed health, and it was within the realm of possibility that her spleen had stopped bleeding on its own without surgical intervention. But he could not, no matter how hard he tried, come up with an explanation for why she could bear weight on her fractured leg.

"I'll tell you what's not kosher," she said, narrowing her eyes at him. "Your diagnosis. Admit your mistake, Doctor. You were wrong about the fracture. Obviously, my leg is not broken."

"Let's check the film."

He stepped to where her X rays were clipped to a fluorescent, wall-mounted box and switched on the backlight. The bulb flickered a minute, then illuminated the view of her right-upper leg.

"See that," he said, pointing to the thin dark line that ran almost the entire length of her long bone. "That's what we call a capillary fracture. The mildest fracture, but a fracture nonetheless. You should be in considerable pain."

"It simply isn't my X ray," she denied.

"It's got your name on it."

"And what name is that?"

"Jane Doe."

"Yes. A name you give all unknown female patients. Correct?"

"There have been no other Jane Does admitted tonight," Tyler replied.

"Are you sure?"

"Positive." But her statement caused him momentary doubt. Could it be true?

"Then someone mislabeled the X ray," she insisted. "You've got me mixed up with another patient. That's all there is to it."

"I want to X ray your leg again."

"No need. It's fine. You saw me walking on it."

"Appease me."

"I see no point. Clearly if I can bear weight on the leg it can't be fractured."

She had a valid argument. Their gazes caught and he couldn't help but feel a flare of heat low in his belly. Her eyes were sharp, intelligent. Nothing got by this one.

"You still can't remember your name?" he asked, flicking off the light under her X ray and coming back to stand beside her.

"No."

"I want to check your neurological signs."

"All right."

At least she hadn't fought him on this. He removed a penlight from his pocket and flashed it in first one pupil and then the other. Equal and reactive.

"Do you know what day it is?" he asked, testing to see if she was oriented to time and place.

"Thursday. November, the seventh," she replied.

He nodded. "And where are you at?"

"St. Madeline's Hospital in Houston, Texas."

"Here," he said. "Squeeze my hands."

She stared at him. "What for?"

"So I can check your grip."

"Is this really necessary?"

"I don't bite."

She sighed and rolled her eyes.

Why was she so reluctant to touch him? He wriggled his fingers. "Come on."

Slowly, she took his fingers in her hands and squeezed.

"Harder," he said.

Her hands were soft and warm and fit perfectly in his. Delicate and feminine hands. She smelled nice, too. Like sunflowers.

"How's that?" she asked, squeezing with all her might.

"Good." He met her challenging glare and swallowed back his awkwardness.

"Sure you don't want it harder?" Her voice held a note of sharp sarcasm. Her stare was disconcertingly intense. His gut knotted.

"That's fine. You can let go now."

She released his hands and although Tyler was relieved, he felt vaguely dissatisfied.

"Lie down," he said. "I want to examine your abdomen again."

"May I leave after this?"

"Perhaps." Boy, was she a tough cookie. He had to admire her doggedness.

Sighing, she stretched out on the gurney, crossed her legs at the ankle and propped the back of her head in her palms.

He moved to her side and palpated her spleen. "Is that tender?"

"No."

"You wouldn't be lying simply to get out of here, would you?" he asked.

"I'm not above fudging the truth in order to get dismissed," she admitted and Tyler suppressed a smile at her honesty. "But I'm sincere. It really doesn't hurt."

When he had examined her previously she'd had marked guarding of the area and had moaned in pain. Now, she seemed unaffected by his probing. Weird. Her spleen must have stopped bleeding spontaneously. He'd never seen it happen, but he'd heard it was possible. He took her blood pressure—116/78. Textbook normal.

"I really think you should be admitted for observation," Tyler said. "We don't know for sure that your spleen isn't still leaking. What happens if you get down the road a few hours and start hemorrhaging internally?"

"Guess that's a chance I've got to take." She shrugged.

Concern kicked him hard in the heart. If she wanted to take that risk, why should he care?

He didn't care.

Yes, you do.

No, I don't.

Come on, you've got to stop being such a crusty old goat eventually. The contrary voice in his head was pure Yvette, goading him to rise to the occasion. She'd always kept him on his moral toes and since she'd been gone he'd slid far down the slippery slope to indifference.

I don't, he mentally argued.

Yes, you do. Because once upon a time you were self-destructive and your friends stepped in. Right now this woman needs all the friends she can get. Whether she recognizes it or not.

Okay. Fine. He would try to cajole her into staying. That way, if she refused, he could let her go with a clear conscience.

"Why are you so adamant against spending the night?" Tyler asked. "What could it hurt?"

"I have an aversion to hospitals." She rubbed her arms and he saw goose bumps rise on her skin. That's when he realized her chemical burns were gone.

He shook his head, blinked and did a double take. He examined her arms and legs. Not a burn insight.

"What's wrong?" she asked.

"Your burns have disappeared." Now that really was strange. He frowned, shoved a hand through his hair and wracked his brain for a plausible explanation. A mistake on the X ray he could buy. Her spleen clotting itself off, while unlikely, wasn't impossible. But now this?

Tyler felt as if he'd just fallen into *The Twilight Zone.*

What kind of chemicals had been in those vials? Curiosity gnawed at him. She was a complicated woman with disappearing symptoms. He told himself he needed for her to stay so he could get to the bottom of her odd healing, but in reality he wanted to find out who she really was.

Gently, Tyler drew the sheet around her shoulders to warm her. She shied at his touch as if afraid he might harm her. Her lip trembled and she turned her head away from him.

"Please, bring me a release form and I'll exonerate you from all responsibility," she said. "I just want to leave."

"You think a piece of paper will keep me from worrying about you?" Tyler asked, disturbed because what he'd said was true. No matter how much a stubborn part of him longed to deny it, he cared about Jane Doe.

And that scared the living hell out of him.

"If you're insistent on leaving can I at least call someone for you?" he asked.

"No." She shook her head. "I…I don't remember."

He saw through her like glass. Whenever she lied, the tip of her nose reddened.

"How do you intend to get home? Your car was totaled in the accident."

"I'll walk."

"Do you even know where home is?"

She didn't answer.

Tyler clenched his teeth. "You didn't have any identification on you. The paramedics searched your car but couldn't find a purse. Do you have any money?"

"Are you offering a loan?" She quirked one eyebrow at him.

"Yes," Tyler said, reaching for his wallet. A wad of cash should take care of the problem. He needn't get anymore involved than that. "Except it's a gift, not a loan."

"Do you often offer needy patients money, Doctor?"

"No." He hadn't ever given money to a patient, but Yvette had. Many times. He'd often joked she was driving them into the poor house with her lost causes. His late wife had been a social worker with a marshmallow heart who'd been unable to resist any stray who showed up on her doorstep. He heard Yvette whispering in his ear, *Help her.*

"I'm special, then." Jane Doe's tone was sardonic but the look in her eyes was one of appreciative surprise.

His chest swelled with an odd emotion he couldn't name. Their gazes locked and he knew it was true. He couldn't say why or how but this woman was special to him and not just because she obviously needed him. Without even trying, she touched something deep inside him. Perhaps it was the sarcasm that hinted at her hidden vulnerability; perhaps it was her nervousness, perhaps it was because she looked a bit like Yvette—blond, petite, fragile.

Or perhaps it was his own loneliness that he saw reflected in those soft blue eyes. Peering through those cerulean depths and on past into her troubled soul was like staring into a looking glass.

"Yes," he admitted. "You are special."

She ducked her head, denying him further access to those tantalizing eyes.

"Please," he said, extending five twenty-dollar bills to her. "Take the cash."

"I can't accept your money."

She glanced up and he caught another glimpse into those too wise yet oddly naive eyes and drew in a breath. What he was about to suggest overstepped all boundaries of the doctor-patient relationship but he could not bear the thought of her wandering the streets hungry and alone.

He remembered the kind man in the desert who had saved his life when he was at his lowest point. Jane Doe was at that threshold now.

Here's your opportunity to repay that karmic debt, Yvette's voice niggled. *Not only that, but giving this woman sanctuary is a chance to get the old Tyler back. I miss him. Don't you?*

Tyler clenched his jaw. Why her? Why now? She made him feel something again when he believed he'd lost all ability to feel tender emotions. And he did long to be the man he was before Yvette had died. Concerned, loving, compassionate. He'd forgotten how to be all those things.

This is your chance at redemption.

Offering Jane Doe a place to stay was the right thing to do, even though he feared prolonged proximity to her might alter his fate in ways he never imagined. He needed to do this. In memory of Yvette. In memory of the man he used to be.

"All right." Tyler pocketed the money. "If you refuse to stay in the hospital and you won't take my cash then there is only one option left."

"And that is?"

It was now or never. If he hesitated, he would back out. Tyler took a deep breath and committed himself. "You'll stay at my secluded beach house on Galveston Island. No one will bother you. You can rest, collect your thoughts and stay until you get your memory back. Is it a deal?"

She had no other choice but to say yes. She couldn't go back home to Austin. It wasn't safe. Daycon's men would be watching her house. And she couldn't talk to the police. They would make a phone call and discover she was the one responsible for torching Daycon Laboratories. Besides, Daycon was buddies with a rogue CIA operative. He would have no trouble locating her if she didn't accept help. She had no money for a motel. She needed food and a good night's sleep before trying to obtain another car so she could get to Marcus in New Mexico. Dr. Fresno's offer was a gift from heaven.

Hannah gazed into Tyler's sincere brown eyes and felt guilty for lying to him. But she didn't know how far she could trust him and as long as she kept her name a secret it offered both of them some small measure of security.

"Why would you do that for me?" she asked.

He shrugged. "Maybe because you're the most interesting case I've ever come across."

She studied him a moment, trying to figure him out.

"Well?" he asked slanting his head and waiting for her response to his proposal.

"All right," she agreed.

"There's just one stipulation."

Hannah groaned. She should have known there would be a catch. "What is it?"

"You allow me to perform a few more tests."

Hannah hesitated. She wanted out of this place. Now. The longer she stayed, the more precarious her position became.

"I've got to know what happened to you," Tyler insisted. "Why your spleen stopped bleeding. Why your chemical burns disappeared."

I could tell you what I think might have happened, Hannah thought, *but I don't fully understand it myself.*

Virusall could be responsible for her stunningly quick recovery. How, she did not know for sure, but the experiences she'd had with the drug in the lab indicated anything might be possible. It was a miraculously healing drug but it was also very unstable.

Fear rippled through her, but she pushed her anxiety aside. She didn't have time to piece together what *Virusall* might have done to her. Not now.

When she'd accused Tyler of misreading the X rays and confusing her with another patient, she had done it to offer him an explanation. A rational possibility his scientific mind could accept. She couldn't tell him the truth—that she had concocted a wonder drug proven to eradicate all viruses. She had scarcely believed it herself.

And then there were the horrific side effects that turned ordinary people with type *O* blood into vicious beasts.

To let Tyler in on her secret would be tantamount to signing his death warrant. If Daycon suspected she told anyone about *Virusall*, she knew the man would not hesitate to do whatever was necessary to protect himself and his CIA cohort.

She had to get to Marcus before Daycon figured out what she was planning, and she had to get out of this hospital before his henchmen discovered she had not died in the car crash.

"Concerning these tests," Hannah asked Tyler. "What do you have in mind?"

"X rays, more blood work."

"How long?"

"Three, four hours tops."

"Sorry. I can give you an hour. That's all. Do what you can in that length of time—after that, I'll be gone."

"Fair enough." He surprised her by agreeing.

Cocking her head, she studied him, wondering what his motivation was in opening his house to her. He had told her she was special. What had he meant by that? Was it because her vanishing illness fascinated him? Had someone helped him when he was down and out? Or was there something more?

He was a handsome man, tall and lean. His hands, long and slender, belonged to a surgeon. His hair was dark brown, his eyes an even darker shade of chocolate. There was a brushstroke of gray at each temple and a few laugh lines creased the corners of his eyes. An air of refinement clung to him and yet at the same time he exuded a rugged masculinity. A hunter who listened to Mozart. A soldier who studied fine art. A man as comfortable skiing in the Rockies as he would be at a wine-tasting party.

She could not deny her attraction to him, but Hannah didn't employ her physical urges to form opinions or make decisions.

Her parents had taught her that nothing was more important than a clear head and a practical mind. Affairs of the hearts were reserved for sentimentalists and fools and she was neither.

Her parents, though they professed to love her, had not been the type to offer kisses, hugs or even many words of praise. Hannah had been expected to perform to the best of her ability and she had strove to please them. She had earned a bachelor's degree in chemistry by age sixteen, had a master's by eighteen and at age twenty had been the youngest woman ever to earn a Ph.D. in pharmacology from the University of Texas. In fact, it had been her burning desire to honor the memory of her parents and the high standards they had set which led her to discover the phenomenal *Virusall*.

She had always been on the outside looking in, the girl who was out of step with everyone else her age. Because of her upbringing, Hannah had never been very good with people, but it was this trait that made her such a dedicated researcher. She possessed an analytical mind and she enjoyed being alone. She didn't easily succumb to the emotional pull of others and she held herself to lofty standards.

But right now Tyler Fresno was tugging at her with the force of a high-powered magnet.

"Do you know where my clothes are?" She ran a hand through her unruly hair. Furrowing her brow, she wished for lipstick and a hairbrush. She must look a fright and although Hannah wasn't given to vanity, she found herself wanting to look nice for him. Why?

"Perhaps they're down here." He turned and bent over to pick up the sack she had been trying to reach when he had come into the room and caught her with her backside in the air.

This turnabout was fair play.

She propped herself up on her elbows and watched with interest as she got a glimpse of his rear-end. Unfortunately, doctors' scrub suits did not offer the same uninhibited view as an open-back hospital gown. Still, she enjoyed running her eyes down the length of his lanky form. She wasn't one for ogling men, but for this guy she would make an exception.

"Here you are." He handed her the paper bag.

Hannah peered inside and was alarmed to see her clothes matted with dirt and blood.

Tyler must have read her mind because in the next minute he said, "Tell you what—I'll get you a set of scrubs to wear. What are you?" He squinted, raking his gaze over her. "An extra small?"

"Yes, but a small will do fine and thank you. That's very considerate."

"Don't mention it." He smiled and Hannah felt warm and tingly all over.

A girl could fall for a guy like him.

She had to be careful. Hannah had spent so much time in a laboratory, she knew very little about the opposite sex or how to handle herself in the presence of a man she found attractive.

"I'll just draw a vial of blood first," Tyler said. He opened a supply drawer. "Damn, we're out of purple-top tubes. Just hang on a minute while I pop over to the lab for the right tube."

"I'm leaving in a hour," she warned.

"Okay, fine. I'll just go ahead and draw your blood and then carry the specimen to the lab in the syringe. I can put it in the correct tube when I get there."

"Thank you." She beamed at him.

He wrapped a yellow rubber tourniquet around her arm and palpated a vein in the bend of her elbow. "Make a fist for me."

After drawing her blood, he then put the syringe into a red bag marked with a biohazard chemical emblem.

It was after eleven o'clock and Danny was getting ready to leave for the night when Tyler walked into the lab.

"Here's the blood on Jane Doe," he said.

"Lad, your timin' leaves a lot to be desired," Danny grumbled good-naturedly and started to shrug out of the coat he'd just put on.

"No, no, go on. I'll put it in a purple-top tube and label it for the next shift," Tyler offered.

"You're a saint, you are."

"Off with you."

Danny headed for the door.

Tyler removed the syringe from the red plastic bag and took off the needle cap. He started to push the needle into the tube's rubber stopper but his hand slipped and he accidentally plunged the needle into the pad of his thumb.

"Yeow!"

"What's the matter?" Danny turned back and paled when he saw the syringe of blood protruding from Tyler's thumb.

"I slipped."

"Ah, Laddie. I shouldna let you done that," Danny castigated himself. "It's my job."

"It's not a big deal," Tyler said, trying to appear casual when his heart was racing. He'd just been stuck with a patient's blood and he didn't even know her HIV status.

Jane Doe wasn't HIV positive.

How do you know? Just because you don't want her to have AIDS doesn't make it so. Her blood work is abnormal.

Danny took the syringe and blood tube away from Tyler. "Go wash up at the sink and mind you fill out an incident report on this. You'll have to get tested and so will she."

"Yeah, yeah." Tyler washed his hands at the sink and tried his best to ignore his throbbing thumb. He would live.

But would his beautiful mystery woman?

By the time the X-ray technician wheeled her back to the emergency room, Hannah was more than ready to see the last of Saint Madeleine's. A knock sounded on the door and she looked up to spy Tyler standing in the doorway, a blue scrub suit in his hands and a smile hovering at his lips.

"Ready to go?" he asked.

She nodded, relieved. "Do I need to go to the billing office?" she asked. "It's going to be tough. I don't have any identification. To be honest, I don't know if I have health insurance or not."

This was the truth. After her run-in with Daycon, she figured her old boss would not be inclined to pay her medical bills. Especially since he would rather cover her funeral expenses instead, but not until he got his hands on *Virusall.*

"Don't worry about it." Tyler said. "I've already checked you out of the hospital."

"How did you accomplish that feat?"

"I told them I would be responsible for your bill."

"Dr. Fresno," she protested, "I can't allow you to do that."

He raised his palms. "Shhh. I have more money than I know what to do with. We'll discuss it later. Right now you need a warm bath, a hot meal and a good night's sleep. Hopefully by morning your memory will have returned and we can piece together what happened to you."

"Why would you do this for me?" she asked. "I'm a stranger to you."

"I'm curious about your condition. About you."

She wasn't buying it. There was something more. Mere curiosity didn't cause a man to open his home to someone he did not know.

"What's the real reason?" she asked.

He looked at her for a long moment and she saw a myriad of emotions play across his face. Sorrow, loss, sadness, regret. By helping her, was he assuaging something inside of him? A long ago guilt? A bad choice made? A wrong turn taken? Was he looking for redemption? Who was she to deny him his salvation?

"A stranger helped me once when I was in deep trouble," he said quietly. She could tell by the way he held himself that the memory of his troubles still haunted him. "I vowed that I would never turn my back on someone in need. And from my vantage point, you're looking pretty needy. Besides, you remind me of someone I once knew."

His voice caught and Hannah realized then he wasn't doing this so much for her or even for his own good karma, but for the person that brought the gravelly, emotional sound into his voice. She shouldn't fight his generosity. She should just accept it as a gift. Why was it so difficult for her to receive help?

Hannah swallowed hard. "I have trouble taking assistance from people I don't know."

"Ah, trust issues."

"You have no idea," she muttered.

"I understand. You're under no obligation to me." The look

on his face was one of utter compassion. He had no ulterior motives. He was simply a nice guy. Why did she have so much trouble accepting that?

Because no one has ever been kind to you without an ulterior motive.

"What about the police?"

"I told them you weren't available for an interview until tomorrow morning."

"What happens tomorrow when they find out I'm not here?"

"We'll deal with that tomorrow."

A lump formed in Hannah's throat. She couldn't believe the kindness of this good doctor. She didn't deserve to be treated so well, particularly since she was lying to him.

In that moment, Hannah experienced a premonition, a spooky sensation that sent goose flesh flying up her arms. By agreeing to go off with Dr. Tyler Fresno and evading the police, was she possibly making the gravest mistake of all?

Chapter 3

"Are you hungry?" Tyler asked as they left the hospital in his silver BMW.

It was either early or late, depending upon your definition. The parking lot lay half-empty. The sky was dark and the street lamps exuded a fuzzy golden glow. Hannah had crashed her car around dusk, now it was after midnight.

"Famished," she admitted and pressed a palm to her belly. She hadn't eaten all day. Between the terror of fleeing Daycon's men, living through a smashup and experiencing a miraculous healing, she was ready for a down-to-earth activity like supper.

Besides, eating might take her mind of this unexpected twist of sexual desire building at a brushfire pace between she and the good doctor. Being in the car alone with him was causing her to think some very unseemly thoughts. She kept getting a flash of what he might taste like. Warm and sweet, she decided. And deliciously sinful. Like Death By Chocolate dessert.

You're just famished. Knock off the fantasy.

"How are you feeling otherwise?" Tyler fretted. "No nausea, no headaches, no dizziness?"

"I'm fine except I could eat a hippopotamus."

"How about a hamburger instead?" He chuckled and pulled through a drive-through fast-food joint.

"Is this your idea of healthy eating, Doctor?" she teased, surprised at her own levity. The truth was, she felt good. Damned good. Happy to be alive and, if she dared to confess it, excited. For the first time since fleeing Daycon's burned-out laboratories, Hannah had hope.

"Normally," Tyler said, "I recommend healthier fare. But considering what you've been through you need the protein and a little fat won't hurt you, either."

She was usually conscientious about what she ate, preferring fruits and vegetables to meat and bread but her mouth watered at the thought of a thick, juicy hamburger. Sometimes junk food was exactly what the doctor ordered.

And what a doctor he was! Tall and lean but muscular. With a dark, brooding quality beneath his professional demeanor. A quality that issued a call to her own sense of isolation.

Stop this, Hannah. Stop it right now. No good can come of your sudden infatuation.

She knew better, and yet she could not stop sending him surreptitious glances over the rim of her thick chocolate milk shake.

Within minutes they were traveling south outside of Houston, the comforting smell of mustard and onions filling the car. After she had polished off the hamburger and the milk shake, she wiped her hands on a paper napkin, sighed her pleasure and leaned back against the leather seat.

What elegance. What style. The car perfectly fit the man. She must have drifted off because the next thing she knew, Tyler was pulling the BMW into the driveway of a dark, silent beach house.

There was no light, save for the full moon overhead and the illumination from the headlight beams. Sitting up, Hannah rubbed her eyes and rolled down the window. The scent of salt air mingled with the sound of the ocean lapping against the shore.

"This is it," he said, coming around to help her out.

Her body had grown stiff during the hour-long drive from the city to the Gulf of Mexico. Stretching, Hannah suppressed a yawn.

Tyler reached to take her arm but she tensed and rejected his extended hand. He shrugged nonchalantly, but evidently she'd wounded his pride. She wanted to tell him it was nothing personal but how could she explain that she didn't like to be touched? Particularly by strangers.

Growing up without much physical affection had caused her to crave a larger than average personal space. She needed distance. Her parents had taught her it was rude and presumptuous to press herself upon people. As a result, she often felt awkward whenever someone touched her. She didn't even care to shake hands.

As for kissing, well, that had proven to be a nightmare the few times she'd tried it. Hannah supposed her less than enthusiastic response to swapping spit was the main reason she'd had a string of first dates but never a steady boyfriend.

And yet, some small part of her desperately wanted Dr. Fresno to kiss her.

She knew she was an oddball. Her parents' negative view of romantic love had colored her outlook. Doctors Eric and Beverly Zachary had been friends and colleagues and little more. They had prided themselves on avoiding the trap of useless emotions in favor of a marriage based on mutual respect. They had even encouraged Hannah to make an emotionless match herself. When they had met Marcus Halpren, they had been hopeful she would choose him as her life mate. He had an IQ of two hundred and ten, and even though Marcus had been interested in her, Hannah had been unable to bring herself to ruin their friendship with a business merger. Although she liked and respected her colleague, she had never been attracted to him. A passionless marriage might have been enough for her parents. It wasn't enough for her. She'd rather remain single.

In college, her roommates had extolled the joys of sex in vivid detail. Hannah had even attempted the act herself but after one or two groping sessions in the back seat of some guy's car, she had come to the conclusion that one, sex was noisy, sweaty and not worth the bother and two, she was in the minority in her opinion.

"This way," Tyler said, leading her up the path to the two-story frame structure built on stilts.

She could see sand dunes beyond, and the ocean shimmering in the distance. It had been such a long time since she'd been to the seaside. The water called to her, pulled at something deep inside her solar plexus. The tide was so elemental, so basic, at once temporary yet enduringly permanent. She was tired of her complex life and had a sudden desperate need for the simple fundamentals.

Food. Water. Love. Not knowing where that last thought came from, Hannah moved toward the ocean.

"Where are you going?"

"Can we take a walk along the beach?" she asked, desperate to clear her head. His proximity was disconcerting. The smell of his woodsy aftershave mingled with the scent of the ocean, creating a powerful draw inside her. A draw she must deny.

Tyler arched his eyebrows at her request. "Sure, if you feel up to it."

Without waiting for him, she trailed over the shifting sand toward the beckoning waves. She needed to put distance between them, needed to get some perspective on what she was feeling. She'd never been this physically attracted to a man before and she didn't know how to handle her body's purely feminine response. Particularly when she could not act on her feelings. The timing couldn't have been worse.

"Jane," he said, and it took Hannah a minute to realize he was speaking to her. "I know that's not your real name, but I don't know what else to call you."

Hannah turned and saw him silhouetted in the moonlight, regal as a mythical knight. His handsomeness took her breath. He possessed an elegant self-assurance and a natural patience. In that instant, she almost told him her name but fear for his safety stopped her. The less he knew about her, the better for both of them.

Wistfully, she thought back to her childhood when her first-grade teacher had read the story of Cinderella to the class. Until that time, Hannah had never heard the tale. Her parents, disdainful of fiction in general and fairy tales in particular, had read only nature stories and biographies for entertainment. Of course, like any little girl, she had been enthralled with the notion of Prince Charming. Excited, she had rushed home to tell her mother what she had learned. Her mother had burst her bubble, telling her that fairy tales were utter nonsense written for silly fools. Then she had pulled Hannah out of public school.

The memory lingered. She wondered why her mother had been so opposed to the romantic story. Now, looking at Tyler, Hannah recalled the joy she had experienced upon hearing that story her first and only time.

What was the matter with her? Why was she thinking these crazy romantic notions when her mind should be consumed by thoughts of *Virusall*?

"Jane will do fine," she said, and wished she could tell him her real name. She would have loved to hear him whisper "Hannah" in his low, sexy voice.

"I want you to know that you're welcome to stay here as long as you need."

"I appreciate the offer, but I'll be on my way in the morning."

"It's not necessary."

Hannah crossed her arms. "Listen, you've been very sweet and I really appreciate what you've done for me, but I've got to be straight with you. I don't 'do' people well."

He cocked his head. The moonlight caught his eyes and they glinted with a dangerous light. "What's that suppose to mean?"

"I'm a loner. I have a hard time with small talk."

"And?"

"I snore."

"Are you trying to tell me that you make a terrible house guest?" He gave her a look that raised goose bumps on her arms. What was it about him that drove her hormones insane? Was this what they called chemistry? It felt wonderful and wild and scary and out of control. She didn't like it. Not one bit. But she loved it.

"Yes," she said. "I suppose I am."

"Don't worry. I live in the city. The beach house is yours."

"I won't be here long," she reiterated.

"Stay as long as you need." Tyler stepped closer and Hannah

felt both fearful and thrilled that he might try to touch her again, but he didn't. Discombobulated, she glanced away.

"Let's walk," she said and started down the beach.

The chilly night wind whipped the thin scrubs around her legs, sliced through her car coat and snatched at her curls. She took a deep breath. It was good to feel cold. She savored being alive with a handsome man by her side. A man she liked more than she had any right to.

These feelings were deadly. She had to be on her way as soon as she got a good's night sleep. For both their sakes. Because she could tell by the expression on his face he was feeling the same powerful push-pull of attraction that was grabbing at her chest.

"I haven't been to the beach house since summer. It's probably pretty musty inside. Salt water takes its toll."

Hannah nodded. Silence elongated between them, increasing their awkwardness with each other.

"Are you married?" she asked at last.

"No. Are you?"

It was on the tip of her tongue to say no, then she remembered she was suppose to have lost her memory. "I don't think so," she hedged. "I don't remember."

"Don't worry," he said. "I'm sure your amnesia is temporary. It's not uncommon in the aftermath of an accident. Spontaneous memory usually returns in a few hours to a few days."

Fresh guilt swept over her. The more she lied to him, the worse she felt.

"I *was* married once," he said quietly. "A long time ago."

The water lapped at their feet. The moon shone down. She could almost palpate his uneasiness.

"You never remarried?" She angled a sideways glance at him. His face was cast in shadows, his jaw ridged.

He shook his head. "No."

"Divorced?" she asked, startled to find her throat thick with an unnamed emotion.

"Widowed."

Then he stopped, turned his back on her and stared out to sea, letting Hannah know the subject was closed. He had loved his wife a great deal, she realized. So much that he still found it hard to talk about her. The knowledge stirred a longing deep within her. Would anyone ever love her with such intensity? Better question, would she even live to see the end of the week?

Not for the first time, she wondered why Tyler had offered her sanctuary. She shivered and hugged herself. If she hadn't been desperate she would never have accepted his offer.

"You're cold."

He slipped off his heavy jacket and draped it gently around her shoulders. He held himself stiffly, making sure he didn't touch her. He was as discombobulated by their attraction and apparently did not welcome it anymore than she did. That was good. If they both kept their distance everything would be all right.

The jacket smelled of him. Of hamburgers and hospitals, soap and antiseptic. She couldn't help herself. She found the scent very comforting.

"Come," he said. "Let's go to the house."

She stumbled in the sand, almost lost her balance. He reached out to take her hand, but she hung back.

"Does touching me make you uncomfortable?"

"Yes."

"I just don't want you to fall, but if you're uncomfortable, I understand." He dropped his hand and seemed relieved she didn't need him.

"I'm fine." But then she stumbled again, belying her statement.

He reached out again. "Come on. Take my hand."

Tentatively, she reached out and slid her hand into his.

Holding his hand was awkward at first. She couldn't deny it. It was as if she didn't belong in this place and had no business touching this man as they walked along in silence under the crescent moon.

His hand was smooth and firm. He held her loosely so she could easily break free if she chose. Hannah liked that. He was offering his support with no expectations. He simply wanted to keep her from falling.

Palm trees swayed. Leaves rustled. The water whispered as

it rolled forward, and then slithered back. Near their feet sea creatures scuttled for safety across the sand.

The bond between them grew. Her hand tingled with a warm glow that increased the longer Tyler held on. Her heart filled with heated syrup. Her mind spun. She felt as if she were falling from a high precipice into a bottomless abyss.

Hannah had never experienced anything to equal the sensation. Her pulse quickened. What did it mean? So many strange things had happened to her over the last few hours that she couldn't unravel the implications.

It means nothing. It couldn't mean anything. She could not act on this attraction. She couldn't trust it. Even if she wasn't on the run. Even if her life wasn't in danger. She simply didn't know how to please a man. She'd spent her life in a lab. She had no idea how to flirt or wear makeup. Had not a clue what turned men on. And most of all, she had no idea how to open her heart to love. And a man as special as Tyler deserved a feminine woman who could give him her all. Especially after he'd been so scarred by life.

So what was she supposed to do about this vibrant electric current running between them?

"Do you feel it?" Tyler asked, his voice a low rumble invading her ears.

"Yes," she murmured.

"My hand's melting into yours."

"Flowing," she said, articulating the word that leapt to her head.

"It's so hot. As if you have a fever."

"I don't."

"What does it mean?" Tyler asked, stopping just short of the house and drawing her into the moonlight. His eyes searched her face. "Tell me, Jane, what's going on?"

Had he guessed that she was lying about her amnesia?

"I can't. Not now. Not yet."

"But soon?"

She shook her head. "It's safer if you don't know."

He raised their joined hands above their heads. "We're connected, you and I, whether we like it or not."

Fear vaulted through Hannah. What he said was true. She felt it. He felt it. And the feeling was almost as terrifying as the knowledge that Daycon and a renegade CIA agent were planning on using her miracle drug as a deadly weapon in a foreign country.

"No," she denied.

She could not be united with this man. She was in this alone. Only Marcus Halpren could help her. Only her ex-partner would understand what was at stake. Tyler was an innocent bystander, sucked by his big heart into something he could not comprehend. She would not allow him to wade any deeper.

With a twist, she jerked her hand from his. It felt as if her arm had wrenched from its socket.

Panic descended upon her. An anxiety so sharp in its intensity she was left breathless. Her chest refused to expand to full capacity. She yanked in small swallows of air and sweat beaded her brow.

"Jane!" he cried.

She dropped to her knees, sand filling her penny loafers. Hannah clasped her hand over her chest and tried to speak, to tell him she was all right, but the words would not come. How could she say she was fine when she obviously was not?

A roaring noise sounded in her ears. Her vision blurred and her stomach burned.

What *was* happening?

A reaction to *Virusall*?

Hannah knew the drug was volatile, unstable and had some serious side effects, but she couldn't tell Tyler about it.

Without hesitation, he bent and scooped her into his arms. "I knew something like this was going to happen," he muttered under his breath. "I knew that you weren't well."

Her chest still encompassed by an invisible band that squeezed tighter with each inhalation, Hannah leaned her head against Tyler's shoulder. Even though she weighed only a hundred and twelve pounds, he was much stronger than she had anticipated. For a lean man, he was quite stout. He carried her as if she weighed no more than thistledown, holding her aloft as he stalked up the stairs toward the house.

If Hannah had thought holding hands with this man had been an earthshaking experience, it was nothing compared to what zinged through her body now.

Desire.

Quick and hot.

Never had she wanted any man the way she wanted this one. Suddenly, the woman who disliked being touched, who hated being kissed, could think of nothing but this man's lips upon hers, his hands tracing a brush fire across her body.

What would he do if she were to kiss his cheek? Why was she thinking like this? She wasn't the sort of woman who fell willy-nilly into relationships. She was cautious, practical, sensible.

Maybe she had a head injury from the accident. Or perhaps she was shell-shocked. She longed to cling to the explanation but she feared her attraction to this man was due to much more than trauma.

And yet, she had waited all her life to feel like this, had waited for someone to unlock her passion. No matter what her parents had told her, deep down inside Hannah had secretly believed in the Cinderella fable. She had hoped against hope that it was true.

Now that she felt these unfamiliar stirrings, she was terrified. This couldn't be happening. Not at this juncture in her life. Not with so much at stake. Not with her future so uncertain. Not when she could drag him down with her.

She clung to Tyler's neck, tossed helplessly by her emotions, more frightened of what she was feeling than the increasing tightness twisting through her chest. Were the two connected? Her emotions and her physical distress?

Tyler sat her on the porch, then reached into the pocket of his scrub pants for the key, keeping one arm curled around her waist.

The door sprang open at his touch. He reached inside, fumbling for the lights. They came on with blinding brightness. Hannah shielded her eyes with her forearm.

Picking her up again, he then hurried inside and kicked the door closed with his foot.

He was right. The house did smell musty. She crinkled her nose against the odor of mildew. Her head ached. The living room furniture was covered with sheets that made it appear like squat, silent ghosts.

Carefully, he deposited her on the sofa, and then disappeared into another part of the house. He returned seconds later with a small black medical bag. He popped an old-fashioned glass thermometer under her tongue and strapped a blood-pressure cuff around her right arm. Hannah peered up at him. His eyes were so filled with concern she experienced an unexpected urge to cry. She was not given to displays of emotion and she fought against the tears.

His bare arm brushed her hand and she lost her breath. She stared at him, unable to look away. He compelled her in a way nothing, beyond her work, ever had.

The green of his scrub suit contrasted nicely with his tanned complexion and straight white teeth. Most people looked blah and shapeless in scrubs, but Tyler Fresno looked astonishing. The cotton scrub top lightly grazed his chest, coyly hinting at the streamlined muscles lurking under the material. Even though he was slim, the man was built like the Rock of Gibraltar.

She felt herself blush. The heat burned her cheeks. What was this? She never blushed. She'd been trained to be passionless, clinical, in control of her emotions.

Disassociate. Disconnect. Disengage. But her favorite mental chant failed to stop the alien sensations from tumbling over her.

His prying fingers were strong yet tender as he examined her. He raised her scrub top, exposing her chest, slipped a stethoscope into his ears and placed the cold bell against her rib cage, his warm hand skimming over her skin. She closed her eyes and battled the hot yearning sensation that surged through her. She ached for him to drop that stethoscope and cup her breasts in his palms.

Why? She had never hungered for anyone's touch.

Tyler told her to take several deep breaths and then cough. Avoiding his eyes, she did as he asked.

He took her blood pressure, then removed the thermometer from her mouth and held it up to the light. "Temp and BP are normal," he proclaimed, his relief unmistakable. "Your breath sounds are clear. How do you feel?"

"Better."

"That's good." He lowered her scrub top and patted her shoulder.

"I'm sorry," she apologized. "I don't know what happened back there on the beach. Or why I collapsed."

"Don't worry about it," he soothed. "You've had a rough day. I think it's past time that you got some sleep. Give me a few minutes and I'll put sheets on the bed in the guest room."

Hannah nodded. She was so touched by his kind heart she couldn't speak. A few minutes later, he returned to lead her upstairs and into the guest bedroom.

The room contained a canopied bed, a white wicker chair and a full-length mirror. There was a dressing table with a round-faced clock sitting on it and a small a.m./f.m. radio. Plain white curtains hung at the windows and several pastoral photographs of the beach adorned the walls. It was an understated but elegant room. Had his late wife decorated it?

Her own domestic genes were nonexistent. She'd been a scientist for so long she had no idea how to simply be a woman.

"You can wear one of my T-shirts," Tyler said, tugging her from her disturbing reverie and handing her a white cotton T-shirt.

She thanked him and when he left the room a forlorn emptiness overcame her. She pressed his cotton shirt to her nose and breathed deeply. It smelled nice and she was surprised to discover the scent comforted her. She took off the borrowed hospital scrubs and pulled the T-shirt over her head. It came to her knees, hugging her in a cloth embrace. Startled, she realized she had never worn a man's garment before.

Hannah tried to sleep but her mind whirled. She closed her eyes and willed her disturbed thoughts away. She dozed for a while, but then the nightmares came. Vivid ugly dreams in which she relived the car crash again and again. Above it all, she kept seeing Lionel Daycon's cruel twisted face laughing at her.

At five o'clock, she jerked awake to the sound of rain hitting the window. Her chest tightness returned along with her labored breathing. She had an awful premonition that something terrible had happened to Marcus. She had to speak to him. Now. He should be home at this hour. It was 4:00 a.m. in New Mexico and although she would probably wake him, she didn't care. She had to know he was safe, plus, she was desperate to get his opinion about the bizarre things that had been happening to her.

Easing out of bed, she tiptoed downstairs, running her hand along the wall to guide her. In the strange house, she was lost and found herself stumbling through the living room before realizing she didn't know where the telephone was located.

Her pulse rate increased. She padded through another room and skipped her fingers along the wall searching for the light plate. Eventually, she found it and flicked the switch, bathing the kitchen in a fluorescent gleam.

It was a nice kitchen. Open, airy, done in blues and yellows, with a wide picture window that looked out over the ocean. She paused a few moments to get her bearings. Cocking her head she listened for sounds of movement upstairs and prayed she hadn't awakened Tyler. She didn't want him involved in this.

A phone was mounted on the wall over the bar. Relief poured through her, and she grasped for the receiver. Sitting down on a bar stool, she punched in the number of her telephone calling card with trembling fingers.

An automated voice came on the line telling her the calling card number was no longer valid. Certain that she had punched the number in wrong, Hannah hung up and tried again.

The same monotone recording greeted her ears.

Damn! Daycon Laboratories issued her calling card and Daycon had probably canceled it the minute she'd left Austin. He had not been idle in the hours she was infirm. She wondered if he could somehow trace her through the card. Terrified at the prospect, she slammed down the phone. She regretted the company phone card, corporate bank account and car they'd leased for her.

Oh, no, what if Daycon had frozen her checking account, as well? A sharp pain rippled through Hannah's chest, then disappeared.

Don't panic, calm down, think. What next?

She couldn't risk dialing direct and having Marcus's phone

number appear on Tyler's telephone bill. She would call collect. Hannah dialed again and gave her name to an automated operator. Nervously she drummed her fingers on the counter.

"Hello," a sleepy male replied.

Relief shot through her, and she unclenched her fists. Marcus was safe.

"Hannah?" he said once the call had been patched through. "Is that you?"

"Listen Marcus, listen to me very carefully—you're in grave danger."

"What's wrong?"

"Something very strange is happening," she whispered. "It's about *Virusall*."

"What's the matter?"

"The drug is amazing. Much more effective than we guessed. It eradicates every virus I've tested it on. HIV, Ebola, hepatitis, influenza, even the common cold."

"You're kidding! That's world-changing news."

"I know, but wait, here's the bad part. There are serious side effects. Everyone with type *O* blood that took the drug during the clinical trials eventually had psychotic breaks. They all became extremely violent."

"But only people with type *O* blood?"

"As far as we know. The effects seem permanent."

"My God, Hannah, that's catastrophic."

"It gets worse."

"How much worse can it get?"

"I went to Daycon with my findings."

"That unscrupulous bastard." There was no love lost between Marcus and Daycon. "What did he do? Try and doctor the clinical trials?"

"He's more unscrupulous than you ever dreamed."

"Tell me."

"I found out he was attempting to sell *Virusall* to overseas terrorists. He wants to create made-to-order assassins." She gripped the receiver hard.

"Did you call the police?"

"I couldn't." She lowered her voice. Paranoia had her thinking Tyler's phone was tapped, even though she knew it wasn't possible. "He has a rogue CIA agent making the contacts for him."

"Hannah!"

"I knew I had to destroy the drug but I also knew I had to find an antidote for those poor test subjects. I packed up a few samples, e-mailed an encrypted version of the formula to you and then I torched Daycon Laboratories to the ground. I'm surprised you didn't hear about it. The fire was all over the news."

"I don't even have a television up here, Hannah, and I haven't checked my e-mail in a few days."

"That's why you're in danger. If Daycon even suspects I sent you the formula…" She let her words trail off. "You've got to download it, put it in a safe place and then eradicate that e-mail."

"I'll take care of it. In the meantime, where are you?"

The tender note of concern in his voice almost had her losing her control. She had to stay calm and not give herself away. While Tyler's phone probably wasn't bugged, Marcus's definitely could be.

"I'm safe for now. It's better if you don't know where I am, but I'll be headed in your direction as soon as I can."

"You sound odd. Is there something else you're not telling me?" he coaxed. Her old friend knew her too well. She was trying to be brave, but it was so tempting to let down her guard just a bit with someone she trusted.

"Daycon's men found me." She gulped, then briefly told him about the accident.

"My God, Hannah, are you okay?"

"Marcus, I'm really scared. Some very bizarre things have been happening to my body." Gingerly, she reached down to rub the leg that had been fractured and then traced her fingers over the right-upper quadrant of her abdomen. "And I think it was because the vials of *Virusall* broke during the accident and burned my skin."

"The drug is toxic?"

"Not exactly."

"What exactly? Talk to me. I want to help."

Deciding to tell him everything, Hannah took a deep breath and related her suspicions that absorbing *Virusall* through her skin had cured her injuries.

"That's amazing," he said.

"But how would it be possible?"

"You said the drug was very unstable and that it did have miraculous healing properties."

"We're talking spontaneous regeneration here, Marcus. It's the stuff of science fiction. And nothing of this magnitude occurred during the clinical trials."

"Did any of the test subjects have *AB* negative blood like you do?"

"No, but would my blood type actually make that big a difference?"

"Look what *Virusall* did to the people with type *O*."

"I can't believe it's simply the drug and my blood type responsible for my healing. There's got to be something more."

Marcus's tone dropped an octave. "I know what it is."

Her heart thundered. She couldn't even believe they were having this conversation. The discussion flew in the face of rational scientific evidence, but she could not deny what was happening to her.

"What?" she whispered, bracing herself for his theory.

"Remember when we were experimenting with radioisotopes last summer?" he said. "And there was a radiation leak at the lab? Daycon hadn't installed the proper safety ventilation and we both got sick."

"But he assured us the exposure was minimal. We were even tested for chromosomal changes and we came up clean."

"And you believed him? You've already learned how ruthless he is. The man would lie about anything to serve his own nefarious purposes."

Hannah sucked in air as the reality of the situation hit her. Inexplicable as it seemed, with the triple combination of her rare blood type, the topical absorption of *Virusall* and her recent exposure to radiation, she'd become her own human guinea pig.

While the womanly part of her was horrified at the realization, the clinician in her recognized what an amazing opportunity she'd been given.

"But, Marcus, what does it all mean?" she cried.

And that was when the line went dead.

Chapter 4

Tyler couldn't sleep.

No matter how hard he tried to quiet his turbulent thoughts, his mind stayed hitched on that fascinating woman sleeping in his guest bedroom right down the hall. It had been an eternity since anyone had entranced him, much less set his soul ablaze.

And he was scared spitless.

He recalled the way her skin had felt beneath his fingers when he had examined her—smooth, cool, creamy. He remembered the way her chest rose and fell with rapid breaths as he had placed his stethoscope above her breasts. He recollected the manner in which she had peeped surreptitiously up at him from behind those long, pale eyelashes.

He thought of the way she'd looked swaddled in his T-shirt that was five sizes too big for her. Her eyes wide and round as she'd studied him. Her blond hair floated softly about her slender shoulders. Her feet were bare, her toes appearing childishly innocent in their unpainted state. She'd looked china-doll fragile, except for the hard set of her determined chin.

Who was this mysterious Jane Doe? More important, why was he so drawn to her? And most interesting of all, how could he explain her instantaneous recovery from life-threatening injuries? Concern for her welled up in him from as far south as his feet and throbbed through his chest.

How had she managed to resurrect his emotions so completely in such a short time? How did he fight these dangerous feelings while at the same time help her?

He felt confused, baffled by both his attraction and her extraordinary afflictions. He found himself caught up in backwash he did not understand, unable to solve his dilemma but equally unable to retreat. Like it or not, he was caught up like a fish in a net. He was involved.

High time you got truly involved with something again, his conscience gloated.

But he feared he was not up to the challenge. It had been a long time since he'd put himself out for another human being and he wasn't so sure he could handle the implications. What had he gotten himself into?

She was an enigma, a riddle, a paradox that compelled him despite his reservations. If only she could remember something about herself. If only he knew what chemicals she had been carrying with her and for what purpose. If only he could explain this inexplicable pull toward her.

Every time he closed his eyes, he saw her face—those vulnerable lips, those wide blue eyes, that mass of golden hair.

After wrestling with the covers for over an hour, Tyler switched on a small bedside lamp, slung his legs over the side and browsed through the books mounted on the shelf over the headboard.

There weren't many medical books here. Yvette had been loath for him to work at the beach, so most of the volumes were either basic textbooks or short paperbacks on first aid. Nothing about chemicals and certainly nothing about spontaneous healings. Then one title jumped out at him, squeezing off his airway.

Healing Your Cancer From Within.

After all these years, any reminder of Yvette still had the power to knock the wind from his lungs. She had been so young, so pretty and full of life, looking forward to conceiving their first baby. It had been during a routine visit to the ob-gyn, in preparation for getting pregnant, that the doctor had discovered she had leukemia. But it had been over four months before she had broken the bad news to him.

Tyler fisted his hand as the familiar anger rocked back into his life. His wife had cheated him of precious moments, all because she hadn't wanted to worry him while he was finishing his surgical residency.

The memory of that awful day when she finally told him the truth was burned into his subconscious. Metastasis. To her lungs and liver. Prognosis poor. Six months to live. With chemo. Four months had already passed and she had decided on her own not to have chemotherapy. Single-handedly she had made the choice without him.

There would be no babies. They would not grow old together.

Shocked, Tyler had slumped into denial. He simply could not bring himself to accept the cruel diagnosis. The doctors had to be wrong. This could not be happening. Not to his young, beautiful, vibrant wife. She could beat it. She would live.

Yvette had handled the news with her usual quiet calm. She had always been spiritual and she turned deeper into her religion. Buying books such as this one that promised if you just prayed hard enough God would heal you.

Rubbish. Tyler jerked the book from the shelf and flung it across the room. It struck the wall with a resounding whack.

He'd lost whatever naive beliefs he'd ever held about miracles.

He was still angry, still very guilty. He should have detected her cancer himself. But no, he had been as useless as a third thumb, and even after the diagnosis he had been unable to do anything but sit idly by and watch her die. There was no greater torture for a physician. Because of his denial, he had never said the things that needed to be said, but he had brought her to the beach in the end, as she had wished.

It was hard for Tyler to come back here. He associated the beach house with her death and could not say why he hadn't sold the place years ago.

It had been too late to save his wife. Maybe he wasn't too late to save Jane Doe. Perhaps that was why fate had deposited her in his emergency room. He was a doctor, dammit. He should be able to save someone.

It frustrated him that the hospital laboratory had been unable to identify the toxic chemicals in Jane Doe's car. Running his hands through his hair, Tyler paced. Over and over he tried to rationalize what he had seen this past evening. How one minute Jane had been broken and bleeding, hovering on the verge of death and later that night she had been in his car wolfing down a hamburger, her battered body completely healed.

There had to be a logical, rational explanation, and he would find it if he just looked long enough.

Then he remembered the symptoms she'd suffered when they were walking on the beach. Obviously, she wasn't completely healed. And what about those lab reports? The ones that indicated she might have cancer?

The conundrum intrigued him almost as much as the lady herself. He had the strangest feeling she was faking her amnesia. But why? What was she hiding from him? Was she in trouble with the law? And how could he get her to trust him enough to give him the answer? She was a very private person and by her own admission, distrustful. Her remoteness evident in the way she held herself aloof, a little shy, as if she wasn't quite sure how to react to people.

What was he going to do with her? What if her amnesia was real? He should report her case to the police but Tyler knew he wasn't going to do that.

An odd excitement raced through him. A sensation of aliveness he hadn't felt since Yvette's death. If he could find out how Jane Doe had been healed, he might be able to heal others in the same manner. The possibilities were mind-boggling and flew in the face of all rational thought, but Tyler knew something miraculous had happened and he intended to find out exactly what it was.

Fingers trembling, Hannah called an operator and had her redial Marcus' telephone number. She held her breath. It rang.

Once. Twice. Thrice. Four times.

"I'm sorry, ma'am," the operator interrupted, "no one seems to be answering."

"Please, could you let it ring longer? My friend was just there. We were cut off."

The operator sighed as if Hannah had asked for the key to Fort Knox. "All right."

More empty rings.

"Your party is simply not picking up."

"Thank you." Hannah cradled the receiver and sank against the wall.

What had happened to Marcus? Why had the line gone suddenly dead and why hadn't he answered when she called back? Her imagination ran rampant as she imagined Daycon or one of his hired henchmen standing in Marcus's bedroom with a gun pressed to his temple, making all kinds of awful threats. She shuddered. By calling him, had she inadvertently placed Marcus in mortal danger?

"What's going on?"

Hannah jumped and clutched a hand to her chest. She had been so concerned about Marcus's welfare that she hadn't heard Tyler come into the room.

His dark eyes were disconcertingly intense, as if he knew exactly what she was hiding. Her stomach churned and for a moment she thought she might be sick.

"I…er…" she stammered, and gestured helplessly. She couldn't explain anything to him without drawing him deeper into her problems. He was a nice man and didn't deserve to be mixed up in this mess. "Did I wake you? I'm sorry."

"Is there something you need to tell me?"

"No," she whispered softly, surprised by the strange look in his deep chocolate eyes.

His gaze landed on hers. Hannah caught her breath. Try as she might, she couldn't look away. He seemed intent on searching her soul, on getting answers to his questions.

"If you tell me the truth maybe I can help you."

"Truth?"

"About those chemicals in your car."

"I told you before that I don't know anything about any chemicals." She hated lying to him, but it was for his own safety.

"Jane, or whatever your name is, whether you realize it or not, you're in serious trouble." His tone of voice suggested he was saddened by her response and disappointed in her.

Hannah's eyes widened. She hated to think that she had displeased him. Perspiration beaded on her upper lip despite the chill in the room. How did he know she was in trouble?

"Come here." He extended his arms to her. "You look as if you could use a hug."

"I'm all right." Hannah shook her head and wrapped her arms around her chest. She wanted to hug him and yet she was afraid. Too many years of keeping her distance from people had held her in reserve.

Plus, she was afraid that if she ever let down her guard, even just a little bit, she would totally unravel and never be able to put herself back together again.

"Are you sure?" His eyes softened. "I've got broad shoulders just perfect for crying on." There was such self-assurance in his voice. He had no clue that crying on his shoulders would not fix anything. He was a doctor, accustomed to performing miracles. How could he know her problems were far beyond his expertise?

She managed to return his smile in spite of her escalating anxiety. How easy it would be to step into his welcoming embrace, and yet how utterly hard. She fought against the attraction urging her to give in and accept his comfort. "I appreciate the offer."

"It's an open invitation." He dropped his arms to his side. "What are you doing up this early? Did you need something?"

"I couldn't sleep."

"Would you like a sleeping pill?"

"No!" The last thing she needed was to be knocked out. Despite the exhaustion permeating her body, she must remain alert.

"Okay. It's probably better to avoid drugs anyway. There's no telling how they might react with those chemicals you came into contact with." His brow knit with concern.

"Thank you for understanding."

"Listen, I have surgery at seven-thirty this morning, so I have to head back to Houston. I'm sorry, there's no food in the house but there's a convenience store at the end of the block that should be open in a hour. Do you think you can walk that far?"

She nodded.

"I'll leave you some cash." He picked up his wallet off the bar and pulled out three twenty-dollar bills and laid them on the counter. "Will you be all right here alone?"

"Yes."

"Sleep, read, rest. Make yourself at home. I should be back by three-thirty since I'm not on call today."

"Thank you so very much. I'll pay you back whenever I can. I promise."

"I'm not worried about it and if you need something else to wear later on, check out the closet in my bedroom. There're some clothes that used to belong to my wife and you're just about her size."

"You're very generous."

Tyler looked deeply into her eyes. "You will be here when I get back." It was a statement, not a question.

"I can't make any promises," she admitted.

"Here's my beeper number." He scrawled the number on a notepad hanging by the telephone. "Page me if you need me."

Unexpected tears misted her eyes. Why was he being so nice to her? She was nothing to him. An odd stranger who had materialized in his emergency room. She didn't know how to deal with kindness. She wasn't used to such an intimate connection with others.

"You're feeling a little emotional," he said as if he could read her thoughts. "It's not surprising, given the circumstances. Come." He held out his arm. "Let me put you back into bed."

Uncertain, she hung back, but Dr. Fresno was not the type to take her hesitation for an answer. Smoothly, he reached over and slipped his hand into hers.

His touch instantly calmed her in a way that confused Hannah. Why should she be so reassured by a stranger? Especially when there was nothing he could really do to help her. And yet she felt safer with him than she ever had with anyone, including her own parents.

What was wrong with her? Why was she so hungry to trust this man?

"Come," he coaxed, drawing her upstairs beside him and draping his free arm around her shoulder.

He was good at handling people. But of course, he was a medical doctor who had been taught the importance of therapeutic touch. She had the strongest urge to lean into his body and absorb his warmth, but she wasn't accustomed to such intimacies with a total stranger, nor was she accustomed to following her emotions.

Instead, she did what came naturally. She kept her shoulders stiff and her attention diverted from the sensation of his warm breath tickling the nape of her neck.

"Here we are," Tyler said gently, leading her into the guest bedroom. "Back to bed."

Hannah's heart did a strange little skip. She couldn't stop looking at him. She admired his strong jaw, the curve of his firm chin, the flat planes of his cheeks. She took a curious delight in the way his hair curled along his collar. She yearned to run her fingers along his neck and knead those corded muscles.

What she wanted was for Dr. Fresno to make love to her. She wanted him to kiss her. She ached to feel his hands at her back, pulling her close, locking her to him. She longed to rip off his pajamas and share with him the hottest, most dynamic sexual passion she'd never had the pleasure to experience.

But were her feelings really based on pure sexual need, as she told herself they were, or was it something frighteningly more? Was she really just seeking to assuage her fear and loneliness through bodily contact?

Earth to Hannah, earth to Hannah. This man is not a potential lover.

He dropped his hand and sadness enveloped her. She did not want him to let go. Where were these feelings coming from? Why the attraction? Was it because he played the knight in shining armor so well? If the truth be told, she was a sucker for Prince Charming.

"Hop in." He turned back the covers and patted the mattress.

Obeying, she slid between the sheets and resisted the urge to pull him down beside her.

"That's right." He raised the covers up to her chin. "There. Snug as a bug in a rug."

Something tore loose inside Hannah. Something she could not identify. She wanted to laugh; she wanted to cry.

"Get some shut-eye." Then he leaned over and ever so lightly kissed her forehead.

Sudden joy rushed through her as she realized what had just happened. Tyler had tucked her into bed. She had never been tucked in. When she was a child she got herself ready for bed and if she was lucky her parents would look up from their research to mutter good-night. There had been no nightly rituals involving bedtime stories or prayers or lullabies.

At last, she was being tucked in like a normal girl. That's all she had ever wanted. To be normal. But her one hundred and sixty IQ and her parents' profession had prohibited any semblance of normalcy in her life. There'd been no slumber parties with friends. Indeed, there'd been precious few friends. No trips to amusement parks or the circus or the Ice Capades.

It wasn't that her parents hadn't loved her, Hannah knew that, in their peculiar way, they had cared. They simply hadn't known how to show affection and they had passed their cold heritage down to her. She had been so isolated from her feelings for so long that the simple act of Tyler tucking her into bed brought forth a string of unknown emotions. Emotions that scared as much as they excited.

She felt as if she were living a weird dream and she worried about the side effects of her exposure to *Virusall*. It hadn't been thoroughly tested. She could not know all the implications, ramifications or adverse reactions associated with the drug. She certainly hadn't expected it to knit her fractured bone in less than an hour. That was something she still hadn't come to terms with, even in the face of Marcus's theory.

This whole thing was uncanny. How could she be sad one minute and euphoric the next? She had no explanation, but surely it had something to do with her exposure to the drug, not her exposure to Dr. Fresno.

Then Tyler was gone, shutting the door softly behind him and leaving Hannah lost. Stacking her hands beneath her cheek, she stared at the pale gray light creeping around the window. Her whole world was changing and she didn't know how to get it back in order.

Nothing would ever be the same again. Absolutely nothing.

Tyler barely made it to the hospital in time to scrub for the scheduled seven-thirty colectomy. While he performed his job with his usual precision and skill, he couldn't stop his thoughts from occasionally wandering to Jane Doe.

He thought of how his desire for her had almost gotten the better of him and it had been all he could do to keep from crawling into that twin guest bed with her. He should never have brought her to the beach house. He'd been recklessly stupid, impossibly insane. He should have just walked away from her. So what if she looked like Yvette. So what if the memory of his wife had prompted him to offer her sanctuary. It had been a very bad decision.

Because he could not stop worrying about her.

He had wanted to drop by the lab for the results of the additional tests he had performed on her the night before, but there simply hadn't been time. After the colectomy came a 10:00 a.m. gall bladder and following that, a hernia repair. It was after one o'clock before he was able to grab a banana and yogurt from the cafeteria for lunch. Then, he stopped off to check on the paramedics that had been admitted the night before.

The men had been dismissed, the floor nurse on duty told him. Both claiming they had never felt so good. Tyler had reviewed their charts, checking their labs. Like Hannah's, their white blood cell count had been low, their platelets high upon admission, but the repeat study done that morning had shown their levels had returned to normal. Puzzling over this, but more optimistic about Hannah's prognosis, Tyler made his way to the lab.

"Afternoon, Danny," he greeted the lab technician.

"And good day it is to you, Doctor Fresno." Danny peered up at him from his microscope. "How might I help you?"

"Remember those chemicals I had you test for me yesterday?"

"From the Jane Doe MVA."

"That's right. Did you have any luck identifying the substance?"

A strange expression passed over Danny's ruddy features. "Some, but not a complete analysis."

"What have you got?"

"Hold on, let me get the results for you." Danny disappeared into the computer room and returned quickly with a computer read-out.

"There's nothing toxic here." Tyler frowned. What had he been hoping for? Some unknown chemical that could have explained Jane's healing?

"Without a bigger sampling we may never known what was in those vials. Too bad she couldn't tell us anything specific."

Tyler sighed.

"Did you fill out an incident report on that thumb?" Danny asked, reminding Tyler that he'd stuck himself with a syringe of Jane's blood.

"No. I'll do it later."

"Don't wait too long," Danny warned. "I don't like the looks of things."

"Don't worry."

"I heard your Jane Doe left the hospital against medical advice last night. Is that true?"

"Yes." Tyler could not say more. For both professional and personal reasons he didn't want anyone at the hospital knowing he was harboring her at his beach house.

Danny clicked his tongue. "That's too bad."

"Why do you say that?"

Danny's bright blue eyes met Tyler's. "You didn't get my message? I called and left it on your machine."

"I'm sorry. I didn't check my messages this morning." He didn't want to admit he hadn't been at his Houston residence. "What was it concerning?"

"That second sampling of blood you had me run on Jane Doe."

"What did you find?" Tyler wadded his hand into a fist. He had a hard, sinking feeling in the pit of his stomach, an ominous sense of déjà vu, but he did not know why. The paramedics' lab results had improved; Hannah's should have, too. "Did her levels correct?"

"No." Danny dropped his gaze. "Not only were her other values unchanged but her hemoglobin and hematocrit had dropped, too."

He wasn't sure he wanted to hear what Danny had to say, but no good came of sticking one's head in the sand. Yvette's death had taught him that. He couldn't help Jane if he wasn't armed with all the details.

"I repeated the test four times, just to make sure."

Tyler shoved a hand through his hair. This didn't make sense. Why had her hemoglobin and hematocrit dropped dramatically? Was she bleeding internally? He swallowed. Had he made a grievous error in taking her from the hospital last night?

The beeper at Tyler's waistband went off. Distracted, he glanced down to see the phone number for the chief of surgery, Michael Ledbetter. Irritated, Tyler switched the beeper off. What now? He didn't have time for Ledbetter. Jane Doe was very sick and he needed to get her back to the hospital ASAP.

"Borrow your phone?" he asked Danny.

The man handed him the receiver.

"Fresno here," he said, when Ledbetter answered.

"Ah yes, Tyler. Could I see you in my office?"

"I was just going off duty."

"I won't keep you long," Ledbetter assured him.

"Can't it wait until Monday?"

"I'm afraid not. You see, there's an angry police officer pacing my carpet and it's your name he's brandishing in unsavory terms."

"I'll be right there," Tyler said through clenched teeth, frustrated that it was going to be just that much longer before he got back to Jane at the beach house.

After Tyler had left for the hospital, Hannah napped fitfully for a few hours, but her dreams had been so plagued with violence and nasty visions of the corpulent Lionel Daycon, she'd jerked awake a little after nine o'clock, achy and hungry.

She had tried three more times to call Marcus but had never received an answer. Her anxiety escalated. What should she do now? Should she try to get her hands on a car and head for Taos? But that scenario worried her, too. What if Daycon was waiting in ambush for her to appear at Marcus's place? But if she continued to stay here, she was putting Tyler at risk. Neither alternative seemed appealing. For the moment, circumstances answered the question. She had no money, no ID and no way off the island. At least, not until Tyler returned.

She tried to refuse the feelings that stirred in her every time she thought about him, but she couldn't quite still the rush of her breath. She couldn't stop her heart from thudding just a little bit faster when she remembered how warm and comforting his hand had felt in hers. No matter how she tried, she could not vanquish this sweet, miserable urge to gaze into his deep brown eyes again and simply drown there.

Keep your mind busy. Find something to do.

Following that edict, Hannah had showered and dressed in blue jeans and a formfitting white cashmere cardigan she had found in a chest of drawers in Tyler's room. He had been right. She and his late wife were exactly the same size.

She walked to the convenience store on the corner, taking in the crisp morning breeze and inhaling the salt air. Seagulls circled and cawed overhead. There hadn't been many people on the beach, nor many cars on the street.

With the money Tyler had given her, she bought not only cereal, tea, coffee, pastries and milk for breakfast, but provisions for dinner, as well. Dried spaghetti, canned marinara sauce, French bread, prepackaged salad. She was optimistic, planning for the evening meal. She shouldn't be thinking about food and cooking dinner but, truthfully, it was a thankful respite from fretting about Daycon and *Virusall*. If she tried really hard, she could almost pretend she was a normal person, engaging in normal activities.

"Yoo-hoo." A feminine voice with a distinctive purr reached

Hannah's ears while she sat at the breakfast table, glancing out the wide picture-window at the ocean beyond. "Tyler?"

Footsteps echoed on the stairs. Seconds later, a slender, dark-haired woman wearing too much makeup appeared on the landing.

The woman spied Hannah through the window and stopped short. Her mouth dropped open. "Yvette?" she whispered, but then she shook her head and quickly recovered from her surprise and waved a hand.

Getting to her feet, Hannah moved to open the door. "May I help you?"

"Oh…" The woman, who was about five years older than Hannah and wore rings on every finger, hesitated a moment before asking, "Do you have any coffee?"

"Just instant."

"That'll do. As long as it isn't decaf."

"It's regular."

"Thank God. You're a lifesaver." The woman was dressed in black skintight leggings and a long orange sweater that suited her dramatic coloring.

Hannah wasn't good in social situations or at making idle chit-chat but she supposed the woman was waiting to be invited inside. Marshaling her courage, she said, "Won't you come in?"

"Thanks. By the way, my name's Margie." The woman extended a many-jeweled hand. "Margie Price."

"Jane," she said using the name the hospital had given her and briefly touching Margie's cold palm.

Her hand melded with the woman's. Hannah experienced an odd swirling sensation in her palm that grew to encompass her entire arm.

"Goodness." Margie's eyes widened and a startled expression crossed her face. "You're so warm. Almost electric."

"I've had my hands in my pockets," Hannah replied quickly pulling her hand away and wondering why she felt compelled to lie.

"That's the oddest thing," Margie said, raising a hand to massage her long neck.

"What?" Hannah experienced something rather unsettling

herself: Her fingers tingled from touching Margie and she momentarily fought a wave of dizziness. She grasped the kitchen counter and the sensation passed as quickly as it had come.

"The crick in my neck just disappeared. I passed out on the couch and when I woke this morning it felt like I'd slept on a coat hanger. Anyway, I was groping around for my coffee and when I discovered I'd run out, I recalled seeing Tyler's light on late last night. So I trotted over, counting on him to have some java stashed away somewhere."

What she hadn't been counting on, Hannah realized, was finding another woman in Tyler's beach house.

"Where is he, by the way?" Margie craned her now-crickless neck and peered down the hallway.

"He's at the hospital." Hannah put a cup of water to heat in the microwave

"And you're here?"

"Yes."

"I didn't realize Tyler was seeing anyone." Margie plopped down at the kitchen table. "We're pretty good friends. He tells me almost everything. And he's never mentioned you."

"He told me he hasn't been to the beach house since summer," Hannah couldn't resist saying and feeling a bit catty for gloating. "I guess you don't get to see him much."

"Oh, I live in Houston, too. On the same block as Tyler, in fact." Margie arched a well-plucked eyebrow. "I see him nearly every day."

Touché. So much for her pathetic attempt at one-upmanship. She was new to jealousy.

Hannah spooned coffee crystals into the heated water and stirred vigorously before passing the mug to Margie. She wished the woman would leave, but then an unexpected thought occurred to her. If Margie Price knew Tyler as well as she claimed perhaps Hannah could tempt her into gossiping about him a little. She was dying to know more about the handsome doctor who had taken it upon himself to offer her shelter during her own personal storm.

"Oh," Margie exclaimed. "You've got Danish. Do you mind

if I have one? Although heaven knows it will doom me to an extra hour on the treadmill."

"Help yourself."

Margie sipped her coffee and happily chewed a pastry while Hannah made herself a cup of tea.

"What's this?" Margie asked, picking up a sheet of paper filled with mathematical equations. Hannah had been trying to replicate the complex formula for *Virusall* from memory and was getting absolutely nowhere. Margie wrinkled her nose. "Ugh. Looks like chemistry."

"It is." Hannah took the paper from Margie, folded it carefully and stuck it in her back pocket.

"What are you? A chemist?"

"Something like that."

"You're a tea drinker, huh?" Margie said, nodding at Hannah's cup. "Just like Yvette."

"Yvette?"

"Don't tell me Tyler hasn't told you about her?" Margie clicked her tongue. "Isn't that just like a man?"

"Who's Yvette?"

"His wife." Margie lowered her voice. "She died of cancer. She was only twenty-five and her death just about killed him. It's been six years and he hasn't gotten over her."

"He must have loved her very much," Hannah said, her mouth suddenly so dry her tongue stuck to her palate.

"Yes."

What would it feel like to be so loved that a man grieved over you for six long years? Whether she had known it or not, Yvette Fresno had been a very lucky woman. And Tyler. What a tragically romantic man.

An edgy panic pushed against her rib cage. How could she be falling for him at the most inopportune time of her life? It was not sensible or smart or safe, but the more she learned about Tyler, the more she liked and respected him.

"You look like her, you know," Margie said. "I suppose that's the attraction."

"Who? Yvette?"

"Yes. Blond. Petite. Curvy." Margie sighed. "You know, I always hoped I'd have a chance with Tyler but no matter how hard I try, I'm tall and flat-chested and brunette."

Hannah stared at her hands. Was it true? Was Tyler projecting his feelings for his dead wife onto her? Was that the reason he had been so eager to help her? It made perfect sense. Unfortunately, it didn't relieve her anxieties.

"I don't mean to be rude," she said, "but I've got a few phone calls to make." Hannah got to her feet. "If you don't mind."

"Oh, sure." Margie got up, not the least bit offended at being tossed out on her ear. Hannah wished she could be so breezy and easygoing. "Well, I'm heading back to the city this afternoon so, if I don't see you again, take care."

"It's been nice meeting you." Hannah smiled tightly.

"Thanks for the coffee." Margie headed for the door but then stopped and turned. "And good luck with Tyler. That man deserves someone to love. Even if it isn't me."

Chapter 5

Hurry up, let's get this over with, I've got to get back to Jane.
Tyler sat in Michael Ledbetter's office watching while the police officer he had spoken to the evening before paced.

"So you say you have absolutely no idea where this Jane Doe might be?"

"None."

He didn't like lying, especially to an officer of the law, but Tyler wasn't going to give away Jane's whereabouts. She needed protection and right now it seemed he was the only one who could give it to her.

"And you'd never seen her before last night?"

"No." At least that was true.

"Yet you agreed to pay her hospital bill. Why?"

Tyler shrugged. "She couldn't remember her name. She had no money, and didn't know if she had any insurance. I volunteered to vouch for her bill until she could regain her memory and take care of it herself."

"Have you ever paid a patient's bill before?" Officer Blankenship narrowed his eyes and placed an oversized hand on the butt of his gun. There was no mistaking he meant to intimidate.

Tyler shifted uncomfortably in his seat. "No."

"Why her?"

"I hope you're not suggesting something unethical." Tyler bristled.

Michael Ledbetter made a calming motion with his hands. "Of course Officer Blankenship isn't suggesting that."

He had overreacted. Why? Perhaps because he felt that his attraction to Jane Doe was unethical? "I felt sorry for her."

"You're absolutely sure you had no idea that she was planning to leave the hospital against medical advice?" Blankenship jotted something in his notebook.

Tyler looked to Michael Ledbetter. "You better tell me what this is all about."

"We ran the plates on Jane Doe's car," Blankenship replied.

"And?"

"The vehicle is registered to Daycon Laboratories in Austin. Ever heard of them?"

"Sure, they're the largest privately owned pharmaceutical company in the country," Tyler said.

"The car she was driving was reported stolen two days ago. Right after someone set fire to the lab."

"Which means?"

"We think that someone was your Jane Doe."

"Oh." Tyler stared at Blankenship. Was he saying Jane was an arsonist and a thief?

"So, if you have any idea at all where she might be…" Blankenship let his words trail off.

Tyler shook his head.

"All right then. Sorry to take up your time."

"No problem." Tyler forced a smile.

"You'll call me if you happen to hear from her," Blankenship said it as a statement, not an option, and handed Tyler his card.

"I won't be hearing from her."

"But just in case," Blankenship insisted.

"Sure." He could feel his collar dampen with perspiration.

"Thank you." Blankenship nodded at Tyler and Michael Ledbetter and then left.

Tyler started to get up.

"Just a minute." Ledbetter raised a hand.

What now, for crying out loud! If he didn't get out of here, get back to Jane and find out just what the hell was going on with her, he would explode.

"What is it, Mike?" Tyler struggled to keep the edginess from his voice.

"The E.R. security guard tells me he saw you leave the hospital parking lot last night with an unknown female in your car."

Tyler took a deep breath. God bless the hospital grapevine. "Listen, Michael."

Ledbetter raised his hands. "Don't tell me, I don't want to know. You're a great surgeon, Tyler, and you've never been one to get overly involved with your patients. That's a good sign. I don't want to hear that you've changed on me now."

"It's not what you think." Great, it sounded as if Ledbetter believed he was having an affair with Jane.

The chief of surgery placed an index finger to his lips. "All I'm saying is be careful. Hospitals are small places. Word gets around. Please, whatever you're up to, be discreet. I'd hate to see you jeopardize your standing in our community for some momentary indiscretion." Ledbetter tried to smile but it came across as a grimace. "You are up for my job when I take the executive administrator's position next year. I'd rather not see Jim Nesbitt get the job over you. He hasn't been here as long, nor is he as gifted a surgeon. But the right candidate must have an impeccable reputation."

You two-faced son of a bitch. You were the one who urged me to put in my bid for chief of surgery.

"Is this a threat, Michael?" Tyler asked, a cold chill running through him. His boss was using this incident with Jane Doe as a chance to play politics. "Because I don't like to be threatened."

"Oh, no," Ledbetter quickly backpeddled. "Not at all. Let's call it a warning. As long as you continue business as usual and don't do anything out of the ordinary, such as harboring a dangerous pyromaniac who's wanted by the police, then there shouldn't be any problems. Are we straight on this?"

"Perfectly." Tyler said through clenched teeth, and then stalked out of Ledbetter's office with one thing on his mind. Jane Doe.

On the drive to the island a thousand awful images flashed before his mind's eye. He had found himself exceeding the speed limit, making the fifty-mile journey in just over thirty minutes, his thoughts occupied with what Danny O'Brien and Officer Blankenship had told him about Jane.

Heart knocking like an engine gone bad, Tyler raced up the steps to the beach house, worried what he would find waiting for him. No matter how robust Jane had appeared that morning, she was very ill. Her low hemoglobin and hematocrit levels in themselves were cause for concern, not to mention her abnormal platelets and white blood cell count.

His gut torqued. He was calling her name before he even pushed the back door open. "Jane!"

"Hi." She stood at the kitchen stove stirring a pot of something that smelled delicious. The shy smile on her face took him completely by surprise.

"Hi," he answered, caught off guard and feeling a little silly for having worried so strenuously.

"I don't usually cook but I think this tastes pretty good. Of course, it's just canned sauce but I spiced it up a bit with chopped onions and diced garlic. Would you like a taste?" She held out a wooden spoon laden with spaghetti sauce.

Tyler stared, unable to believe what he was seeing. She appeared the picture of health, her cheeks rosy, her blue eyes shining brightly. Relief surged through him. "You're all right."

"Why, yes—why wouldn't I be?"

"I don't… I thought… I was afraid." His knees trembled. He sank into a chair.

"You look as if you've seen a ghost."

Her hair was feathered about her face in an unruly tangle that flattered her high cheekbones. She had on a pair of Yvette's faded blue jeans that cupped her bottom in an enticing manner and caused his heart to flutter. She wore a frilly apron knotted around her narrow waist and filled out a fuzzy white sweater that molded provocatively over her breasts.

Her feet were bare. The sight of those tiny naked toes did unexpected things to him. Tyler was so thankful at finding her healthy that he had a strong urge to get up, cross the room and kiss her.

Urges like that are what's got Ledbetter issuing threats and Officer Blankenship eyeing you with suspicion.

"We've got to talk," he told her.

"Yes." She nodded and set the wooden spoon on the counter. She turned off the flame under the spaghetti sauce. "I've got a huge favor to ask."

"You don't understand. Please, sit down." Tyler pulled out a chair for her.

She removed the apron and draped it over the back of the chair before seating herself beside him. She turned her eyes his way, giving him her rapt attention and he had the overwhelming urge to kiss her and run his hands up underneath her soft, fuzzy sweater. Purposefully, he ignored the high-voltage spark of energy surging between them. He would not give in to his baser instincts. No matter how much he might want her.

"A police officer was at the hospital this afternoon asking about you," he said.

"Oh?" She tried to appear nonchalant but he noticed her hands were shaking.

"They ran the plates on your car. Turns out it belongs to Daycon Laboratories."

"Does it?" She wouldn't look him in the face. Bad sign. Maybe she *had* torched the place.

"Uh-huh. And strangely enough there was also an arson fire at Daycon labs."

"Really?" She didn't act surprised.

"There's more."

She laughed uneasily. "The suspense is scaring me. Just come out and say it."

"I got the results back on the last round of blood tests we drew on you last night." He fisted his hands. He wanted to pummel something. Wanted to curse the unfairness of life. Instead, he bit down hard on the inside of his cheek to stay his anger. She would need him to be calm and in control of his emotions.

"And?"

He reached across the table and lightly touched her hand. The contact produced a curious warmth that grabbed at his belly. Tyler inhaled sharply. "Your hemoglobin and hematocrit levels are very low. You might even need a blood transfusion. You have to go back to the hospital. Right away."

"I can't."

"Because the police are looking for you?"

She said nothing.

"Jane, this is serious business. You have no choice."

"There's always a choice."

"I can't stand by and watch you do yourself in." He gritted his teeth. Didn't she understand? It was all he could do not to take her by her sweet shoulders and shake some sense into her. He was that concerned.

"Couldn't I just take some iron pills or something?"

He removed a pill bottle from his jacket pocket and set it on the table. "I assumed you would say that, but the iron tablets might not be enough. It takes a while to start reproducing new red blood cells. Besides, I need to find out why your blood values keep dropping."

"But I feel great. So good in fact I took a two-hour walk along the beach this afternoon." She ran a hand through her hair and he couldn't help noticing how the lush strands tumbled about her shoulders in sexy disarray. She looked positively luminous.

Tyler shook his head. "Something very bizarre is going on here and as your doctor I strongly urge you to admit yourself into the hospital so you can be closely monitored. Please. Do it for me."

"You can't cure me," she said. "Going to the hospital is a waste of time."

"I think you'd better tell me what you're hiding. You don't really have amnesia, do you?"

"No," she admitted, lowering her gaze to the floor and slipping her hand from under his.

"You owe me an explanation," he demanded.

He almost lost the battle and kissed her. Rough and hard and punishing. Anything to get through to her. He even leaned close and lowered his head, but somehow, he managed to stop himself just short of his intended target. Her lush beautiful mouth. Sweat beaded above his upper lip. He felt his control slip further and further away.

"I can't say anything."

"Why not?"

"It's too complicated."

"Can you at least tell me your real name?" he growled. Her distrust was twisting him inside out. Couldn't she see that?

For the longest moment, she didn't answer. Then, at last, she said, "I suppose it won't hurt. My given name is Hannah."

"Hannah." He tried it on his tongue and liked it. Old fashioned, but feminine. "No last name?"

"Listen." She met his gaze and ignored his question. "You're in over your head."

"Yes, I am in over my head." His tone was angry but he wasn't mad at her. He was frustrated by her evasiveness and her refusal to trust him. Hadn't he proved himself to her by offering her shelter, by not turning her in to the police?

"I'm bewildered and curious by both your symptoms and the things the police had to say about you. What's going on?"

"I'm trying to protect you."

"Protect me from what?" Agitated, he shifted in his chair. He didn't appreciate being kept in the dark. How could he help her if he didn't know what was going on?

"There are people who wish me harm. That's what I wanted to talk to you about."

"Who are these people?"

Was she involved with gangsters? But what would that have to do with her horrific lab values and the chemicals in her car? Nothing made sense and nothing was following his expectations. He had entered a whole new dimension and he didn't know how to navigate this unknown territory, but his medical training urged him to investigate and get to the bottom of her mystery.

"I can't tell you."

"Why don't you just go to the police?"

She ran a hand through her hair. Tyler watched the gesture, felt his heart plunge. Suddenly, she looked weary. He wanted to wave a magic wand and make everything perfect for her.

"They wouldn't believe me. You told me yourself they think I started a fire and stole a company vehicle. That's why I need to borrow your car. I can't say for how long, but I've got to leave the state as soon as possible. Please?"

"It's my professional opinion you need to be hospitalized."

"Don't speak to me as a doctor. Speak to me as a man," she beseeched.

Nothing else she could have said would have worked like that statement did. Because all he'd wanted from the time he'd first met her was for her to see him as a man. He studied her face. Took in her flawless skin, the shape of her enticing lips, the proud tilt of her nose.

"Where do you need to go?" he asked, knowing he was probably making a grave mistake, but unable to give her any other answer except the one she needed to hear. Once he'd committed himself to traveling down this road with her, he knew there would be no U-turning when things got hairy. He had to prove to her she could trust somebody in this world.

"New Mexico." She exhaled her relief.

"Since you refuse to check yourself into the hospital, I'll take you there. It's dangerous for you to be alone. At least with me along I can keep an eye on your symptoms and be your bodyguard."

"You're a doctor. You've got responsibilities, patients who are counting on you. Besides, I simply can't allow you to put yourself in danger for me."

Don't you understand? I want to go with you. I need to take care of you. For my sake as much as yours. "Hannah, whatever is happening to you is beyond the realm of medical science. How did your broken bone heal last night? And please don't tell me I looked at the wrong X ray. How did your ruptured spleen repair itself? How did those chemical burns vanish? How can you be so damned healthy and yet so sick at the same time? I'm not a fool. Just exactly what was in those vials?"

"You wouldn't understand."

"Then help me to understand."

"If I tell you, they'll kill you, too."

"Who are *they*?"

She brought her hands to her face. "Please, don't ask."

Tyler immediately felt contrite for browbeating her and raised his palms in a gesture of defeat. "Okay, I'm sorry. Have your secrets. It's just damned hard for me to sit here knowing you're ill and not being able to do anything about it."

"I'm not your responsibility. You don't even know me. Why do you care?"

"Because I'm a doctor. I'm supposed to heal. It's my job. And…"

"And?" she repeated.

"I care what happens to you," he said gruffly. *And I want to make love to you so badly I can taste it.*

This was seriously twisted. He should back out, mind his own business. But he simply could not.

She cleared her throat. Her jaw tightened with resolve. "If you want to help, then you'll let me handle this my way. In fact, that's why I have to leave. There's a man in New Mexico."

"Family?" he asked, swallowing hard. Then, before he could stop himself, he asked, "Your husband?"

Fool. Wise up. She doesn't want you along because she has someone else.

"No, a friend."

"But he can help you and I can't." God, he sounded like a jealous jerk! What was the matter with him?

"Yes."

"Your hands are trembling." His heart wrenched, even at the same moment the sexual tension between them sizzled.

"Okay, I admit it—I'm scared."

"But you still don't want to talk about it?"

She shook her head.

Tyler blew out his breath. His emotions were in a peculiar scramble. He felt angry, confused, worried and worst of all, desperately attached to this woman. He didn't want to feel anything for her other than a detached clinical interest. But he did. For the first time in six years he was attracted to a woman and she was dying. God must be quite a jokester to so cruelly twist Tyler's fate. A smart man would let her walk right out of his life.

But he didn't want her to walk out of his life. Whenever he was around her, he felt alive and whole again. Plus, she needed him. He hadn't been strong enough for Yvette. He had been so wrapped up in his own denial, his own fear of her disease that he hadn't been there for her. He did not want to make the same mistake with Hannah.

"May I please borrow your car or will you rent one for me? I really hate to ask, but I have nowhere else to turn. I lost my purse, all my identification and my money."

He held up a palm. "It's all right. You can take my car."

"I can? Thank you, thank you so much." Hannah pushed back her chair, rose to her feet and held her hand out for the keys.

"You're leaving now?" Why this tearing sensation inside him? As if he were being split in two pieces? Why the deep abiding ache far too similar to what he'd felt when he'd lost Yvette?

"I shouldn't have stayed here this long."

"But your spaghetti." He gestured at the stove. "You need supper."

"So do you."

She looked at him. Were those tears shimmering in her eyes? Was she as loath to leave as he was to have her go?

"You've been very kind. I can't thank you enough."

"Stay," Tyler whispered, hating himself for pleading. "Just for another hour. And eat something. We can have a nice polite conversation that has nothing to do with the people who want to harm you or dangerous chemicals or freaky lab values. We'll talk about music and art and movies. We could even take one last walk along the ocean."

Why he was begging her to stay, Tyler couldn't really say, but he wanted to be with her. More than he had wanted anything in a very long time.

You're just looking for a way to make amends to Yvette. That's it. You're still feeling guilty after all these years.

Maybe that was true. But maybe it wasn't.

Hannah hesitated. He saw her dilemma written on her face. A face that was so beautiful it broke his heart. She needed to go, but she wanted to stay. "I suppose another hour wouldn't hurt."

"Great." Tyler smiled but he couldn't stop thinking that his elation was short-lived.

Fear and common sense prodded Hannah to take the keys to Tyler's flashy BMW and run as fast as she could. She needed to get to New Mexico and find Marcus.

You are dying and Marcus is the only one who can save you. That is, if Marcus was still alive.

But something quite different urged her to linger with Tyler—physical attraction and the nonsensical but unshakable notion that he could protect her.

You never needed anyone to protect you before, Hannah Marie. Why him? Why now?

She couldn't allow illogical sensations to dictate her actions. Time was of the essence and it wasn't smart for her to stay, but she couldn't seem to help herself. She had never experienced these emotions before—the longing, the anxiety mixed with wonder and trepidation. And since she might not have much longer to live, Hannah ached to explore her budding feelings while she still had the chance.

Just one more hour in Tyler's company. She would probably never see him again. If she had to die, then an hour more with him was worth the risk.

Her stomach twisted at the thought, but it was true. If Daycon didn't get her, the side effects of her accidental exposure to *Virusall* and the radioactive isotopes from last summer surely would. When Tyler had shown her the printout of her lab results, Hannah's heart had skipped several beats. No wonder he had been so concerned. Never in her wildest imagination had she anticipated a reaction like this. Spontaneous regeneration of tissues and cells while at the same time gross alterations of her blood values. How was her body functioning under those conditions?

And oddly enough, she felt better than she had before the accident.

Except it had been no accident. Daycon's men forced her off the road. Not to kill her. Not yet. Not until Daycon got what he wanted. They'd meant to get her to stop, but traffic and rain had foiled their attempt. If Daycon got his hands on her, got the formula for *Virusall*, then he would have her killed. There was no way out of this mess. If she went to the police claiming her prestigious and powerful boss was trying to murder her, they would not only think she was crazy, but they would arrest her for setting fire to Daycon Laboratories.

She couldn't even go to the press as she had intended upon fleeing the lab, because she no longer had proof. The vials had shattered in the accident and she had destroyed all written evidence of the formula to keep Daycon from getting his hands on it. Nothing existed to substantiate her claims except for the e-mail she'd sent Marcus.

Fear for her friend rose fresh in her mind. What *had* happened to Marcus? Why hadn't he answered his telephone?

She kneaded her brow with two fingers. *Don't panic, Hannah, there could be a very logical explanation. He lives in the mountains. Bad weather could have knocked out his phone lines. It's probably something as simple as that.*

If only she could believe that was indeed the case, but she couldn't afford the luxury of assumptions. Hannah finished preparing the spaghetti dinner but, when they sat down, it was apparent neither of them could eat.

"This is killing me," Tyler said, pushing pasta around on his plate. "Having to let you go."

Hannah raised her head and met his eyes. The look shining there was honest, sincere and full of tender emotions. No man had ever looked at her like that.

She caught her breath.

A shiver passed through her. Surely she was imagining things. They barely knew each other and, according to Margie Price, Tyler was still in love with his late wife. She had misread his signals. If he was concerned about her, it was as a medical doctor, not a man.

She knew better than to trust her feelings. The few times

she'd followed her emotions, they had led her straight into trouble. She pushed back her chair, feeling suddenly claustrophobic in the room's confines and desperate for a rational blast of cool air. "Let's walk the beach."

"I'll get your coat."

Why did his caring gesture make her want to cry? Hannah bit down on her bottom lip. *Knock it off, Hannah. His thoughtfulness means nothing more than that. And even if it did, it's not like you have the luxury to investigate a future with his man.*

While Tyler went to retrieve her coat, she stared out the window and watched a seagull hopping along the porch railing. How peaceful and quiet it was here. If she closed her eyes and shut down her racing mind, she could almost convince herself that she wasn't Dr. Hannah Zachary, scientist on the run from a megalomaniac who wanted to use her discovery for mercenary means, but a normal woman on vacation at the beach with an attractive man.

Yeah, right. Like you've ever been normal.

When the other kids had been learning to swim and going to summer camp, Hannah had been memorizing the periodic table and conducting experiments in her own lab. She'd never learned the things most teenaged girls did—how to dress to catch a boy's eye, how to wear makeup, how to giggle over your guy's bad jokes. Face it. She didn't have the faintest clue how to be appealing to a man. Her lack of expertise in the sexual confidence department had secretly nagged at her, but until now, it hadn't bothered her enough to want to take a crash course in Femininity 101.

"Here we are."

She opened her eyes, dissipating the ridiculous fantasy before it had time to take root and grow. Tyler helped her on with the coat, then led her outside. The air was damp and cool. The setting sun hovered just above the horizon, casting the ice blue ocean in a tangerine glow. She swallowed and wished sentimentally that she could stay here forever.

When Tyler reached to take her hand, she did not resist. They walked without talking down to the rock pier jutting out into the Gulf of Mexico. They had no need for conversation. Words were merely words, and the communication between them went far beyond speech.

It was a strange sensation, the realization that he understood her. He had not pressed her for more information. He let her keep her secrets.

Tyler Fresno was a rare man. Patient, kind, trusting. It was a shame that she would not get to know him better.

But she had now, this moment and Hannah reveled in it, savoring his touch, the feel of his long fingers laced through her own, the reassuring smile he gave her each time she hesitated.

He guided her slowly after him, picking the way over the slippery stones. The wind stung Hannah's cheeks, and blew her hair back off her face. The air smelled fresh and new with twilight. Stars sprinkled the sky. Hannah went quiet inside. Cut off from her past, insulated from the future, for this fraction in time, she was happy.

She studied Tyler as they walked, admiring his tall silhouette, his broad masculine shoulders. He still wore his green hospital scrubs and white-leather running shoes. Dark hair curled around his ears in a boyishly endearing manner. She shocked herself by wondering what he was in like in bed. He looked as if he could be either wildly passionate or exceptionally controlled. Then she wondered why she was wondering.

They reached the end of the pier just as the sun settled against the lip of the earth and side by side they stood looking out to sea. Tyler wrapped his arms around her, holding her close.

Her shoulders were pressed into his chest, her head resting against the hollow of his neck. To a casual observer, they must have looked like an affectionate couple in a Hallmark greeting card. It was an illusion, this picture of domestic tranquillity. There was nothing tranquil or loving about Hannah's world.

And she was the cause of her own problems. If she hadn't been so determined to discover a cure for Ebola in the wake of her parents' deaths, she would never have stumbled across *Virusall*. Persistence was not always a virtue.

They watched until the sun was almost gone and the emptiness in Hannah widened to a gaping chasm. She did not belong here. This wasn't right.

"I must leave," she said. "I've already stayed far too long."

"Will I ever see you again?" Tyler murmured, hooking an index finger under her chin, tilting her head and forcing her to look at him. His dark eyes were murky, disturbed.

"Probably not."

"Then this is goodbye."

"Yes."

The word brought a grimace to his handsome face. She had the strongest urge to reach up and wipe the pain away with her hand.

"This may sound illogical but in a very short time I've come to care about you a great deal, Hannah."

"It's an illusion, Tyler. What you're feeling isn't real. We're caught up in this craziness together but if we'd met in a different context, would you have been attracted to me?"

"I don't know," he admitted. "But I didn't meet you in another context and I can't deny the way I feel right now. Whether it's real or not, who can say?"

"And how do you feel?" she asked, curious and yet dreading to hear his answer. All her life she had suppressed the quiet internal stirrings that whispered to her that she was not like her parents. She wasn't meant to stay cloistered in some lab, forever peering down a microscope. She had wanted nothing more than to live a normal life, to have friends, go to parties and yet, she had never acted upon these buried desires.

Because deep down inside she was afraid that she could never belong in the ordinary world. That she would always be on the outside looking in. She feared she did not possess the social skills to have a regular life. She'd spent so many years living in the safety of her own mind, she had no idea how to break free.

"I feel like kissing you," he whispered.

"Oh." The sudden heat pushing from inside her contrasted with the cool ocean air blowing against her skin.

"Would you mind if I kissed you, Hannah?"

His dark eyes burned with a feverish intensity. An intensity that raised the hair on her arms, and dried her throat. Her pulse hopped. Mind? Would she mind a drink from heaven's cup? Would she mind an eternity in paradise? Would she mind flying to the stars?

"I don't know if a kiss would be prudent," she said rather primly while her thoughts raced in the opposite direction. She ached for him to scoop her into his arms and kiss her so hard that she forgot about Lionel Daycon, *Virusall*, her spontaneous healing and all the strangeness. She forgot about everything but the taste of Tyler's lips and the feel of him pressed against her.

"Do you want to be prudent when we might never see each other again?" The wind snatched at his clothing, billowing the tail of his white lab coat around him.

"What would be the point?" she asked, knowing she spoke like a true scientist, detached and analyzing everything to death, but that's not what she felt. Yet for so many years she had been trained to ignore her emotions and focus only on facts. How did one go about changing their entire personality? If only she could.

"Pleasure. A deadening of the pain, a filling of the emptiness you carry here." He lightly tapped her chest. "My gift to you. A parting kiss. Something to remember me by."

"I couldn't forget you if I wanted to."

"Nor I you." He caressed her cheek with the back of his hand and lowered his head. The sun had gone completely and only the silvery moonlight illuminated them.

His lips were warm. Much warmer than she had expected. And buttery soft. Rocked by incredible sensations, Hannah closed her eyes and tilted her head farther back.

He tasted unique and when his tongue skimmed over her lips she became a part of his taste, blending with him until they were a flavor unto themselves. He held her tightly, one palm pressed against the back of her head, the other resting at her waist. This was pleasure of the most remarkable kind.

Unbidden, her arms reached up and wrapped around Tyler's neck, drawing him closer. She hadn't meant to do it but she could not seem to halt her mad rush toward intimacy with this man.

In the past, she had always found kissing rather distasteful, but, then again, she had never kissed Tyler. Instead, Hannah wanted more. She wriggled impatiently, going up on her tiptoes, opening her mouth wider, egging him on.

He groaned and increased the tempo. He seemed as hungry as she.

Kissing him was foolish, rash, an action that simply begged for trouble and yet, once started, she could not stop.

She sank against him, melting, wielding, gluing her mouth to his. Mine, she thought greedily. Mine.

"Sweet," he whispered. "You taste so damned sweet."

He kissed her eyelids, her cheeks, her chin and jaw. He ran his mouth up and down her neck, over her forehead, nibbled her earlobes. He feasted on her neck with wet, burning, openmouthed bites. The need was savage, driving, and she ached for him.

Finally, Hannah drew in a wobbly breath. She was burning up inside, her body a virtual pressure cooker of desire. Never, ever had she suspected that sexual passion could feel like a thunderous waterfall tumbling headlong into rapture. She had secretly dreamed of such passion, had prayed for and fantasized about it, but now that it was within her grasp, she could not keep it.

She had to pull away. Had to put a stop to this while she still could.

"Tyler," she said panted, "I have to go."

He stopped kissing her and just held her tightly. "Are you sure?"

"Yes."

They could have been Cathy and Heathcliff on the windswept moors or Rick and Ilsa at the airport hanger, so tragically bittersweet was their parting. She was Hannah Zachary, a dying research scientist who didn't know how to love and he was Tyler Fresno, a dedicated doctor who wanted to help her but couldn't; a man who was still in love with his dead wife. The scenario didn't bode well for a happy ending.

She looked at him. Were those tears shimmering in his eyes? Hannah's heart wrenched and she felt her own tears swell close to the surface.

"I'll never forget you," she said softly.

Lifting his hand, he pressed his fingertips lightly against her lips. "Shh. You'll come back to me," he murmured softly, but in their hearts they both knew it simply wasn't true.

Chapter 6

Hannah looked away from him and gazed toward the sea. While she still had the courage, she had to leave before she begged him to kiss her again. Turning, she hurried back down the pier, heedless of the treacherous rocks beneath her feet.

Her mind raged with thoughts of all she had lost, all that she could not have. She and Tyler would never be lovers. They would not court, they would not fall in love, they would not get married and have children. Hannah would never find out if she was even capable of sustaining an intimate relationship.

Who was she kidding? She didn't have the vaguest idea about how this man-woman thing worked. And if her relationship with Tyler was taken out of this current context, what were the chances they'd feel the same way toward each other?

Slim. Very slim. She knew their parting was for the best. No sense pining for something she could never have.

"Hannah!" Tyler called. "Please, be careful. Wait for me to guide you."

She ran. She'd never needed anyone's help. Never wanted it.

Her entire self-image was based on her deep-seated desire to be competent, capable, self-contained. Her soft-soled shoes smacked against the wet rocks. The evening tide rose and slapped against the pier, splashing her with cold, salty water.

Hurry. Run. Go. Forget about Tyler. Forget about these feelings that will only betray you in the end. Concentrate on Marcus.

If she could find Marcus and replicate *Virusall*, perhaps they could reverse the damaging effects she had suffered by creating an antidote for herself and the people in the clinical trials who'd been given the drug. Maybe then she could return to Tyler, see where they stood.

Face facts. You're really very good at seeing the truth, the niggling voice in the back of her head insisted. *You and Tyler were never meant to be. He was a temporary port in a crazy maelstrom and that was all. Anything else was pure wishful fantasy.* And how often had her parents ridiculed fantasy?

"Hannah!" He sounded father away, his voice muted by the rushing wind.

Don't listen to him, don't think about him, she urged herself but it was an impossible task, especially when her mouth still burned from the power of his kisses and her blood sang with the heat of his embrace.

She ran on, urgency pushing her into a dim future, away from the man who stirred her in alien and wondrous ways. She hit the beach. Sand flew from beneath her feet and shifted into her shoes. His porch lamp glowed up ahead in the darkness, lighting her way.

Behind her, she heard Tyler mutter a curse but she did not look back. She could not afford to entertain the sentimental sensations growing inside her.

Disassociate. Disconnect. Disengage.

She chanted the lifelong mantra, a technique her mother had taught her for controlling her emotions. But this time, it proved ineffective. She thought only of Tyler's kisses, his lips.

Forget it. Their relationship wouldn't last. Even if she wasn't being chased by a megalomaniac bent on filling the world with drug-induced assassins. Even if she wasn't slowly dying. Tyler was still longing for his dead wife. She still had no confidence in her femininity. She was his rebound woman. He was her stop-gap man.

Well, the gap stopped here. Before either one of them got hurt.

She sprinted up the steps and into his house. Frantically, she grabbed her change of clothes, Tyler's car keys and the rest of the money he had given her that morning. Whirling on her heels, she turned to escape but his looming presence in the doorway stopped her.

"Hannah," he said, breathing heavily, "don't leave like this."

"Tyler, I…"

That's when she saw the blood streaming from his right hand. His surgeon's hand, cut wide open at the juncture between his thumb and index finger.

"What happened?" she cried, dropping everything and springing to his side.

He stared at the cut, at his own blood, as if noticing for the first time that he was injured.

"I fell on the rocks," he said, "and I cut my hand on some broken glass, but that's not important."

"Not important! You're gushing like a waterfall."

Tyler blinked and Hannah realized he was in shock. Oh, God, and she had left him out there alone in the dark.

Quickly, she scanned the room for something to stanch the bleeding and spied a clean dishtowel draped over the oven door handle. Springing into action, she pushed him into a chair before his legs buckled, and then snatched the towel from the door handle. She sank to her knees before him and twisted the make-shift bandage around his hand.

There was a lot of blood, on the floor, on his clothes. Tyler's face was pale, his breathing shallow.

"It didn't hurt at first," he said. "Now it's throbbing like hell. I'm going to need stitches."

Hannah wrapped her hand over the bulky towel, applying pressure. The bleeding slowed immediately.

An odd heat flooded her palms and radiated out through her fingertips. Then the tingling started.

First it was just in her hands. Then both arms. In a matter of seconds the tingling accelerated, engulfing her entire body in a white-hot hum. She felt like a high-voltage wire vibrating with raw energy. Hannah inhaled sharply.

Exhilaration built in her solar plexus and tickled her insides with an unbelievable dynamism. She wanted to laugh, but was too startled to do so. She felt breathless, excited and uncertain. Looking at Tyler's hand she saw blood no longer oozed through the towel.

"Hannah?" His voice sounded strange, dreamy.

Her gaze met his. Tyler's eyes widened. She smiled shyly, as if she had the most awesome secret.

"What's happening?"

Her elbow rested on his thigh. She felt his leg muscles tense. She shook her head, her hand still pressed firmly against his wound. "I don't know."

"I feel…" He hesitated as if unable to fully express what he was experiencing.

"Hot?"

"Sweltering."

"Light?"

"Like a helium balloon."

"Tingly?"

"Electric."

"Dizzy?"

"Tilt-A-Whirl muzzy."

"I know." She smiled again, knowing she must look like the crazed Cheshire cat but unable to stop herself.

"You feel it, too?"

Their gazes were locked. She could hear him thinking. He was astounded, caught off guard and nervous. She had never felt so connected to anyone.

"Yes."

"My hand doesn't hurt anymore." His tone was incredulous.

"It's stopped bleeding."

"You're not going to believe this," he murmured.

"What?"

"It feels as if my skin is actually growing back together."

A knot of trepidation formed in Hannah's stomach pushing aside her earlier euphoria.

"Shall we look?"

His breath warmed the nape of her neck as she leaned over his hand. Fear clutched her heart. She sat back on her heels. Slowly, she peeled back the towel soaked with drying blood.

And gasped.

The wound was completely healed. All signs of damage gone. No cut. No blood. Not even a scar. Simply smooth, uninterrupted skin.

Dubiously, Tyler raised his hand before his face, staring at the wound that wasn't. His jaw dropped.

He looked at Hannah and held her eyes prisoner with his bewildered stare. "Just what the hell is going on here?"

Panic bloomed in her chest. Shaking her head, she rose to her feet and backed away from him, not believing what she was seeing.

Tyler was healed.

Just as she'd been mysteriously healed of a broken bone and a ruptured spleen.

The implications hit Hannah dead center between the eyes.

Her touch had cured him.

But how? She could marginally buy into the spontaneous regeneration theory in her own body—she'd been exposed to a volatile drug and radioactive particles. But healing Tyler's wound was something else entirely.

He stalked across the floor and grabbed her by the shoulders. "Tell me, dammit. What's happening? I've got a right to know."

It was a mind-boggling concept with no answer based in her scientific experience.

She, Hannah Zachary, had the power to heal with a single touch.

"No more evasiveness, Hannah. You've got to tell me everything."

The look in Tyler's eyes was like flint. She hadn't known he could be so determined. His fingers dug into her shoulders, not hurting her but firmly insistent nonetheless. Her own knees quaked at the magnitude of what she had just done and her pulse hammered.

"I can't."

"I won't accept *no* for an answer."

She tried to move away but he blocked her with his powerful body, pinning her beside the kitchen cabinet, his pelvis pressed flush against her hips.

"Please," she begged.

"The issue is nonnegotiable."

His physical energy was overwhelming. It would be so simple to crumble and tell him everything. But she didn't even know him. How could she trust him with her secret? She tried to shift away, to distance herself from him but he held her trapped.

"Hannah." He held up his right hand that was miraculously whole. "I want an explanation for this and I want it now."

"You wouldn't believe me."

"Is this believable?" He ran a finger along the spot where his cut had been moments before. "One minute I'm pouring blood like a fountain and the next minute—after you touch me, I might add—full skin integrity is restored. It's bizarre, it's supernatural but it *happened* and I want to know how."

"You don't understand," she said desperately. "Time is running out. I have to leave. Now. This minute. I may already be too late."

The truth was, she didn't know how the healing power had been transferred from the broken vials of *Virusall* to herself. Nor did she know how to control her newfound power. Could she manifest this ability at will or did it appear only when she needed it?

Suddenly, she remembered Margie Price. The woman had spoken of having a painful crick in her neck that had disappeared right after Hannah had shaken her hand. And at the time, Hannah had experienced that same tingling, the same warmth as when she had healed Tyler, except on a smaller scale. Had she healed Margie's stiff neck, as well?

"Why is time running out? Because of your dwindling health?"

"Yes," she admitted.

"This inexplicable healing power has got something to do

with your abnormal blood values, and don't try to deny it. The two things have got to be connected."

A pounding headache built behind her eyes. Reaching up, she massaged her brow. Okay, if she could cure Tyler and Margie, then why not herself? Was she immune to her own cure? Her broken leg and ruptured spleen had healed spontaneously in the emergency room, so why the headache? What was different? Hannah willed the headache away but it persisted, gathering strength.

Her mouth was dry. She moistened her lips and narrowed her eyes against the kitchen lights that seemed intolerably bright. "Those people that I told you about. The ones that want to harm me. They're the reason I'm on the run. I have to find my friend, Marcus, before he, before they do something…." Her throat constricted cutting off the rest of her sentence.

"You're talking in riddles. I want the whole story. From the beginning and I want it now."

"Can't." It was all she could manage. The throbbing in her head increased. Nausea swept through her. She had to sit. Blindly, she reached out.

"Hannah?" His hand was at her hair, gently stroking her, while his other arm went around her, pulling her against his broad chest. In an instant he was as soft and caring as, earlier, he had been forceful and determined. "Sweetheart? Talk to me—what's wrong?"

When she could not respond, he swept her into his arms and carried her upstairs to the bedroom where she had spent the previous night. She watched the carpet flow away beneath his feet as he climbed the stairs, her head whirling and her vision playing tricks.

He laid her beneath the sheets and pulled the covers to her chin. Her shaking increased until she was trembling so violently her teeth clattered and she began to hyperventilate.

She didn't have time for this. She had already stayed here far too long. And yet, more than anything, she wanted to block out the rest of the world and stay forever in this man's arms.

"Hang tight," Tyler said, dropping a quick kiss on her forehead. "I'll be right back."

Scarcely able to nod, Hannah curled into a fetal position and struggled to breathe.

He returned a moment later with a brown paper bag, a cool damp washcloth and his black medical bag. He slipped the paper bag over her mouth and nose and held it in place with his hands.

"Shh, slow down."

Panic tightened her chest.

"Breathe deeply. That's it. In through your nose and out through your mouth."

She obeyed.

"That's good."

In a few minutes, she felt herself relax and the tension ebb.

"Okay." He removed the paper bag. His eyes were bright with concern. Tenderly, he ran the damp cloth over her face, soothing her. "How does that feel?"

"Nice."

He checked her vital signs. "Both your blood pressure and temperature are low and your pulse is fast. Can you describe your symptoms?"

"Headache," she whispered. "Nausea. Weakness."

"This started right after you healed me."

"Yes."

"Do you have a history of migraines?"

"No, I never get headaches. In fact, it used to be a joke back at the lab."

"Lab?"

Hannah propped herself up on her elbows and met his kind gaze. She saw nothing but openness, a willingness to hear her out. She owed him the truth. No matter how far-fetched, he had to know what he had gotten himself involved in because there was no denying, the minute she had reached out and healed him, Tyler had become a player in this drama. Without meaning to, she had tied him to herself irrevocably.

"I'm a research scientist at Daycon Laboratories in Austin."

"Does this have anything to do with the chemicals that were found in your car?"

She nodded, her gut squeezing with fear as she remembered

the accident. Then bit by bit, she told him everything. About her parents and their dedication to eradicating disease, about their deaths in Africa of Ebola, about her own quest to cure the virus. Tyler listened while Hannah cleared her throat and told him everything she knew about *Virusall*.

"And this extraordinary drug cures all viruses?" He shook his head, a stunned expression on his face. "How is that possible?"

She gave him detailed information on her seven years of research and the particulars of the various chemical compounds.

"You're a little over my head," he admitted.

"It's truly a miracle drug. I can explain the properties but I can't tell you why it works on every virus every time, but it does."

Tyler whistled. "If I hadn't seen the results myself, I wouldn't have believed it." He stared at his hand. "Wait a minute. You said you discovered this antiviral agent, but it was your touch that healed me, plus you cured a cut not a virus. How is it possible this happened?"

That's when she told him about her contact with the radioactive isotopes and Marcus's theories. "But honestly," she said, "I'm just as confused about this latest development as you are. I didn't even know I had the capacity to heal until I touched you. I'm guessing when *Virusall* got into my bloodstream it reacted with the radiation stored in my cells and somehow I took on the healing properties. The trouble is, I don't know if the manifestation is long term, short term, or if healing your hand was a one-time thing."

"And your lab values? Your symptoms? What's causing that?" He sat on the edge of the bed looking like he had been poleaxed. He was a man of science and the magical quality of the things she was relating took time to absorb.

"I have no idea. I knew the drug was unstable, possibly even dangerous, despite its positive aspects. Then when I got the results back from the clinic trials, I knew we were in deep trouble." She told him what had happened with the test subjects.

"Were there any side effects in people with other blood types?"

"I don't know. I was so upset by the other findings I didn't have time to investigate those."

Tyler scratched his head. "You're AB negative, right?"

"Yes."

"It appears to me that your immune system is reacting adversely to the combination of radiation and *Virusall* exposure, turning your own body against you."

"While at the same time giving me supernatural healing abilities," she finished his thought for him.

"I didn't want to be the first one to use the word supernatural."

"It's the right word. We both know it."

Their eyes met.

"The drug may be killing you, Hannah, even as it gives you this incredible power." His voice was serious and tinged with sadness.

"I know. Do you think that I might pass these symptoms on to you?" The thought terrified her.

He shook his head. "There's no way to know for certain, but I doubt it. Even if you had administered the drug to me, my body might have responded differently and I wasn't exposed to radiation like you were. Did you see any other anomalies?"

"Well, with everyone in the study there was an initial dip in white blood cell count and platelets, but the lab values quickly returned to normal. Usually within an hour or two after administration of the drug."

"Just like with the paramedics," he mused. "Yes, I believe your particular immune system response is tied in with your radiation exposure. Please, don't worry that you could have passed it on to me just by touching my cut."

"I did more than touch your cut. I healed you. Did you feel anything afterward? Sudden weakness, headaches?"

"No. I felt intensely energized."

"That's good."

"How about you? How are you feeling?"

She licked her lips. "A little better."

"Let me check your vital signs again." He performed another blood pressure, pulse count and temperature check.

"How are they?"

"You're still tachycardic, but your blood pressure's coming up," he said.

"There's something else I don't know. How long do the effects of these healings last? Is it permanent or temporary?" Hannah worried her bottom lip with her teeth.

"Only time will tell."

"I've opened a Pandora's box I can't close." Her weakness seemed to be passing, her headache lessening, but she felt exhausted straight through her bones.

"You haven't told me the whole story. What are you running away from, Hannah? Who are these people that are out to harm you?"

She hesitated before speaking. She still wanted to spare him the details, but like it or not, he was a part of this. "If I tell you, then you're in danger, too."

"How can you not tell me, Hannah? You've got to have help. You can't do this alone."

His words, the tenderness in his eyes, caused her heart to race and the light-headedness to return, but this time she knew it had nothing to do with low blood pressure and a rapid pulse.

"You would do that for me?" Emotion caught in her throat at the reality of what he was offering. At long last. Someone to lean on.

But as much as she might ache to let down her guard and trust him, she could not. She had to protect him. She would not endanger his life by letting him get too close to her.

"I can't accept your offer."

"Hannah, I need to help you as much as you need the help. For the past six years I've been holed up in my grief. A virtual zombie, dead to life. Until you. Please, let me help you. For my own selfish reasons."

"Wait until I tell you what's at stake. Then you can make a decision whether I'm worth the risk or not."

"I'm listening. Although I can tell you right now, you're worth whatever it takes."

She smiled, heartened by his response. "What I did was precipitous and presumptuous. My idealistic enthusiasm has cost me a great deal."

"Idealism is never a bad thing."

"Ha. It is when you work for Lionel Daycon." Hannah heard

the bitterness in her own voice and realized she was very angry with Daycon. He had not only spoiled everything she had worked seven years to create, but he had jeopardized her life, making her future shaky at best.

Tyler waited for her to go on. He was leaning above her, an arm placed on either side of her shoulders. She looked up at him, remembering the incredible kiss they had shared on the beach. Her anger dissipated and was immediately replaced by sadness. Without a future, she could promise him nothing.

Even if things were different, he was obviously placing unrealistic expectations on her ability to heal his broken heart. She swallowed hard. She wished she could whisper rash, romantic promises that she knew she couldn't keep, but she'd never been that kind of person. Her word was gold. She did not give it capriciously. She could make him no vows.

Slowly, he lowered his head and traced his lips along her mouth. Hannah did not resist. He deepened the kiss, but it was not demanding. He meant it to comfort, not arouse her, but instantly she felt rejuvenated and her headache vanished. She felt as if she were a car with a new battery. Her heart fluttered.

"You taste nice." He pulled back to study her face. "I could get seriously accustomed to doing that."

Me, too! That's why she had to stop this. Now.

Tyler reached out a hand and brushed a strand of hair from her forehead. Hannah sucked in air. Every time he touched her with an affectionate gesture she experienced a jolt of pure rapture. Healing him had drained her, but kissing him revived her. She had the strangest urge to bounce around the room.

"Your cheeks are pinking up," he said and she hated to tell him she was blushing. "But I didn't mean to interrupt. Go on, tell me the rest of the story."

"I've been such a fool," she whispered, desperate to shake off this bittersweet desire for him. "I thought I was going to save lives. Me, Hannah Zachary. Single-handedly I was going to eradicate all viruses and make the world a better place." Then she grimly told him everything about Daycon's criminal intention to supply terrorists with the drug and his dark association with the rogue CIA insider. "So you see, I had to keep the formula for *Virusall* away from Daycon."

"How did you manage it?"

"I set fire to the lab."

"Hannah! You could have been hurt or killed."

She stubbornly hardened her chin. "I did what I had to do."

"How did you get your hands on the vials you were carrying in your car?"

"I kept a few samples at home. I also have a computer linkup to Daycon Laboratories. I went home and deleted all my computer files. I destroyed everything."

"Everything?" he echoed.

"Well, except for a copy of the formula I e-mailed to my friend Marcus in New Mexico. That's where I was headed when Daycon's men caught me and forced me off the road, causing me to crash. Do you see now why I can't go to the police? I'm wanted for arson in Austin. Daycon's got the CIA in his pocket and he's telling everyone I'm crazy. It's his word against mine. Who do you think they'll believe? An eccentric scientist or a rich and powerful man? I can't even go to the media as I'd first intended before the car wreck. I no longer have proof of my discovery. At least not until I find Marcus."

Silence elongated in the small room. She peered up at Tyler but his face was unreadable. What was he thinking? Had her act of arson put him off? Was he disappointed in her? Did he consider her a lunatic, a zealot? She hated to think of his judgment.

"You're very courageous," he said at long last.

"Or very stupid. My principles have often gotten me into trouble." She smiled wryly.

"Daycon's men left you for dead on the roadside? Why didn't they finish you off?"

"I've been thinking about that," she said, "and I figured they were suppose to bring me back to Daycon, but eyewitnesses arrived so quickly they were unable to get their hands on me. Without me, Daycon can't reproduce the formula. Now, with the vials gone, neither can I. Not alone. I need Marcus for that, but he's something of a hermit. He lives in the mountains and keeps to himself."

"Your friend is familiar with the drug?"

"Yes. In the early days, before he left Daycon, we were working together on the formula. But I'm worried about him." She told Tyler about the phone call to Marcus, the line going dead, and then being unable to reach him again.

"There could be a logical explanation."

"Yes—Daycon's men have already gotten to him."

"What are you saying? That Lionel Daycon is capable of murder?"

"I think he's capable of hiring it done." Hannah shivered. She felt very tired.

"You're serious."

"There's a lot of money at stake and Lionel Daycon is a very greedy man. Do you see why time is running out? I'm sick and getting sicker. Marcus is the only hope I've got and I'm not even sure where he's at. Right now, I'm all alone."

"That's not true, Hannah."

Their gazes locked. She saw something in Tyler's eyes that gave her hope—strength, determination and devotion.

"You've got me," he said and squeezed her hand.

Chapter 7

What had he committed himself to? Tyler felt as if he's taken a header off the Empire State building. He braced himself as a tidal wave of emotions hit. Panic, resolve, elation, apprehension. His mood ran the gamut.

Hannah's eyes had shuttered closed for a brief moment and she had immediately fallen asleep. Tyler sat for a moment watching her, trying to get his bearings. Trying to decide what was real.

He was reassured by her slow steady breathing. Poor kid. She needed rest and lots of it. Softly, Tyler eased off the bed and turned out the light to let her sleep while he struggled to come to grips with what had just happened.

Tiptoeing downstairs to the kitchen, his mind reeled from the events she had just relayed to him. Magical healing potions that drove test subjects insane, radioactive isotopes, homicidal pharmaceutical owners, dangerous henchmen, a renegade CIA operative and a mysterious hermit living in the mountains of New Mexico.

It was a lot to absorb.

And he might have suspected Hannah had a psychotic break with reality except for one thing.

His hand.

Tyler held his right hand up to the light and studied it carefully. Not a trace of the cut. Not even a scar.

Impossible. His scientific mind rebelled, not wanting to accept the truth, but there was no other explanation, rational or irrational. He could not cling stubbornly to denial.

Stupefied, he poured himself a glass of water, then sat at the kitchen table and tried to make sense of everything that had occurred that evening, from kissing Hannah to his wound healing to her sudden illness after the cure.

Confusion clouded his brain and dulled his thought processes. He didn't like the feeling. As a surgeon, Tyler was accustomed to identifying problems and dealing with them. If someone had a tumor, he took it out. If someone got stabbed, he repaired the damage. Everything in his world was tangible and sensible, if at times tragic. The world Hannah painted for him was a world too foreign to ponder.

From the time he was a small boy and had saved his grandfather's life, Tyler had known he was destined to be a doctor. It was his calling, his identity and one of the reasons he'd had such a hard time accepting Yvette's terminal diagnosis. He was meant to rescue the infirm, not lose a young, vibrant patient.

What of the healing power Hannah now possessed? How far did it extend? How many lives could she save?

Had Hannah thought through the ethical dilemmas inherent in her abilities? Did she realize this healing power essentially made her God, giving her jurisdiction over life and death? Power was ultimately what Daycon wanted. Power other people would want, as well. She would be inundated with the infirm seeking healing. Her life would never be her own.

"If indeed she even survives this," he whispered and stared into the water glass.

He thought of Yvette.

A lump rose in Tyler's throat. He removed his wallet from his back pocket and slipped his dead wife's faded picture from the plastic folds. She smiled up at him, her arms draped around a carousel horse on the merry-go-round at the county fair. He remembered the day the picture was taken. Their third anniversary. They had acted like children, giggling together, eating cotton candy, taking their turn at games of chance. Even though they hadn't known it at the time, it was one of the last happy, carefree days they'd had left.

"Why did you wait so long to tell me about the cancer?" he whispered. "Why did you cheat me out of those precious months?" A tear slid down his cheek. He would have given his own life for Hannah's healing touch six years ago.

Closing his eyes, Tyler swallowed back the pain. For six years, he had been performing his duties, doing what was necessary but never really enjoying life.

He dated occasionally because those in his social set expected it, especially as the years had rolled away and Yvette's death had slipped further into the past. But Tyler was a loyal man and he did not easily forget. The women who escorted him to hospital functions soon discovered he rarely called them for a second date. It wasn't that they weren't nice women, it was just that none of them sparked his interest.

That is until Hannah Zachary.

He recalled the odd feeling of panic he'd felt when he first examined her in the emergency room, and now he understood what his intuition had been trying to tell him. Here was a woman he could fall in love with. A woman who could help him overcome the pain of the past and redeem him by showing him how to live again.

Except that she was quite possibly dying.

Tyler groaned low in his throat and bit down on his hand to silence his agony. He did not want to feel the things he was feeling—desire, concern, worry. He ached to run back into his familiar shell and hide behind work.

But he could not.

Hannah needed him and he would not let her down the way he had let Yvette down. He regretted staying in denial so long that he had wasted the time he'd had left with his wife.

Besides, there was hope, albeit a small one.

If he could halt Hannah's immune system response to the drug, could he save her life? It was a question he could not answer. Not now.

He started to put Yvette's picture back into his wallet, but stopped. "You'd like her," he murmured. "I know you would. You two could pass for sisters."

Yvette kept smiling.

She would have wanted him to go on, to love anew. She had told him so many times in those last days but he hadn't wanted to listen. He'd had his love, but it had come and gone.

But Hannah made him hope for a second chance. Could fate grant her a second chance, as well? Tyler knew there was only one thing to do. Take Hannah to New Mexico. Become her protector. Help her find this Marcus fellow and, at all costs, keep her safe from Lionel Daycon.

He got to his feet, kissed Yvette's picture one last time, then put it away in a drawer. It was time to let go of the past. He would never forget her, but now his responsibility was to the living.

Picking up the phone, he called his medical partners, then took a deep breath and rang up Michael Ledbetter at home.

"What is it, Fresno?" Ledbetter asked, coming to the phone after his wife had answered.

"I need a leave of absence, sir."

Ledbetter made a noise of exasperation. "When?"

"Immediately."

"Don't you have surgery scheduled for next week?"

"Yes, but I've already made arrangements with my partners to take over for me."

"This is highly irregular."

"I appreciate that, but I've never made such a request before. This an emergency situation."

"Does this have anything to do with that Jane Doe case?" Ledbetter asked suspiciously.

"I'd rather not say."

"You're putting your job on the line, Fresno."

"I'm aware of that, sir." Tyler tightened his grip on the telephone receiver. He hated supplicating himself before this hard-headed man, but he had to do it. For Hannah's sake.

"When will you be back?"

"I don't know."

"Not good enough."

"I'm sorry, I simply can't say how long this will take."

Ledbetter was silent for a moment. "All right. I'll give you seven days. If you're not back in surgery a week from Monday, your hospital privileges will be rescinded."

"Thank you, sir."

"And, Fresno…"

"Yes?"

"This little episode will go into your file. Don't think it's not going to come up when it's time for promotion."

Tyler's gut squeezed. For years he had had his eye on Michael Ledbetter's job. He had wanted nothing more than to be chief of surgery at Saint Madeleine's. But now, it suddenly didn't seem to matter.

"Very well," he said. "I understand." Tyler hung up and experienced a peacefulness he hadn't felt in a very long time. He'd done the right thing.

The phone jangled. Surprised, he picked it up thinking it was one of his partners calling back for particulars on a patient's condition. "Dr. Fresno here."

"Is this Tyler?" The woman's voice was muffled, as if she had been crying.

"Hello?"

"It's me, Margie Price."

"Margie," Tyler said. "What's wrong?"

"I'm afraid I've done a terrible thing."

"Talk to me."

"Some men came to your house."

"My house?" He didn't understand what she was talking about. Margie was sniffling so hard he could barely hear her.

"One of them came over to speak to me. He wanted to know where you were. He was looking for Jane."

"Jane?"

"Except he called her Hannah."

"Margie, are you all right? You sound pretty shaken up."

"I would never have told them where you were, but the man pulled a gun on me. He was very mean, very nasty. He looked like a TV gangster."

"Margie!"

"Who are they, Tyler? What do they want? I was scared and I'm so sorry I told them where to find you, but he threatened to do awful things to me if I didn't talk."

Daycon's hired thugs. The ones who'd caused Hannah's car wreck. "It's all right, Margie," he soothed, trying to calm the hysterical woman. "Can you tell me how long ago this was?"

"An hour, maybe more. I was too shook up to call for awhile and then when I tried, the phone was busy."

Hell, they could be pulling into the driveway right now. Tyler's gut tensed. He didn't own a gun.

"You did fine—don't blame yourself. I'll take care of everything. You lock your doors, take a sedative and go to bed. I've got to go now."

"Tyler."

"Yes?"

"Be careful. Those men are very dangerous."

Get her the hell out of here.

Not knowing how much time he had before two armed toughs showed up on his doorstep, Tyler raced through the house gathering what they might need for an extended road trip. Panting, he stuffed the supplies into the trunk of his BMW and then dashed back inside and up the stairs to where Hannah slept, oblivious to the fact her pursuers were minutes away.

He tried to rouse her but she slumbered as deeply as if she'd swallowed a double dose of Ambien. Having no choice, he threw her over his shoulder and hauled her to the car.

Her hair swung against his back. She was soft in his arms, her smell delicate.

Poor kid. She's got no one except me.

He was taking her on the road to the devil only knew where,

away from the devil only knew what. It wasn't prudent, it wasn't smart, but this Tyler knew from the bottom of his heart—he would do anything to protect Hannah. He had let Yvette down when she needed him most and he would not repeat his mistake.

Somehow, he managed to maneuver Hannah into the passenger seat and get her buckled up.

He slammed her door, then ran around to the driver's side, got in and started the car. His breath was a visible white cloud in the frosty night air. He fumbled for the headlights as he put the car in reverse. Revving the engine, he backed up and to his dismay saw a car turn off the main street and onto the beach road leading to the house.

There were only two cottages on this lane. His and Margie's. And he knew Margie was in Houston.

His blood chilled. Were these the men who were after Hannah? For the first time in his life, Tyler wished for a handgun.

He slammed the gearshift into drive and trod on the accelerator as if he were an action-movie stuntman. He shot past the oncoming battered white sedan, his BMW bottoming out in the low driveway, jostling him and his passenger. But Tyler never eased off the gas pedal. Hazarding a glance in the side-view mirror, he saw the sedan brake suddenly and spin around to follow them.

Son-of-a-bitch!

"Tyler?" Hannah mumbled. She was sitting up, her eyes wide. "What's going on?"

"We're being followed."

"Daycon's men?"

"I'm assuming."

"A white sedan." She turned and looked over her shoulder out the back window. One hand clenched the armrest. Tyler saw her knuckles had gone pale from gripping so hard.

"Yeah."

"It's the same car that ran me off the road."

"Let's see 'em outrun this baby," he said and pushed his foot to the floor.

They flew without being airborne.

Hannah raised a hand to her throat. Flashes from the accident flickered through her mind and fear spilled a bitter taste into her mouth. In an instant, she was reliving the car crash.

Except, this time, she was not alone.

With the intent expression of a man on a sacred mission, Tyler kept his eyes glued to the road, his hands on the wheel. It was Hannah who kept peering back at the sedan.

He burst from the beach road onto Seawall Boulevard, thick with evening traffic. Cars honked and swerved to get out of their way, but he never slowed, driving as calmly and skillfully as a professional race-car driver.

Hannah's breath hovered in her lungs, barely slipping in and out through her nose. The ocean lay to their left. Restaurants and clubs extended out over piers, neon lights burning brightly. Shrimp boats bobbed in the Gulf. A few tourists, bundled in coats, strolled the sea wall.

"They're still following," she said, sneaking yet another glance over her shoulder.

A signal light turned yellow and Tyler sped through the intersection. "That ought to slow them down."

"No, it didn't. They ran the red."

"Damn."

"They're not going to stop."

Hannah shifted in her seat to study Tyler's profile. He was incredibly handsome, especially with that determined look on his face—his jaw resolute, his lips pressed into an unyielding line—as if nothing could stand in his way. His strength gave her courage.

"What are we going to do?"

"I don't know."

The traffic thinned the farther west they traveled, the city giving way to more condos, beach resorts and long stretches of sand. Tyler increased his pace and continued to zigzag between the lanes.

"We're going to run out of island soon," Hannah said.

"Don't worry, I'll think of something." His tone was adamant, leaving no doubt to his commitment.

Why is he doing this? she wondered. She'd had few true friends in her life. Hannah wasn't the type to cultivate lasting relationships. She had her work. It had always been enough. Until now. In an instant, she realized what she had been missing all these years. Someone to confide in. Someone she could count on through thick and thin. Someone to share her life with.

Someone to love.

Did she dare to trust him completely? Heart and soul?

The questions scared her. She wanted someone to love, but at the same time she was afraid that if she let herself hope it would all slip through her fingers.

"How far are they behind us?" Tyler asked.

"You've outpaced them a little. There are three cars between us and them."

"Good."

Up ahead, the road curved. Two lanes went right. The third, the lane they were in, continued straight to the ferry landing.

There were no other cars in line. Hannah saw the ferry lights winking in the harbor and her stomach sank as she realized the ferry was just about to pull away from the dock.

"We're too late." Dismay shot through her as the slender mechanical arm began to descend across the lane.

"Hang on!"

She sucked in her breath when it dawned on her what he intended. "Tyler, no!"

He floored the BMW and they shot through just as the mechanical arm grazed the trunk. The ferry was a good foot from the dock, but they were traveling too fast to stop. The road ran out and they were airborne.

Hannah screamed.

For one awful split second that seemed to stretch on into infinity, they hovered above the Gulf of Mexico. Hannah gazed down at the dark waters below and thought, *We're going to die together.*

Wham!

The BMW landed with teeth-jarring impact on the back of the ferry, thankfully empty of cars, and immediately the engine died.

Ferry workers were shouting and running toward them. People got out of their cars to gawk. Hannah trembled, all the air expelled from her lungs.

"Are you all right?" Tyler asked.

"Uh." She placed a hand to her chest.

"Hannah?" Panic laced his voice.

"I'm okay," she managed. "Knocked my breath out of my lungs. Are you all right?"

"Yes."

"I'm a little dazed," she admitted, leaning her head back against the headrest.

"I'm sorry I had to do that."

She nodded.

"We gave them the slip." His smile looked as shaky as hers felt. They both turned and glanced out the back windshield.

Under the bright dock lights, two stocky men were standing beside the white sedan with arms akimbo and wearing incredulous expressions on their heavy faces.

A ferry worker jerked Tyler's door open, startling him and Hannah. "Just what in the hell do you think you were doing fella? You coulda gotten yourself killed."

Hannah sat shivering on the upper deck of the ferry, a cup of steaming black coffee clutched in her hands. She wasn't shivering from the cold, although the night air was nippy. Rather, she was suffering a delayed reaction to the car chase and the clear fact that she and Tyler had almost lost their lives.

Tyler was below with the ferry workers, trying to talk his way out of trouble. It was nice, she thought, to have a man handle things for her. A simple luxury. Even as a child, she had taken care of herself, often fixing her own meals because her parents were too wrapped up in their work to spare time or attention to something as mundane as food. She had often been jealous of her classmates who came home from school to houses warm with the smell of baking cookies and welcoming hugs.

He makes me feel safe. Hannah marveled at the unique sensation. *He makes me feel special.*

But could she trust these feelings? Could she trust herself?

Instantly, her old self-esteem issues raised their ugly head. Why would a vibrant, successful man like Tyler be interested in a woman like her? A woman who had spent her life in front of a microscope. A woman who had no idea how to have fun. A woman who was a cold fish in bed.

Hush, she warned that nay-saying voice. *Shut up and let me relish him while I can. It'll end soon enough.*

Finishing off the coffee, she disposed of the plastic cup in a nearby waste receptacle and went to stand at the railing. The coffee worked its magic, giving her energy while at the same time paradoxically soothing her frazzled nerves. She tilted her face to intercept the cool night breeze.

Several people were clotted in groups, staring at her and murmuring under their breath. She and Tyler had certainly given them a show. Hannah smiled as she imagined what the crowd had seen as the BMW sailed toward the moving ferry.

"What's so funny?"

She raised her head and met Tyler's gaze. He wore a half smile of his own, but his dark eyes were serious. Running a hand through her hair, she wished for a comb and some lipstick. Funny, she wasn't usually given to vanity, sometimes going months between haircuts, but with Tyler around she had a sudden desire to look her best, to prove she was worthy of his attention.

"This whole situation. It's like something from an Ian Flemming novel," she said.

"Bond." Tyler affected a British accent, moved beside her and gave her a naughty wink. "James Bond. And you're…" He raised a finger. "Let me guess. Ravishina Beauty."

"Are you telling me I'm pretty enough to be a Bond girl?"

"Oh, most definitely."

Hannah surprised herself by laughing at his flirtation. She should be worried and frightened and scared. Instead, all she could think was—*he's got the most gorgeous eyes.*

His pupils widened as he stared at her. Hannah got lost in his stare and momentarily forgot to breath.

All of the extreme emotions—the yearning, the fear, the guilt, the passion—of the past two days were flung together inside her in a huge, expanding whirlpool of desire. She was swept away, disconnected from her rational brain and all she had left was her hungry, desperate need for this man.

She was so woefully unprepared. No one had ever coached her on what to do when faced with such stark, hormonal urges.

"We've shaken the baddies, Ravishina," he whispered, lifting a finger to caress her cheek. "And Benjamin Franklin talked the ferry workers out of reporting me to the port authorities."

"You bribed government employees?" She pretended to be aghast.

"Bribery is such an ugly word. I prefer the term 'persuaded.'"

"I've got to hand it to you, Mr. Bond, you're slick, very slick." He bowed low. "Compliment accepted."

"You know," she said, "I've seen every Bond movie ever made. I'm a sucker for the gadgets."

"Have you?" He seemed surprised. "Me, too."

"So you know what happens when the baddies have been properly shaken?"

"And not stirred?" His mouth quirked in amusement. "Of course I know, but why don't you tell me anyway."

"James and the Bond girl take a much needed break from non-stop danger."

"Oh?" He rubbed a strand of her hair between his thumb and forefinger. "And how do they achieve that lofty goal?"

"In each other's arms."

Her boldness at once titillated and thrilled her. She was almost dizzy from their teasing banter and surprised by her own unexpected wit. It felt dangerously illegal and infinitely compelling.

"Like this?" he asked and drew her to him.

"Mmm, there's usually a little more to it."

"You don't say."

"Stress reducers for Bond and his girl usually involve a few kisses," she ventured.

"I see." He hooked a finger under her chin and lowered his head. "And are these kisses of the French variety?"

"Most assuredly."

Hannah let herself be swept away in the fantasy. She forgot about Lionel Daycon and the formula. She ignored the gaping passengers, tossed caution to the chilly breeze and indulged in the most luxuriant kiss she had ever experienced.

Tyler shifted closer.

She nestled against his broad chest, fully, acutely aware of him. From his crisp white shirt redolent with the scent of spray starch, to the way his beard stubble tickled her chin, she took stock of every nuance, focusing on him in the same intense manner she tackled a chemistry puzzle.

He was quite a bit taller than her own five foot two and a half inches, long-limbed and long-waisted, so she went up on tiptoes.

His mouth pressed hers, soft at first, testing, then growing bolder. He tasted just as good as when he had kissed her on the pier outside his beach house, but this time there was something more.

Heat swirled through her solar plexus. Energy surged through her like Popeye after eating a can of spinach. She could not explain the occurrence but every time Tyler kissed her she grew stronger.

Hannah could not put a name to it but the experience they had just shared, running from Daycon's men and leaping onto the departing ferry had stirred their already simmering desire for each other. This kiss was hotter, more urgent, the direct results of heightened fear, excitement and danger. She was alive with sensation and hungry for more.

Under different circumstances, would Tyler have been attracted to her? Were her perilous troubles what drew him to her? Did he find her neediness compelling? Did he see himself in the role of great protector?

That notion dampened her ardor despite her renewed vigor and true to her nature, Hannah broke their connection, gently pulling her mouth from his and withdrawing, putting up her guard, stepping back, rescuing her heart.

Tyler stood looking at her, his eyes murky with passion. "Well," he murmured, tracing a finger along his lips. "Well."

Hannah inched over to the railing and peered down at the water churning beneath the bow of the ferry. She turned and stared out to sea for a long moment, then glanced at the port ahead.

The harbor lights blinked. Red. Green. Red. Green. Stop. Go.

She felt the same quixotic push-pull. Her chest tightened. She had already begun to care for Tyler more than she should.

"Hannah," he spoke softly and took her elbow. "We'll be going ashore soon. It's best we head back to the car."

She nodded, slipped her hand in his and allowed him to lead her to the BMW.

Chapter 8

They drove throughout the night, avoiding the interstate, opting instead for back country roads. Out here the sky was darker, the stars brighter, the road virtually empty. Tyler took an unusual route, hoping to stay one step ahead of Daycon's men.

Try as she might, Hannah could not forget the kiss they had shared on the boat. Every time she would hazard a glance over at him, the memory plagued her. She had played the radio for a while to fill the silence and forced her mind away from the thoughts that kept popping into her head. Dangerous thoughts of what it might be like to make love to this handsome doctor.

After fiddling with the radio dials, she discovered to her delight that they both shared a love of Country and Western music, though he preferred the golden oldies while she liked the emerging new stars.

Their conversation drifted along those lines for awhile, then wanting to get to know him even better, Hannah asked, "What made you become a doctor?"

Tyler shrugged. "The typical reason I suppose. I wanted to help people."

"Were your parents in the medical profession?" Most doctors she knew went into the field because it was a family tradition. Just as she had done.

"Yes. They're retired now and live in Florida."

"Is your family close?" she asked.

"I suppose you could say we are. We get together for holidays, call each other every two or three weeks."

"Brothers or sisters?"

"One sister. Younger. Joanne is a dietitian. She's married and lives in New York State with her husband and three kids. I don't get to see them as much as I'd like. How about you?"

"Only child," she admitted. "How come you stayed in Texas when everyone else moved away?"

"It's home and when my parents moved, I was in medical school and married to Yvette."

"Am I like her?" She dared broach the question she had been itching to ask since Margie Price had told her she resembled Yvette Fresno, even though she dreaded the truth. "Do I remind you of your wife?"

Tyler glanced over at her. "Physically, there's some similarity."

"That's why you decided to help me, isn't it?"

"Maybe at first it was," he admitted. "But you're nothing like her personality-wise. The more I get to know you, the more apparent it becomes. Don't think I compare you to her, because I don't."

"I'm sure there's no comparison."

"No," he said. "There's not."

Emotion knotted in Hannah's throat. Of course she could never fill a dead woman's shoes. Why would she want to try?

"Yvette was sunny and outgoing. She had a very accepting nature. Nothing ever bothered her. She wanted a home and kids. Those were her only ambitions."

She ducked her head. Yvette was her exact opposite and the kind of woman Hannah had always privately envied. She was serious and introverted. She never accepted anything at face value, always questioning the status quo. She'd lain awake at night worrying about the world and its problems. She had no time for a husband and children. Her ideals were much loftier. She had wanted to cure disease and she had succeeded. But success had come at such a high price.

Deep inside she feared she would never find a place in the world or with people. She'd withdrawn from the pain of her doubts into her own head, telling herself she actually preferred living in her head to hanging out with others. But now here she was, hoping for something she had no business hoping for.

"I loved Yvette," Tyler said. "But she's gone. I've finally comes to terms with it."

"It must have been very hard for you."

"Unspeakably."

"When did you first know you wanted to be a doctor?" she asked, anxious to get off the topic of his late wife and trying to figure out how someone made their career decision independent of parental influences. There had never been any discussion in her family. Her folks had simply assumed she would follow in their footsteps and like the good little girl she'd always been, she had done what was expected.

She watched while Tyler's face grew animated in the ghostly illumination of the dashboard light. She studied his firm jaw, admired his strong chin. Her heart caught in her throat as a melty sensation dissolved in her tummy and her pulse flamed through her veins.

He glanced over at her, giving her a slow, thorough once-over. Shivers skipped down her spine. And when a slight smiled tipped up the corners of his mouth, Hannah found herself moistening her lips with the tip of her tongue. The look in his eyes told her all she needed to know. He felt the sexual tension, too, and was just as afraid to act on it as she was.

"When I was twelve my grandfather had a heart attack while we were out fishing together," he said. "I'd learned CPR in Boy Scouts and I started cardiac compressions on him. He survived. I saved his life."

His voice cracked. Hannah felt his emotions straight to her marrow. What an unselfish man, she thought, and swiped a stray tear from her eye.

"That's a touching story."

"It was only later I learned that I couldn't cure everyone. In fact, the hard truth comes to all physicians sooner or later. Ultimately, you can't defeat death."

"Until my healing touch," she said softly.

He inhaled sharply. "It's an unbelievable concept."

"But it happened."

Tyler glanced at his hand. "Yes. You could change the world, Hannah. Does that scare you?"

"I'm terrified."

He reached across the seat for her hand. Hannah hung on tightly, wanting to never let go.

Guilt dogged Tyler. His job was to protect Hannah and through his own foolishness, he could have gotten her killed. He had always been a careful man, choosing to err on the side of caution whenever a difficult choice had to be made. This sudden reckless streak surprised and concerned him.

I wanted to impress her, he realized. *I wanted her to know that I would take care of her.*

But why? Tyler wasn't ready to examine his motives that closely. Instead, he turned his head to study the woman beside him.

Hannah dozed in the passenger seat as he headed northwest toward New Mexico. To stay alert, he'd stopped for coffee and while he was at it, filled up with gas at a small roadside convenience store. The car was a little worse for the wear, the vault onto the ferry having created an odd rumbling beneath the carriage. He air-pumped the tires, washed the windows and peeked under the car but saw nothing suspicious dangling.

Exhausted, Hannah had slept throughout the entire stop. Every so often, a breathy sound, like a contented kitten purring, would emerge from her slightly parted lips. It was, Tyler decided, a very sexy noise.

The plush bucket seat was tilted as far back as it would go. She lay on her left side, knees curled to her chest, her hands stacked beneath her cheek, her blond hair spilling over the headrest like a halo.

His gaze traveled over her. Studying her delicate bone struc-

ture and childlike sleeping position and listening to that soft
feminine snore, Tyler experienced an unusual heaviness in the
general region of his heart. Probably indigestion from the greasy
donut he had bought at the convenience store, he told himself.
At least that's what he hoped it was. He hated to think it might
mean something else.

He wasn't ready for it to mean something else.

You want to make love to her. The thought floated to him from
the ether.

"Don't be silly," he muttered out loud, but it was true.

Back there when he had kissed her on the ferry, he had grown
hard with desire. He wondered if she had felt the evidence of his
desire and that was why, flustered, she had turned away from him.

Did she want him or not? Her kisses seemed to suggest that
she did but then just as quickly, she had withdrawn.

*She's got a lot of problems, Tyler. A lot of things on her mind.
People are trying to kill her.*

Yes, and the last thing he wanted was to add to her troubles.

But he still wanted her.

She looked as innocent as Goldilocks in Papa Bear's bed, and
good enough to eat whole. He shouldn't be thinking about her
like this but he was. He should be trying to figure out what to
do, how to elude the men hunting them, how to heal her mysterious disease, but he couldn't seem to think about anything except the way she made him feel.

Strong. Manly. Virile.

He hadn't felt like this in years.

"Is that what this is all about, Tyler? Saving Hannah in order
to assuage your guilt?" he mumbled under his breath.

Maybe, in the beginning, that might have been true, but not
now. Not since he had come to know and care about her. The truth
was, he didn't want to see her hurting or in pain. Even the mere
thought of her discomfort sent arrows of unhappiness shooting
through him.

Without meaning to, Tyler reached out a hand to stroke her
arm. Her skin was soft as butter. She mumbled in her sleep,
stirred, then leaned over and kissed his hand.

Shocked at the intense tingles resulting from her lips on his hand, Tyler froze. He stared out the windshield, barely aware of where he was headed, his heart jerking like a jumping bean.

"Nice," Hannah murmured, eyes closed and patting his hand.

God, he thought and held his breath. *She's so beautiful.*

She didn't possess that stunning gorgeousness of a runway model but who in the hell wanted a bag of bones anyway? Hannah was round and firm. Her loveliness was all natural. She had no need for makeup. Her skin was creamy, flawless, her lips a rich salmon color. Her eyelashes were pale but long, her cheekbones a study in perfection.

In Tyler's opinion she was a quintessential knockout—smart, sexy, gorgeous and modest to boot. He couldn't believe she had spent her life buried in a lab, hiding behind Bunsen burners, metric scales and chemical formulas.

He wanted to kiss her again. Taste her sweet, original flavor. He had kissed a few women in his life and none had tasted like Hannah. She had a full, rich flavor that stirred him the same way a fine, earthy wine might.

His reserve melted like chocolate in the sun. She had tucked his hand under her chin and every so often she would move her cheek back and forth over his skin.

Goose bumps fled up his arm. He darted a glance at her and mesmerized, could not seem to look away.

She had arched her upper body and her chest was elevated. Through the fluffy material of her blue sweater he spied the delineation of her breasts. And her nipples. They were beaded into hard peaks.

Blood emptied from his head, swamping his groin. He felt the pull of her like a thousand tiny vacuums turned on at once, sucking him into her aura, bathing him in a hot, white glow of intense energy. His body was an inferno, burning for her.

Tyler gulped and whipped his hand from beneath her cheek. The front and back tires on the right side of the BMW ran off the road, spewing gravel. He wrenched his gaze from Hannah, twisted the wheel to get back in the lane and forced his attention on the white stripes zipping by the window.

Hannah never woke.

The pressure in his lower region was unbelievable. This wasn't right. He was supposed to be protecting Hannah, not lusting after her.

But he was only human.

Faced with a beautiful, sexy woman sleeping beside him, his body had behaved accordingly. It was a natural response. He had nothing to be ashamed of.

He ached with the need to touch her. He wanted to make love to her. Long, slow and perfect.

Tyler shook his head. There was no excuse for this wayward fantasy. He had to get himself under control. He was a doctor. A surgeon. An educated man. He would not succumb to physical urges, no matter how normal they might be. Hannah needed him to be strong and dependable, not to paw her in her sleep.

Clenching his jaw, he vowed to keep his eyes on the road and his hands to himself. No matter what.

At dawn, unable to drive any farther without at least a few hours of sleep, Tyler pulled into a motel on the other side of Abilene. They ate breakfast at a twenty-four-hour Waffle House across the street, both of them yawning and struggling to stay awake long enough to swallow eggs, waffles and orange juice. At this hour of the morning the place was packed with early-rising farmers and bleary-eyed travelers who had wandered off the main highway.

"How are you feeling?" he asked her

She noticed shadows under his eyes. If he appeared that tired, she probably looked ten times worse. "Actually, pretty good."

"No weakness or vertigo?"

"I'm fine, doc. Truly."

"I worry."

"I know."

"Occupational hazard."

Self-consciously, Hannah ran a hand through her hair and grinned sheepishly. "As soundly as I was sleeping, I'm surprised I don't have drool on my face."

"You look perfect."

Shyly, Hannah turned her head.

"I would like to get a fresh set of labs on you, though. Check your hemoglobin and hematocrit levels and see exactly where we stand."

"How?"

"We'd have to find a hospital. I could speak to a staff physician, have them order the tests."

She shook her head. "No. No more hospitals."

He started to say something but held his tongue.

"If it makes you feel any better, Marcus has a fully equipped lab. When we get to Taos, I'll let you do the blood work yourself," she said.

"You're forgetting, it has been a long time since I was in medical school."

Tyler admitting a weakness? She smiled. "I'll do it then, or Marcus will." If Marcus was there. Her smile disappeared.

They finished their breakfast and walked across the highway to the motel.

"I hope you don't mind," Tyler said. "I booked just one room for us because we won't be here long. I'll only need a few hours of sleep."

"One room?" Her voice squeaked, surprising her.

"But it has two beds," he added quickly.

Sleeping in the same room with Tyler? Her heart beat faster. Alone in a bedroom with the one man in the world who had the power to shake her resolve and melt her knees?

"And I used an alias, just in case Daycon's goons come looking for us, but I'm afraid I wasn't terribly original. Mr. and Mrs. Smith."

Unlocking the door, he ushered her over the threshold and into a sparse but clean bungalow. Tyler kicked off his shoes and dropped to the twin bed closest to the door. An unwieldy silence filled the tiny room.

"If it's okay," Hannah said. "I'd like to take a shower."

"Of course it's all right. You don't have to ask my permission. I'll get the suitcase from the car. I packed Yvette's clothes for you. I hope you don't mind." He was looking everywhere but at her.

"If you hadn't, I'd be naked," she said, then immediately regretted her word choice.

Fire heated her cheeks and she fled for the bathroom. Escaping.

Closing the door behind her, she sagged against it and caught a glimpse of herself in the mirror. Her hair was disheveled, her clothes wrinkled. She looked road weary and worse for the wear. How was it possible that Tyler found her attractive when she resembled something the cat had dragged in and chewed on for a while? Shaking her head, Hannah peeled off her sweater and wriggled out of her blue jeans.

The hot water massaged her tired body and by the time she had finished her shower and wrapped a towel around herself, she was feeling a lot better. Tiptoeing, she inched into the other room, clutching her towel closed with her fingers. Tyler had drawn the heavy curtains, and only the cracks around the windows and door offered much light. He was stretched out in bed, sleeping.

At least Hannah hoped he was asleep.

She located the suitcase situated on a straight-back chair beside the thirteen-inch television set resting on a scarred bureau. She rummaged through it in search of undergarments, her damp hair splattering water droplets across the worn carpet.

At the sound of the bathroom door creaking closed, Tyler opened his eyes and started to call out to her, but the sight of Hannah wrapped in nothing but a skimpy white bath towel, tiptoeing around the bedroom, stilled his tongue.

She was the most exquisite thing he had ever seen. Bar none.

Her movements were graceful as a dancer's. With her ivory skin and mass of blond hair shining in the darkness she could have been a moon goddess. Her body was slim but well-rounded in all the right places. Even from this distance he could smell the fresh, clean scent of her soap.

His mouth watered and his body hardened.

God, how he wanted her. More than he had any right to want her. Tyler was faced with the most gorgeous, sexy woman conceivable and he could not have her.

She was vulnerable. He had promised to help her and she

trusted him to do just that. He could not betray that trust by acting like some sex-crazed caveman.

He thought of all the women he should have wanted. Of all the women who wanted him. Society women like Margie Price, who would make a perfect doctor's wife. But he had not been interested in Margie or any of those other women. Unable to stop himself, Tyler watched as Hannah dropped the towel and shimmied into her panties, unknowingly exposing her naked backside to him. He knew it was wrong to watch but he was only human.

Too human, it seemed.

Those lush, lovely hips. That firm bottom. Those shapely thighs.

He almost groaned aloud at the pressure building inside his groin. He could still taste her tongue on his as the sharp memory of their hot kisses aboard the Galveston ferry flashed through his mind again.

She pulled one of his T-shirts over her head. Having her covered should have eased his suffering. It did not. Because he knew what forbidden treasures lurked beneath that thin cotton shirt.

When she slipped into the other bed, the springs groaned loudly. Tyler closed his eyes against the erotic image those creaking springs produced and forced himself to breath slowly and deeply.

She rolled onto her side.

Squeak.

A few minutes later she flopped onto her stomach.

Squeak. Squeak.

The tightness in Tyler's groin grew into an almost unbearable throbbing.

Squeak. Squeak. Squeak.

Hannah sighed.

"Is something wrong?" he asked.

"Did I wake you?"

Not wanting her to know he had been observing her in the buff, he lied. "Yeah."

"I'm sorry."

"Can't sleep?"

"No. It's this bed. Apparently, the coils in the box springs are busted and the mattress sags in the middle. I'm having trouble getting comfortable."

"I'll switch beds with you."

"Oh, no. At least I got a nap in the car. You need your rest. We've got a long day of driving ahead of us."

"You could share this bed with me," he said, instantly wondering why he had made such a rash offer. The idea of Hannah curled up beside him on the narrow twin bed was pure torture. If she spooned that fine fanny against him he could not be held responsible for his actions.

"Would you mind?" Her voice was wavery, indecisive.

He scooted over until his back touched the wall and he raised the covers for her. Like a little girl crawling into her parents' bed during a thunderstorm, Hannah climbed in beside him.

No matter how badly he might want to make love to her, Tyler knew he could not. She trusted him. He had never taken unfair advantage of a woman in his entire life and he wasn't about to start now.

"Thank you," she whispered.

Her damp hair tickled his face. Her body heat warmed him. It had been a very long time since he had lain beside a woman. Especially a woman as beautiful and sexy as Hannah. A very long time indeed. He had forgotten how wonderful it felt.

The sweet scent of her filled his nostrils. Her bottom brushed against his belly, setting his torso ablaze. To keep from touching her, he curled his hands into fists.

Don't do it, Fresno.

He was mahogany-hard and very close to losing the last shred of his control.

For a woman who disliked being touched she was enjoying this way too much. How she had come to spend so many years denying herself the tactile pleasures of another person's body, Hannah did not know.

But this wasn't just any body. This was Tyler.

She realized that by climbing into bed with him she was playing with fire, but she had such a desperate need to be close to someone. A need that had lain dormant for thirty-two years.

She was tired of being distant, repressed and aloof. Tired of living her life according to outdated expectations. Her parents were gone and she was free to make her own way. She ached to unleash her passion, longed to lose herself in the reckless abandon of physical desires. Her body blistered with yearning. She had spent way too much time locked up in a lab, smelling of chemicals and living like an old maid.

Besides, this might be her last chance.

If she did not find Marcus, her chances of surviving the combined exposure to *Virusall* and radiation and her body's subsequent radical-immune response to the drug were nil. And even if she were to find Marcus there were no guarantees they would be able to reverse the deadly effects.

Hannah rolled over onto her back and when her hip brushed against Tyler's, she realized with a start that he was completely naked. His breath tickled her cheek. Under the sheets her bare feet grazed his.

He inhaled sharply.

Palms sweaty, heart roaring, blood pumping, she held her breath and waited.

"Tyler," she whispered, too excited and nervous to look at him. Instead, hands folded across her lap, she stared up at the ceiling. "Are you awake?"

He did not answer.

Hannah knew he was awake. He was breathing too fast to be asleep.

"Tyler?" She laid a hand on his chest and he jerked.

"What is it, Hannah?" he asked in a heavy voice.

How did a girl go about seducing the man of her dreams? She had no clue. On the job, when she had wanted something she was accustomed to coming right out and asking for it, but somehow that approach seemed unromantic. She did not want to make any mistakes.

And she was terrified of disappointing him, but her body's

urges were too strong to be denied. She worried her bottom lip
with her teeth.

If she made the first move would he consider her too bold?
She knew he was attracted to her. His kisses left no doubt to the
power of the chemistry undulating between them. The way his
lips, his touch, seemed to revitalize her was startling. It had to
mean something.

But he didn't have to be in love with her. She wasn't asking
for that. Truth be told it would be much simpler if he wasn't in
love with her. She would hate to die and break his heart the way
his wife had.

"I was wondering…"

"Yes?"

"If you…er…if we… Oh, I can't say it." Embarrassed, she
covered her face with her hands.

"You can say anything to me, Hannah, and I won't judge you
harshly. I want you to know that."

His words melted her.

"I want to make love to you," she whispered.

"Are you sure that's what you really want?" he asked huskily.
"Are you strong enough?"

"Touching you makes me stronger. Every time you touch me,
I come alive. But, Tyler, do you really want me?" Every doubt
she'd ever had about her abilities to please a man knotted inside
her chest, making it hard to breath. Her muscles bunched from
the tension of wanting and waiting and worrying that she wasn't
woman enough for him.

"Silly woman, do you even have to ask?"

And then he was pulling her into his arms, holding her close,
his mouth covering hers with fierce kisses.

Hannah moaned softly and pressed her feverish body against
him. His skin was as hot as hers.

"You're so beautiful," he murmured, kissing her throat. "I can
hardly believe this is happening."

His long fingers skimmed over her skin, sending tremors
throughout her body. Her muscles dissolved into mush as she
gave herself over to him heart and soul.

Tyler gently lifted her shirt over her head and tossed it to the floor, then cupped a breast in each hand. "Perfect," he pronounced, before lowering his head and taking first one beaded nipple into his mouth and then the other.

Hannah hissed in her breath at the warm moisture of his tongue. It felt so good.

"Relax, sweetheart," he soothed, rubbing one hand across her belly, stoking the fire already glowing there.

Easy for him to say. She was wound tighter than a top and ready to explode. She laced her fingers through his dark hair and softly called his name.

"Yes?" Propping himself up on one elbow, he looked down at her.

"Nothing. I just wanted to say your name."

In the faint light oozing around the curtains, she saw him smile. She absorbed the beauty of that smile, committed it to memory before shifting her gaze from his face to his body. She had to seize this moment and pour everything she had into it, because she knew this miniscule window of time was all she possessed. Relaxing a little, she allowed herself to enjoy him.

His broad shoulders progressed into a smooth chest. His dark nipples had turned to pellets as tight as her own. His ribs, waist and stomach were compact planes of lean muscle and sinew. The bed sheets hid him from his hips downward and Hannah was dying to see what treasures lay beyond.

She wanted him more than she had ever wanted anything in her life, and that included avenging her parents' deaths by developing *Virusall*.

"I want to see all of you," she said, and pulled back the covers.

Her hands trembled with desire and her eyes widened. The wall of his flat abdomen gave way to slim hips. The part of him that was distinctly male stood at erect attention amidst a triangle of dark hair flanked by light-colored skin. His thighs looked firm and powerful. Hannah's throat constricted and she wondered if she had bitten off more than she could chew.

While she was perusing him, he was studying her just as intently. His gaze traveled from her breasts to the rounded curve of her hip and on down into the blond apex that housed her parts most feminine. If possible, the flag of his arousal seemed to grow taller.

"Oh, Tyler."

He embraced her again and they kissed, their gazes locked the entire time. Their moans mingled and vibrated inside their kiss, over the sizzling shock of their bodies touching intimately for the first time.

A hundred fires leapt to life in a thousand different places throughout her tingling body, whooshing together, fusing into one magnificent all-consuming inferno. Tyler's hands were gentle and firm, massaging her tender flesh in a way that promised more sinful indulgence to come.

Every cell inside her hummed and vibrated, bustling with life. When she was lying in his arms it was hard to believe she could be dying. She felt as invincible as superwoman.

Caught between his pleasing hands and his teasing lips, Hannah had never felt so drunk with need and want. She clung to him, running her hands down his knotted back muscles, squeezing his buttocks as his shaft pulsed against her thigh.

"Are you absolutely sure this is what you want?" he whispered.

"Oh, Tyler, it's so much more than that. You're everything I ever hoped for and never expected to get."

"Hannah." His voice was choked with emotion.

Birth control, she thought for the first time since starting this. "I don't suppose you have a condom?" she ventured.

Tyler groaned. "No."

Why was she worried about birth control when she didn't know if she would live from one day to the next? Why? Because she could not risk bringing a child into the craziness of her life when her body was unpredictable, her future so uncertain.

Hannah swallowed. "I'm sorry, I never even thought."

"Shhh," he whispered. "It's okay."

"No, it's not. I got you stirred up. Gave you promises I couldn't keep." She was almost crying.

He stroked her hair, kissed her forehead. "Shh."

"I'll go get in the other bed."

"You'll stay and I'll put on a pair of pants."

"It's not fair," she whimpered. "I wanted you so."

"Not any more than I wanted you, sweetheart. Don't worry. I'll buy some condoms at our next stop. We can do this later."

"But I want you now."

"We've waited this long to find each other, a few more hours is nothing."

"You say the sweetest things." She traced a finger along his cheek and laid her head on his shoulder.

"That's because I mean what I say."

Tears stung her eyes. In her wildest imagination she had never dreamed a man like this could exist, much less care for her.

At that moment there was a loud banging on the door. Hannah clutched the sheet over her nakedness and stared at Tyler.

"Who's that?" she whispered.

The knocking came again, urgent, insistent.

"Who is it?" Tyler called, and climbed over Hannah. He picked his jeans off the floor and slid into them.

"Mr. Smith?" came a worried masculine voice from the other side of the door.

"Yes?"

"Are you by any chance a doctor?"

"Just a minute." Tyler pulled his shirt over his head and moved to open the door.

Early-morning sunlight poured in. Hannah craned her neck to peer at a middle-aged, apologetic-looking man standing in the doorway wearing blue jeans, a flannel shirt and a shapeless beige work coat. He worried a battered cap with his stained, gnarled fingers. "Sorry to wake you folks."

"That's all right," Tyler said. "What can I do for you?"

"Me and my wife, we saw the M.D. plates on your car and the medical bag in your back seat. Are you a doctor?"

"Yes," Tyler said, raking a hand through his unruly hair. "I'm a doctor."

"Thank the Lord." The man placed his palms together and glanced heavenward. "The nearest hospital is in Abilene thirty miles away and Angie, my four-year-old, is so sick I don't think she can make it that far. Would you come have a look at her, please?" The man's homey face wrinkled with concern.

"Sure, sure. No problem," Tyler replied. "What's wrong with your daughter?"

"She's got a high fever. A hundred and five. And a real bad headache. She's been throwing up...." The man consulted his watch. "For over an hour now."

"I will be right with you. Let me get dressed."

The man nodded and Tyler shut the door behind him.

Hannah looked at him, her eyes wide. "It sounds serious."

"I'll be back soon," he said.

"You're not leaving me behind."

"Yes. Get some rest."

"No way," Hannah said and sprang from the bed. "I'm coming with you."

Chapter 9

"No."

Fear chilled his blood. If Hannah came with him, Tyler had no doubt she'd try to cure the little girl with her touch. Healing his cut had compromised her health. A niggling suspicion told him the more she used her uncanny healing powers, the weaker she would become as her immune system warred with the irradiated chemicals inside her body.

Already she had jerked on her blue jeans and was searching under the bed for her shoes.

"Hannah, you must stay here." He put steel into his voice.

She raised her head, met his gaze, her blue eyes ablaze with determination. "A child's life is in danger and I can help."

"So can I," Tyler said firmly. "Allow me to do what I was trained to do."

"You can't ask me to stand by and watch a child suffer when I can do something about it." She shoved her feet into her loafers and raked a hand through her tangled tresses.

Just minutes ago he had been inhaling the scent of that hair, kissing those determined lips. It seemed as if eons had already passed since that tender moment. Another time, another century. Harsh reality had come screeching back, jerking him from the soft, fuzzy afterglow of their intimate physical contact.

"That's why you should stay here," he said. "So you won't see her suffering."

"My imagination will be worse than any actuality."

"If you see her, you'll want to touch her."

"Yes."

"I can't let you harm yourself." He crossed his arms and moved to block the door. "Admit it. You lose strength when you heal."

Her jaw tightened; her nostrils flared. "It's not your decision to make."

"The child probably has nothing worse than the flu. Is it worth harming yourself over?"

"What kind of person would I be if I refused to help simply to save myself some discomfort?"

"It's more than mere discomfort, Hannah. This healing power of yours is killing you, or hadn't you noticed?" Even though he was frustrated with her, Tyler couldn't help admiring her stubborn resolve to do what she considered was right.

"I'm dying anyway."

"We don't know that for sure," he protested.

"I'm prepared to take the risk."

"As your physician, I will not allow it."

"You're no longer my physician."

"What am I then?"

Hannah said nothing, silent and immovable as a brick wall. "You're the guy who's driving me to Taos."

"Is that all I am?"

She didn't answer. Her silence sliced crueler than angry words. She still didn't trust him. He'd proven himself to her time and time again and still she held part of herself in reserve, unable to fully surrender her faith to him.

"I care about you, dammit!" His words echoed in the small room. "Doesn't that mean anything to you?"

"Keep your voice down, her father is right outside." Hannah shushed him.

He saw her clench her jaw, hardening her resolve, denying her feelings. He wouldn't get away by force. Not with her, but for her own good, he must convince her to stay behind.

"Hannah." He changed his tactics, lowering his voice and softening his gaze. "Please, be reasonable. You've barely regained your strength from healing me and we've got a long, arduous trip ahead of us."

"I have to do this."

"Why? I can help the child. The old-fashioned way. There's absolutely no need for you to take such a chance."

"I have to test myself and my abilities." She stood staring into his face, beseeching him to understand with those hauntingly blue eyes. "I have to know what I can and cannot do. Tyler, don't deny me this."

Tyler sighed, knowing he was defeated. Fear coiled like a leaden snake deep inside his center. "All right." He put on his own shoes and shirt then opened the door.

Hannah was scared. Terrified, in fact. For the same reason Tyler hadn't wanted her to come with him.

Today, she might die.

The motel owner, weathered by many years of scratching out a living in the barren west-Texas land, led them toward the office. Tyler carried the medical bag he had retrieved from the BMW.

"My name's Will Henry," the man explained. "We live around back of the motel. My wife Rosie runs the place while I farm the fields." He gestured at a pasture of freshly tilled dirt, separated from the motel bungalows by several hundred yards and four strands of barbed-wire fencing. "We're gettin' ready for spring planting."

Hannah took a deep breath of the chilly morning air and wondered if she would live long enough to see the spring plants ripen into summer produce. She watched Tyler as he walked, shoulders rounded, head lowered, a serious expression on his handsome face.

He seemed so isolated, so encapsulated within himself. A man alone. A man apart. Had she done this to him? Forced him to mirror her own desolation? She knew she had displeased him by refusing to stay behind, but she'd truly had no choice. How could she cower in the bungalow when a child's life hung in the balance? She might be a lot of things—antisocial, idealistic and obstinate—but she was not a coward.

"Rosie," Will Henry called, pushing open the screen door that moaned on its hinges. He motioned them inside the overly warm kitchen. "We hit the jackpot. Got two doctors instead of just one."

A pale, narrow woman with pinched features appeared from the hallway. She dabbed at her watery gray eyes with a tissue, her nose red from crying.

"Thank the Lord," she whispered in a wobbly voice.

"Where is your daughter, ma'am?" Tyler asked with his most polished bedside manner. Hannah admired the respectful smile he gave the harried woman, the gentle way in which he took her hand.

"Follow me."

Mrs. Henry led them down a short hallway and into a child's room decorated with nursery rhyme characters painted in bright primary colors—Mary and her little lamb, Old King Cole with his pipe and fiddlers, the cow jumping over a smiling crescent moon. It was a cheerful room meant for laughter and kisses, not worry and fear.

In the middle of the bed lay a tiny red-haired girl curled into a tight knot, her pallid cheeks stained with tears. A worn teddy bear with one button eye missing was tucked in the crook of her arm. Hannah's heartstrings pulled taut as she watched Tyler settle himself beside the child.

"Hello," he soothed. "My name's Doctor Fresno. Your mommy tells me you've been very sick."

The child possessed hardly enough energy to nod. Her face was scarlet, her skin extremely dry.

Dehydrated, Hannah thought.

"I'd like to listen to your chest and take your temperature," Tyler explained.

"Mommy?" Her voice was weak. She cast dull green eyes toward the doorway where Mrs. Henry stood beside Hannah.

"It's okay, Angie. Let the doctor examine you."

"Tell me about your headache," he said, carefully raising the top of her Barbie pajamas and laying his stethoscope over her frail chest.

"It hurts real bad," the child whispered and clutched a hand to the back of her head.

"Could you take a deep breath for me?" he asked softly.

The girl complied.

He took her temperature and frowned over the results.

Watching in awe as Tyler worked, Hannah's throat collected a thick coating of emotion. She felt at once impressed, overwhelmed and contrite. He was so good with the child, touching her gently, explaining everything before he did it, trying his best to extract a smile from her. Why had Hannah presumed she could do better? His healing gift was natural, not chemically induced like hers. He truly cared. More important, he knew how to listen to people, how to relate to his patients. Hannah was nothing but a fluke.

She was out of her element and over her head. She was the woman who had so disliked touching others. She had no business being here. She should have listened to him and stayed in the bungalow. Turning, she stepped from the room.

"Hannah," Tyler called.

She looked back. He was rising to his feet, draping his stethoscope around his neck. "Yes?" she murmured.

He crooked his finger at her. "Come here."

"Me?" she asked, even though she was already moving toward him, anxious to help.

"Why don't you sit here with Angie while her mother and I have a talk."

"Do you want me to hold her?"

A nervousness as shocking as biting down on a piece of aluminum with a mouthful of metal fillings took hold of her. Touch this child she did not know? Heal her? Would her abilities work? Did she still possess the healing power or had her talents dissipated as ephemerally as the paradoxical drug that had leaked from the vials in her Fiat? Now that the pressure was on, could she actually deliver?

Their eyes met. Tyler's expression was grave. "Yes."

Hannah wandered over to the bed. "Hi," she said breathlessly. She hesitated and peered over her shoulder at Tyler.

He nodded.

"My name's Hannah," she continued, "and I'm sorry that you're feeling bad."

Tyler took Mrs. Henry by the shoulder and ushered her from the room, quietly closing the door behind them.

"Are you the doctor's wife?" the girl asked.

"No," Hannah said. "I'm his helper."

"Like a nurse?"

"Yes. Something like that."

The girl nodded acceptingly.

"You look thirsty. Would you like something to drink?" Hannah asked noticing a glass half filled with what appeared to be 7UP sitting on the bedside table.

"Every time I try to drink sumpin' I throw up," the girl said. Her breath was warm—too warm.

Hannah sat on the edge of the bed and fingered the bedspread. Touching the child was harder than she expected. Tentatively, she reached out.

Her hand trembled.

The child smiled.

It's all right. Touch her, Hannah.

The voice seemed to come from nowhere and everywhere at the same time, stoking her courage.

Heal her.

Drawing a deep breath, Hannah braced herself and brushed her fingers along Angie's brow, pushing back the straight curtain of her auburn bangs. The ardent tingling began immediately.

The tips of her fingers were at once alive with a bright flaming sensation that quickly spread through her hands, to her wrist, forearms, elbows and beyond. Stretching, flowing, blending. Encompassing her entire body in a throbbing inner heat.

Angie gasped in wonderment, her eyes growing rounder, her mouth opening in a startled circle. "Mommy," she whispered.

"It's okay," Hannah reassured her. "Everything is going to be all right. I promise."

Then she scooped the girl into her arms and pressed her against her chest.

She had never held a child before. Had never had the opportunity to do so. She had no siblings. No close women friends. She'd had no younger cousins or neighbors.

In truth, she had never really thought about children before. How it would feel to hold them close, smell their hair, hear their velvety intake of air as they breathed. She had always assumed motherhood was for other women. Women not obsessed with a career. Women who liked to touch and be touched in return. But not for her. Not Hannah Zachary. She was too strong-minded, too independent, too focused on inventing a cure for viruses to pay attention to her biological urgings.

She wanted a child.

The realization took her aback.

Slowly, she began to rock back and forth, a soft soothing lullaby pouring miraculously from her lips. She hadn't been aware that she even knew any lullabies. Hannah clung tightly to the small form in her arms and tried her best not to become overwhelmed with the disquieting changes in her own body. Her blood turned to sludge in her veins. Her tongue grew thick and her pulse slowed to a crawl.

As her stamina ebbed, Angie grew stronger right before Hannah's eyes. The redness drained from her cheeks. Her skin turgor improved. Her eyes brightened.

"My headache's gone," Angie cried in amazement.

Hannah's arms had turned to lead. They were as heavy as her head was light. Her vision blurred. She heard a far-off rushing in her ears, like the sound of heavy road traffic on a distant highway. She felt at once hot and cold. Paralyzed. Deadened. Numb.

I touched her and she's healed. It was worth it.

Angie squirmed from her arms, rolled off the bed and sprang to her feet like a gymnast at the Olympics. "Mommy, Mommy," she exclaimed, running for the door. "I'm all better now."

Hannah closed her eyes, overcome by a staggering desire to

sleep for a hundred years. Through a fog, she heard the door open and listened to cries of joy from Angie's mother and father. She also heard Tyler's voice, deep and nearby.

"Are you all right, sweetheart?" he murmured, his lips pressed close to her ear.

She tried to speak, to tell him about the extraordinary occurrence that had happened between her and Angie, but Hannah's tongue lolled against the roof of her mouth and refused to articulate sound. She attempted to open her eyes, to peer into his face but it took too much effort to raise her eyelids and focus beyond the gathering nebula.

Tyler's arms went around her. Arms that had become so familiar in such a short amount of time. Arms she longed for, even in her dreams. Hannah smiled faintly. If she had to die to gain this sort of treatment, then fair enough.

"What's happened to her?" Mr. Henry asked Tyler. "Is your wife okay?"

"She suffers dizziness from time to time."

His wife. Mrs. Henry had assumed they were married. If only it were true.

"She made me feel so much better," Angie chattered. "She touched me and my headache went away."

"It's a miracle," Mrs. Henry said.

"No," Tyler said and she heard him speak his second lie of the morning. "Your daughter's flu has simply run its course. But it wouldn't be a bad idea to take her to see your regular physician as soon as possible. To make sure she's made a full recovery."

"We will, Doctor. Thank you."

"If you'll excuse us." Holding Hannah tightly in his arms, Tyler carried her from the house and back to the motel room.

"Hannah?" Tyler bathed her face with a damp cloth. "Can you hear me? Speak to me, sweetheart." Blood moved through his body in a slow, sticky thickness.

You've got to distance yourself. That's what she did with you. You can't let yourself feel too much.

Easier said then done, especially when she looked so helpless, so lifeless. If he had forced her to stay behind in the bungalow she would not at this moment be lying cold and prostrate in the shoddy twin bed. Dammit.

But if you'd forced Hannah to stay behind, little Angie Henry would be dead.

Tyler closed his eyes, rocked back on his heels. It was true. The child did not have the flu as he had told her amazed parents, but a virulent form of bacterial meningitis. He had seen a few cases in his career. A child as young and weakened as Angie had been could die in a matter of hours. By the time Tyler had gotten to her she was close to death. If her parents had made the trip with her into Abilene in all likelihood she would have succumbed to the disease on the road.

But Hannah had saved her. At the expense of her own health.

Biting down on the back of his knuckles to stay the despair rising inside him, Tyler knew there had been no choice. Neither one of them could have allowed Angie to die when Hannah held the key to her survival.

No matter the price.

He was scared. Damned scared. He suppressed a desperate urge to flee. He felt pulled in two directions at once, torn between his need to take care of her and his fear of losing her. For a fleeting moment, he imagined himself jumping into his car and speeding away, justifying her lack of trust in him.

Stop it!

He had to shut down his panic. Quick. Had to gain control. He could not let her condition get to him. He would not collapse in the face of adversity. He would persevere.

"Tyler?" Hannah's voice was raspy as a file against rocks, but filled his spirit with instant thanksgiving. Her eyelashes fluttered open, revealing those incredible ocean-blue eyes.

He sat forward and smiled down at her. "Hi."

"Hi, yourself." Her eyes crinkled slightly at the edges. "How's Angie doing?"

"Out playing with dolls in her front yard. You saved her life, you know."

"Did I?" Hannah brightened.

"Absolutely."

"It's a pretty great feeling. I see why you doctors get a rush from saving lives."

"Us doctors are not usually as effective as you were."

"I cheated. I had a secret weapon."

"A secret weapon that you created."

"It's not as much fun as it sounds."

He held himself back, afraid to touch her, afraid he'd stir up more feelings he wouldn't know how to deal with. "I know."

"How long have I been out?" she asked.

"Three hours."

Hannah groaned. "More time wasted."

"You're not superwoman. If you insist on going around healing the sick then you've got to rest up and save your own strength."

She lifted a hand and lightly traced his cheek. Her touch sent a shiver of longing through him. His need for her bothered him. He hated being so susceptible. He stepped back, moved away.

"You're too good to me." She dropped her hand heavily as if her arm weighed a hundred pounds.

"Too good? How do you suppose?" He forced out a dry chuckle when the last thing on earth he felt was lighthearted. But he had to pretend, for her sake, that everything was okay.

"For taking care of me. Standing by me. Even when we argue."

"We don't argue." Guilt was an arrow through his chest. Just a minute ago he was thinking of running out on her. He wasn't a coward. He could deal with this. He could.

"What do you call that fight we had a while ago, when you didn't want me to go with you to see Angie?" she asked.

"A mild difference of opinion."

"That's a nice way to put it." Sudden tears misted her eyes.

"Hey, hey." Similar tears choked his throat and he fought to keep them from spilling down his cheeks in a sloppy display. "What's all this?"

"No one's ever treated me the way you do."

"Well, all I've got to say is that you've been hanging out with the wrong people."

"That's the truth." She smiled wanly.

Touch her, comfort her, his physician's voice demanded. But he could not. His hands seemed frozen at his sides.

"We've got to leave soon," Hannah said.

"Not until you're better."

"Did you ever get any rest?"

He waved a hand. "Don't worry about me."

"Did you?" she insisted.

"I dozed maybe an hour."

"Liar. That's your third lie of the day. Keep it up and you're going to give Pinnochio a run for his money."

Ignoring his fear over touching her again, Tyler helped her out to the car. His heart swooped with the rich sadness he'd been seeking to avoid and he swallowed hard against the pain. They hadn't driven ten miles down the road when Hannah fell asleep again. Tyler gazed over at her. Had it only been a few short hours since they had almost made love? He blew out his breath, relieved to discover his panic had disappeared and he was once more committed to seeing this through to the end, no matter what happened.

Healing little Angie had taken a lot out of Hannah. She was more drained than when she had cured his cut. His cut had been a fairly minor wound, however, while Angie's meningitis had been life-threatening.

Did the ebbing of Hannah's energy directly correspond to the extent of the disease process she healed? Would curing say, a massive heart attack take more out of her than treating a hangnail? Or was her waning endurance progressive? So that the more she healed, the weaker she would become, no matter what the illness?

There was no way to know for sure unless she kept healing people. Tyler could not allow that to happen. But how could he prevent it? For instance, what if Hannah inadvertently shook hands with someone who had cancer? What then?

Fine. He would run interference. Keep her out of a crowd and away from everyone.

And if another Will Henry comes knocking on the door?

What if the word somehow got out about her abilities? What

if people with every ailment under the sun came looking for her, seeking a miracle cure? She would be bombarded, chased, harassed. Worst of all, she would be unable to refuse.

Tyler stared at the road stretching before them, realizing there was no way he could protect her. Just as he had been unable to protect Yvette. All his years of medical training and experience were completely useless.

Reaching over, he trailed a finger across her arm and breathed in her heavenly aroma. He had to be proactive. Had to do something.

But what?

He had to think rationally, objectively, ignoring all feelings, all crazy impulses. He had to think like a man of science. If he detached from her emotionally, he would make better decisions. He could prevent his fears from governing his actions.

Hannah's situation was not only far beyond his expertise, but beyond that of any doctor he knew. They were treading new ground, stepping about in a brave new world without a road map. How did he even begin to develop a cure for what was ailing her?

He mulled the question over in his mind. Before he could proceed he had to know what her lab values were like.

Except Hannah had refused to have her blood tested at a hospital.

Hannah doesn't always act in her own best interest, Tyler. It's up to you. You're driving the car and she's so tired she probably wouldn't even notice you'd taken a detour until it was too late.

The thought was enticing. Take Hannah to a medical facility. Where?

The Dallas–Fort Worth Metroplex was about two hundred miles east. Out of their way for sure but Tyler knew an excellent hematologist who had an office in the area. It was dishonest to change plans without Hannah's permission but once he got her there, Tyler had confidence he could make her see things his way.

He simply had to do something.

Because he could not live with himself if he didn't try.

Oblivious to his underhanded tactic, Hannah slept on as Tyler turned the car east toward Dallas–Fort Worth.

How would Hannah react when she discovered that he had betrayed her?

Tyler grimaced and mentally sought to defend himself. He wasn't betraying her. Taking her to see the hematologist in Dallas was for her own good. Eventually, she'd see things his way. He was sure of it.

Oh, yeah? Remember what happened with Yvette? Admit the truth for once. She didn't tell you about her cancer for so long because she knew exactly what you would do.

Licking his dry lips, Tyler's mind jettisoned to the past. He recalled his anger with his wife when she'd finally told him she had cancer. He'd felt so dishonored. Why had she kept her illness a secret from him? Why hadn't she trusted him with the most important event in her life?

Yvette, always the peacemaker, had tried to smooth it over, telling him she'd remained silent because he was completing his medical training and she hadn't wanted to worry him. It was partially true and the excuse had appeased him.

On the surface.

But something inside him had died. He and Yvette weren't as close as he'd believed. She'd carried a great burden, stoically, silently. And once he found out about it, he'd taken over her care, practically forcing her to have chemotherapy when they both knew it was futile. But he was a man of science and had put little stock in faith.

Before telling him about the cancer, Yvette had handled it her own way. Through alternative medicines, prayer, massage therapy, and while those things had not extracted a cure, she had been peaceful.

Tyler had changed all that. He'd taken her to M. D. Anderson Cancer Center and hired the biggest guns in oncology. She'd been poked and prodded and filled with chemicals. She'd vomited and cried. Her hair had fallen out. But Tyler had had his battle with death.

And lost big.

On her deathbed, Yvette had confessed the truth. She hadn't told Tyler about the cancer because she knew what he would do and she had wanted to die in peace.

He had wrest control of his wife's disease away from her. He'd taken over. For her own good, of course. Or that's what he'd told himself. Had it really been for Yvette's own good? Or had he persuaded her to endure chemotherapy to assuage his own fears and sense of helplessness?

Tyler gulped as the realization hit him.

In taking Hannah to Dallas was he committing the same mistake he had with Yvette? He had to turn around.

"Tyler?" Hannah sat up and blinking, peered out the window. "Where are we?" she frowned.

Uh-oh. This was the moment he'd dreaded since making his decision.

"We're just east of Ranger."

"Texas?" She yawned. Her hair was rumpled and there were creases on her cheek from where she'd lain against the seat's upholstery. She looked, incredibly endearing to him. "Shouldn't we be in New Mexico by now? And where is Ranger, anyway?"

Tyler took a deep breath and keep his gaze firmly fixed on the road. "It's halfway between Abilene and Dallas."

"Excuse me?"

He heard the confusion in her voice as she processed what he had told her. Guilt lay like a rock in his belly.

"Hannah," he said, "I made a big mistake."

"I don't understand. Did you take a wrong turn?"

He chanced a glance at her. "No."

Her face was expressionless, as if she had shut off all emotions, her mouth pressed into a thin, hard line. Gone was the sleepy young woman and in her place was a sharp-edged scientist. "Are you telling me you changed our destination without consulting me?"

"It's not what you think."

"How do you know what I'm thinking?"

"You're right. I don't know what you're thinking. Would you like to tell me?"

"Are you working for Daycon?" she demanded. "What's he paying you?"

"Come on, Hannah. How can you ask me that with a straight face?"

"What am I suppose to think? You change our course behind my back. You deceived me and for what?"

"Calm down."

"Oh, I'm quite calm," she said but her voice dripped fury.

"Listen, I have a friend in Dallas who's a hematologist. I'm taking you there for a complete examination."

"I told you. No hospitals. Is this the way you take no for an answer, Dr. Fresno?"

He'd never seen her angry. Her eyes spit fire, her jaw was clenched, her arms wrapped tightly around her chest.

"I did it because I was worried about you."

"Be honest," she snapped. "You did it because you like to be boss. You have to be in charge."

"That's not true."

"Then why did you disobey my wishes? This is happening to me, dammit. Not you."

"I don't want you to die."

"For your information, the longer it takes me to get to Marcus, the closer I may come to death. By taking us on this wild-goose chase you've wasted precious time." Her words rang in the dead silence that followed her declaration.

"It was a mistake. I admit it."

Hannah shook with rage and her voice quivered. "Is that all you have to say for yourself?"

"I'm truly sorry."

She swiveled her head away from him and peered out the window at the dreary yellowed landscape beyond. He slowed the car and headed for the median.

"See. I'm turning around."

"I think maybe you better take me someplace were I can rent a car of my own," she said.

"You're not serious."

"Oh, deadly serious."

"Hannah, you can't do this alone."

"And I can't do this with a companion who defies my wishes," she replied.

"Think this through. I made a mistake, yes, and I'm sorry. But you do need me. You said Daycon's men are ruthless. What happens if you run up against them alone?"

He reached over and touched her melded hands. "Look at me," he urged. "Please."

"I'll stay with you, but from now on, I'm completely in charge of my own care. If you do anything else to betray my trust, I'm leaving you flat. Is that clear?"

"Crystal," he said and goosed the car faster down the road, headed once more for New Mexico.

Chapter 10

They arrived in Santa Fe sometime after midnight the morning after Hannah had healed Angie Henry. Hannah's strength had slowly been restored and along with it, her sense of urgency. She sat in the passenger seat beside Tyler, her body tuned tight as guitar strings. The tension between them was wearing on her. She wanted to forgive him. He had, after all, only been thinking of her health, but she was afraid to let go of her indignation. If she released her anger, she would be forced to confront the other emotions lurking inside her and she simply wasn't prepared to do that.

Disengaging from her emotions came easily to her. Examining them was what she found difficult. She told herself that she didn't need Tyler. Not really. But the lie was so blatantly desperate she couldn't kid even herself.

And she hated that she did need him so badly. That's what kept her staring silently out the window at the frosty landscape, arms folded stoically across her chest.

"Shouldn't we stop for the night?" Tyler said. "And save finding Marcus for the dawn?"

"No." Taos was only thirty miles away. She couldn't stop now, not when they were so close. "Keep driving."

Tyler did not argue but guided the car through the quaint town's empty main streets. Hannah peered out the window at the snowcapped mountains rising up in the darkness. The scenery was so different from the barren landscape they had left behind.

Hurry. Hurry. Hurry.

Tyler's sneakiness had put them behind and she felt as if she would never catch up. The same anxiety had pushed her forward on the day that she'd discovered Daycon's fax.

"Drive faster."

"Hannah, the road is dark and there are icy patches. I'm not going over the speed limit." Tyler spoke calmly, the voice of rationality.

It's what she needed to hear, but Hannah responded petulantly, lashing out at him, displacing her fear. "Just whose life is at stake? Mine or yours?"

He deflected her anger with a smile. Reaching over, he rested a hand on her thigh. "I know you're scared."

"You don't know anything about me," she said coldly and immediately regretted it.

She wanted to ask him to forgive her. To tell him she was sorry, but something inside her reverted to childhood and she did not know why. She had a deeply ingrained habit—one born of the type of work she performed—of detaching from her feelings in order to observe. She was a watcher, an observer, a witness to events but not a participant. She had always kept people at arm's length, and Tyler had already transgressed against her once. Life was safer when you didn't place your security in the hands of another. She might need him to help her reach her physical goals but she did not want or need his comfort. She had survived for thirty-two years without him.

Survived, yes, but that was all.

"If it makes you feel better to rake me over the coals, then go at it. I'm not going to abandon you."

Then Hannah realized what she was really afraid of.

The warmth of his hand seeped through her blue jeans, caused her skin to tingle. Whenever they touched she never failed to feel that enigmatic heat that always increased her stamina. What was it?

Affection?

Or something more?

Why was she so terrified of being hurt?

Because the idea of being helpless, useless, incapable made her mouth go dry and her heart race. She feared losing control more than she feared anything.

Briefly, Hannah closed her eyes, as memories of the past flitted through her mind.

"Don't ever fall in love, Hannah," her mother had told her on more than one occasion. "It will only cause you pain."

"Don't you love Dad?" she had asked.

Even now, Hannah remembered the faraway look in her mother's eyes. A longing look of something lost forever. "I respect your father and admire him a great deal. And, yes, I love him. But with a controlled, rational kind of love. What I want you to avoid is that messy rush of chemicals so many people call love but is actually just lust."

Hannah had never understood what her mother was talking about. Messy rush of chemicals? She looked over at Tyler and in that moment she grasped the obscure meaning of her mother's admonitions. Her mother had been in love with someone else once. Either before her father or during the time they were married, and the affair must have ended badly. How else to explain her mother's opinion on love?

No Cinderella. No Prince Charming. No soul mate. No happily-ever-after.

"Talk to me, Hannah," he soothed. "Tell me what's going on inside that complicated head of yours."

She shrugged. "There's nothing to talk about."

"Don't shut me out."

"I'm not."

He snorted. "Woman, you couldn't be farther away from me right now if you were holed up in a lead bunker in Siberia."

"You exaggerate."

"And you don't trust me."

She notched her chin up. "Why should I?"

"Why shouldn't you?"

"You betrayed me by trying to take me to a hospital."

"I made a mistake. I apologized. I did not betray you." His nostrils flared and he gripped the steering wheel tighter. "Dammit, Hannah. Look at everything I've given up to help you. Isn't that proof enough I'm on your side?"

"Nobody asked you to help."

"You're right. I did it of my own free will. So if you want to stay clammed up, then fine with me." He smacked the dashboard with his fist.

She'd really hurt his pride. Hannah swallowed. He was right. He had given to her unselfishly. She was the one building the walls.

Just talk to him.

"I'm afraid," she whispered at last. "Afraid Marcus won't be there or, worse, he'll be dead. I'm afraid we won't be able to find the copy of the formula I e-mailed him and that all my work will have been for naught. I'm afraid this healing power transferred to me by *Virusall* is going to kill me. I'm afraid that Lionel Daycon and his cohort in the CIA will do something drastic." She drew in a deep breath and met his eyes. "But none of those things are what I fear most."

"No?" His voice was soft. He took his eyes off the road only briefly but, when he met her gaze, invisible sparks arched between them. "What scares you most?"

"You."

"You're scared of me?"

Unlike most women, Hannah avoided talking about her feelings. Emotions were, well, emotional. They didn't mean anything, really. Feelings had no place in a scientific mind. They only caused problems, introduced clutter and self-doubt. It was difficult for her to say what she said next.

"I'm scared for you. Terrified I've placed you in jeopardy right along with me. You don't deserve that, Tyler."

"You let me worry about me, okay?" He reached over and gently stroked his index finger along her cheek. She did not pull back.

They drove on into the night. The mountain rose closer and

the air thinned as they approached Taos. The growth of pines thickened, the snow covering the ground grew deeper. She shivered and hugged her thin coat around her shoulders. Without a word, Tyler leaned over and turned the heater up a notch.

He was so solicitous of her needs. So caring. She wasn't sure how she felt about it. On one hand, she had never been treated so courteously. On the other, his concern was a little too intimate. A little too possessive. Why did she perceive his attention as restriction? What was the matter with her? Any number of women would be overjoyed to have a handsome man devoted to meeting their needs.

Hannah remembered her one and only lover. He had been a brilliant boy from her graduate school chemistry class who had taken her virginity in the back seat of his car. A Volvo, she recalled. Silver. With cloth seats. The seatbelt had kept stabbing her in the back during the entire passionless process. After it was over, feeling completely empty inside, she had calmly gotten dressed and asked him to take her home. When he had tried to kiss her again, she had turned away.

"You're one cold fish, you know that?" he had said. "You have no passion. You make a man feel small."

She had known right then she could never be a great lover. She didn't feel the things other people felt.

Was she a cold fish? Did she make men feel small? What was the matter with her? Why was she so different from the other members of her sex?

Except Tyler made her question those old assumptions about herself. Lying in his arms in that motel outside of Abilene had been an eye-opening experience. That's what truly scared her. Knowing she had been wrong about herself all these years. That her mother had been wrong. That there might just be such thing as true and lasting love. Discovering the need inside her, learning she indeed possessed a passionate nature, shook Hannah to her very core.

"You don't have to know all the answers," Tyler said softly. "There's no pop quiz. No right or wrong response. You aren't required to be head of the class."

They passed through Taos, the small town sleeping quietly in the snow. Tyler slowed the car. "Where to from here?"

Hannah frowned into the darkness. She'd visited Marcus only once. "Take a left at the bakery on the corner."

The bakery was the only building on the whole street with the lights on. The rich smell of yeast permeated the air, adding a cozy warmth to the otherwise dreary night.

Tyler turned onto the side road and drove past a hostel and a campground filled with motor homes. The farther they went, the narrower the road became until at last it was just a thin snake of pavement etching its way up the mountainside.

"Are you sure we're going in the right direction?" Tyler asked.

Taos was behind them. They met no other vehicles, nor were there even any other houses along the roadside.

"Yes. Keep going. I told you he's a hermit."

After another ten miles the road ended abruptly in front of a six-foot-high padlocked iron gate. Tyler's headlights reflected off a metal sign posted with the unfriendly advice—Keep Out! Trespassers Will Be Prosecuted. This Means You!

"This is it," she said. "We walk from here."

"But we're not dressed for hiking in the mountains. No parka, no hiking boots. You don't even have any gloves."

"I know of no other way inside, unless you can pick locks," Hannah said.

"How far to his house?"

"A mile." She guessed. "Maybe less."

Tyler frowned. "You've just now recovered from healing Angie Henry. I hate to think of you traipsing through knee-high snow in the wind and the cold."

His concern was touching but she would not depend on him. "I'll be fine."

"Let me go alone," Tyler urged. "I'll introduce myself to Marcus, explain what happened and have him bring me back down here to pick you up in a vehicle."

She shook her head. "You don't know the way."

"Dammit, Hannah, would you listen to my advice for once?" His nostrils flared in anger.

"I'm not accustomed to being taken care of," she said.

"As long as you're with me, get used to it."

"I'd rather go with you," she stubbornly insisted.

"You'll be safer in the car."

"And lonelier," she admitted.

That must have gotten to him. "All right. You can come. But I'm wrapping you up in the blanket that's in the back of the car. No discussion."

"Okay."

"We'll need a flashlight." Tyler leaned over Hannah to open the glove compartment. His shoulder brushed against her knees. Her pulse scrambled wildly at the contact.

His profile was shadowy in the wan moonlight and his breath came in frosty white puffs. She had an almost irresistible urge to kiss him but managed to squelch it by telling herself that within a few minutes she and Marcus would be face-to-face.

But even that couldn't stop a hot flush of sexual excitement from racing through her body.

He got out, went around to the trunk and retrieved the thick blanket. He helped her from the car and wrapped the blanket around her until she felt as cozy as a papoose.

"What next?"

"We climb the fence."

They scaled the fence and started up the long driveway to the house. Already, Hannah's feet were soaked from snow, but she wouldn't worry Tyler with her minor discomfort.

He kept his arm draped around her shoulders as they walked in step together. It was the dead of winter in New Mexico, but with this exceptional man at her side, her blood flowed so hot it could have been August in the Amazon. In that odd moment, on a mountain in the Rockies, under a starry night, Hannah felt happy for the first time in a very long time. And Tyler was responsible.

How had she managed to stumble through her life for so long without his fingers at her elbow, his strong presence enveloping her in a warm cocoon? Ah, if she could only hold on to this precious moment for all eternity.

"You're excited," Tyler commented. "And walking fast."

Hannah grinned at him. She was optimistic, yes, now that she was in touching distance of her old partner, Marcus, but that wasn't what lifted her spirits and revived her soul. Rather it was the sensation of Tyler's hand moving to the small of her back, where it felt so strangely right, it gave wings to her heart.

Tyler guided her around a fallen log. Snow crunched as it packed beneath their shoes. Up ahead a gabled roof rose from the darkness, sharp and imposing as the House of Usher. Two tall stone pillars stood sentinel, glaring down at them like nightmarish creatures from a murky lagoon.

The gloomy structure dispelled her earlier pleasure.

Until recently, Hannah would not have entertained such foolish notions about inanimate objects. As it was, she was seeing enemies hiding in every corner.

"Hannah?"

It wasn't until Tyler spoke that she realized she had stopped walking and was hanging back, staring at Marcus's house. A bitter, metallic taste flooded her mouth and an eerie premonition of impending danger lifted the hairs at the nape of her neck.

They had arrived.

Hannah was afraid to go in.

"Something's wrong," she whispered.

Tyler squeezed her waist. "It's all right. I'm here." He moved her toward the front porch, pushing her the way a fall breeze pushes autumn leaves from a tree.

She stood at the door, huddled beneath the blanket. Forcefully, he stepped forward and banged on the door.

They waited.

And waited.

No answer.

Tyler knocked again. Hannah's nerves stretched taut.

The door swung open of its own accord, creaking on its hinges like a ghost-house portal.

He strode forward.

"No." Hannah grabbed for his wrist. "Don't go in."

"What's the matter?"

"Danger."

"You wait here. I'll check it out."

"Please," she whimpered, but he was already inside the house. Hannah brought a hand to her mouth, swallowing her fear.

"Hello!" Tyler called, his voice echoing hollowly. "Anybody home? Marcus Halpren?"

No answer.

He must have found the light switch for the entry way was suddenly awash in illumination.

"Geez-us," he exclaimed.

"What is it?" Hannah cried, rushing headlong inside, awful images of Marcus' murdered body running through her mind. Blinded by the brightness, she charged straight into Tyler's back.

"Whoa." He caught her, pulled her against him to keep her from falling.

Blinking, Hannah steadied herself against his lean body and stared at the mayhem surrounding them.

"Oh my," she whispered.

Marcus' living room, which was not decorated like most living rooms with couches, chairs and television sets but rather resembled a miniature lab with sturdy tables, microscopes, computers, printers, Bunsen burners and the like, had been completely demolished.

Shattered glass lay embedded in the short Berber carpet. A large poster of the periodic table had been ripped in half. The smell of chlorine and sulfur filled the room. Purple solution used for gram staining was splashed across one wall, looking obscenely like splattered blood. The legs of a stool had been broken, as had a chalkboard covered with chemical symbols. The chalk itself was crushed to powder on the floor.

"Marcus," she whimpered and nausea filled her throat with harsh brackishness.

Terrified for her friend, Hannah ignored her earlier cautiousness. She raced from the living room to the adjoining dining room, which also held experiments and laboratory accoutrements instead of a dining table. This area, too, had been ransacked.

Tyler followed as she went from room to room, surveying disaster after disaster. The bathroom pillaged—towels in the bathtub, toilet paper unrolled across the floor, toothpaste squashed from its tube. The bedroom despoiled—feather pillows sliced open, clothes torn from the closet, the bureau mirror smashed. The kitchen plundered—food flung from the refrigerator onto the floor lay rotting. Dishes were broken, chairs overturned, the flour bin upended in the sink.

Dizziness assailed her at the savagery of the damage.

This destruction had been more than a mere search. It had been malicious and mean-spirited. Whoever had wrecked Marcus's house had done it for fun.

"The lab!" Hannah ran for the door leading from the kitchen into the basement. She flung it open, turned on the light and took the steps two at a time.

Stunned, she stopped and turned in a slow circle. This was where Daycon's men had done their worst. Hannah had no doubt Daycon was responsible for this. Everything had been annihilated. Marcus's computers lay smashed, books and papers had been set afire in a trash can in the middle of the room. Microscopes were dismembered, scales broken, tubing severed. There were fresh scars on the heavy Formica tables. Numerous vials lay overturned, the contents spilling onto the cement floor. The odor of a dozen different chemicals metabolized into one odious, overpowering stench that made her nose burn and her eyes water. A lifetime worth of work had been senselessly ravaged.

And all because of her.

She was dazed. Numb. Dumbfounded.

Hannah felt the same way she had at age six when she had fallen backward off a swing and knocked the air from her lungs. She had lain on the ground, twigs and dirt in her hair, staring dizzily up at the frothy white clouds floating against a background of blue sky. The memory came with startling clarity. Her mother, squatting beside her, a chiding expression on her angular face. "That's what you get, Hannah, for playing instead of doing your homework. I told you not to go outside. Now get up." Her mother had not held her, nor comforted her. She had stood and walked away, leaving Hannah alone.

Gulping, she splayed a hand over her heart. Her breath hissed inward with a rattling wheeze. Hannah burst into tears.

"Aw, honey. I'm so sorry."

She hadn't even noticed that Tyler had come downstairs to join her. He pulled her to him and held her while she wept against his chest. After several minutes of serious sobbing, she raised her head, accepted the handkerchief he offered and blew her nose.

"I'd hoped against hope that Daycon didn't know about Marcus," she said, sniffling.

"You've been through so much."

"Look what I've brought down on my friend. If Daycon would do this to Marcus, I hate to think what he would do to you." Her bottom lip trembled.

"Don't you worry about me."

"How can I not worry? You can see for yourself what they're capable of." She swept a hand at the room.

"Why would they wreck the place? What were they looking for?"

"Me? The formula? I don't know. But I do know Marcus wouldn't tell them anything. He hated Daycon. That's why he quit." She met his eyes. "Oh my God, Tyler. Where is Marcus?"

Exhaustion claimed her. The pent-up adrenaline that had kept Hannah running from Austin to Galveston and on to Taos dissipated as reality dawned. She sank to her knees amid the chaos and anxiously twisted the tail of her shirt around an index finger.

It was all over. Marcus was gone, his computers destroyed. For all she knew, Daycon's men had found what they'd come searching for. Her e-mail. She could not come up with an antidote for *Virusall* alone, nor could she even replicate the drug. Not without the formula. She would not be healed, nor would she be able to heal those afflicted test subjects.

She was going to die and there was nothing she could do to alter her fate. Even now her strength ebbed, her spirits spiraling downward into depression.

The worst part of it was that she was going to die without helping anyone else in the process. Oh, she'd had so many dreams.

In hindsight, they seemed silly and idealistic. Had she really believed she could eradicate all viruses and put an end to so much suffering? She had lived in her ivory tower, spinning her fantasies, completely unaware of the evil that existed in the hearts of men like Lionel Daycon.

She was a ninny and the sad thing about it was she had dragged poor Tyler along on her fool's quest. He had jeopardized his own career to assist her and she could reward him with absolutely nothing.

Hannah had reached her goal only to discover it did not hold the key to her success. For the last several days she had clung to the hope that Marcus would be here, that he would help her re-create *Virusall* and manufacture an antidote, cure the test subjects and suspend her own death sentence. But that wasn't going to happen. There would be no celestial reprieve.

What now? She had no options left. She felt like a tightrope walker crossing the Grand Canyon on a string of dental floss.

"Don't despair," Tyler said.

They were so connected that he seemed to know exactly what she was thinking. It unsettled her. She had never been this close to anyone and that knowledge alone set off warning bells in her head.

He moved to embrace her in a hug, but she stepped back, breathing hard and fighting off the urge to fling herself into his comforting arms.

"Hannah," he whispered and patiently kept his hands extended. "Come here."

"I'm okay."

"You're bottom lip is trembling," he gently pointed out.

She clamped down on her lip with her top teeth.

"Come." He motioned to her with his fingers.

Drawn by the force of his presence, she took a faltering step forward.

"That's it. You gotta trust someone, babe. Come on," he cajoled again.

And then she was in his arms clutching him around the waist as tightly as she could. He wrapped his arms around her shoulders and softly kissed the top of her head.

"It's okay. We're going to get through this," he said. "Together."

How she wanted to believe his promise! But it was not within his power to grant such a wish. She shook her head, pulled back and stared up into his face. "Can't."

"What's that? You're giving up?"

"No use."

"That doesn't sound like the Hannah Zachary I've come to know," he said.

"Don't you understand? It's hopeless. Marcus has disappeared. His computers have been destroyed. I can't retrieve the formula from his e-mail and I can't create an antidote alone."

"You're not alone. I'm here."

"Yes, but you don't know anything about chemistry."

"I am a doctor."

She waved a dismissive hand. "I know you mean well but it's not the same thing." Her voice dropped in despair. "I'm doomed."

Tyler pulled back and leveled her a stern stare. "I never would have figured you for a quitter."

"And I never would have figured you for an ostrich."

"What's that suppose to mean?"

"Don't you get it, Tyler?" She shook her head, then immediately stopped and placed her hands at her temple to steady herself. She felt as dizzy as a drunk taking a spin on the Tilt-A-Whirl. "I'm dying."

"And don't you realize that I'm going to fight for you, fight with you until the bitter end? It's not over until it's over, Hannah."

She stared at him in disbelief. "Man, are you ever a glutton for punishment."

"That may be." He sank his hands on his hips. "But I'm here to stay. Now, are we going to sit here and feel sorry for ourselves or are we going to solve the problem?"

A tentative hope flickered inside her. Maybe, with Tyler's help, she could come up with some sort of antidote.

"Well? What's it going to be? Are we having a pity party or are we going to fight?"

She smiled at him. A little wavery, a little uncertain, but still, a smile. "Fight."

Tyler took her palm, squeezed it, and then raised their joined hands in the air like a manager and his prize fighter.

"Good choice," he said. "Let's start going through this mess and see if we can find any clues."

A few minutes later, Tyler cocked his head to one side. "Do you hear that?"

"Hear what?" She looked up from her crouched position on the cement floor where she had been desperately searching through Marcus's scattered research material, hoping against hope to find a printout of her e-mail.

"Shh." He raised a finger to his lips.

His hair glistened like a raven's wing in the light from the bare bulb overhead. Hannah's heart caught in her chest at the sight. He was incredible. Strong, devoted, determined, loyal. She couldn't look at him without this warm, mushy feeling squishing around in her stomach. Flustered at her thoughts, Hannah frowned in concentration and forced herself to listen.

"Sounds like an engine."

"A car?" Hannah leapt to her feet, surprised by the mix of apprehension and anticipation rampaging through her. "Do you think it could be Marcus?"

"No. Not a car," Tyler said. "It's a smaller engine. Like a motorcycle."

"Who would be riding a motorcycle way out here at three o'clock in the morning?"

"Snowmobile. And there's not a good answer for that question."

"What do you mean?"

Their eyes met. Hannah's heart sank.

"We better get out of here. Fast."

"You don't think it could be whomever it was that trashed the place, do you?"

"I don't intend on waiting around long enough to find out." Tyler reached for her hand and tugged her toward the stairs.

"What if it's the same guys who were following us in Galveston?" She asked.

"It very well could be.

They scrambled through the kitchen and out the back door.

The air was frigid but unnaturally still. A sprinkling of stars carpeted the sky but the moon had disappeared. They could hear the engine more clearly from out here and the sound was definitely drawing nearer.

"Come on."

"But the car is over there." Hannah pointed south.

"No time." Tyler dragged her toward a clump of trees a few yards away.

The snowdrifts were high. If it hadn't been for Tyler hauling her along beside him, she didn't know if she would have made it.

"Get down."

Gently, he thrust her behind a cedar tree and with his palm, pushed her head down, tucked her head under his arm and shielded her with his large frame.

Hannah found herself on her knees in the snow, her head resting on Tyler's bent thigh as he crouched above her, her gaze pointed directly at his crotch.

Strange time to notice, she thought inanely, *how the part of him that was strictly male strained against his blue jeans.* But notice she did and with a vigor that surprised her. She should be terrified, frightened by their grave situation. Instead, she was thrilled, invigorated by the cold, the danger and Tyler's awesomely masculine presence.

Her blood pumped. Her pulse roared in her ears, loud as the ocean's surf. She tasted the sharp flavor of adrenaline underneath her tongue, inhaled the stimulating aroma of savory pine, wet snow and manly man.

Seconds later a snowmobile slid into view with two burly men astride. Hannah tensed and caught her breath between clenched teeth. The driver killed the engine. She watched as both men pulled guns from their coats and advanced upon the house, their weapons clutched in two hands just like actors in a cops-and-robbers drama.

Except this wasn't a television show and those dangerous-looking men weren't fictitious villains. The tallest one kicked down Marcus's backdoor and they both sprang through the gaping entrance.

"Good thing they were so intent on getting inside the house that they didn't see our footprints," Tyler whispered.

"But they'll come back. They'll figure it out. Tyler, we're trapped here!"

"Not trapped." He nodded at the snowmobile that sat where the men had left it, keys dangling in the ignition.

"You don't mean…"

But he had already snatched her hand and was dragging her toward the snowmobile.

Chapter 11

I'm going to save Hannah. No matter what. If it means hand-to-hand combat with those two goons inside, then that's what I'll do.

For six years Tyler had been adrift, going through the motions of life but not really feeling anything. It seemed as if he had been waiting. Waiting to be truly needed. Waiting for his emotions to come alive again.

And come alive they had. With a vengeance.

His entire body pulsed with primal energy. Awash in adrenaline, he had no choice but to act. Swift and stealthy as a predator on the prowl, he stalked the snowmobile.

The keys glinting in the porch light swayed like a prize, enticing him. Tyler sprang across the snow and vaulted onto the thick cushioned seat.

"Climb on," he called over to her his shoulder. "Wrap your hands around my waist."

In an instant, she was behind him, her delicate arms squeezing his midsection for all she was worth.

He started the engine. The sound seemed deafening. He knew the men would hear it and come running. There was no time to waste. Fumbling momentarily as he figured out the shifting mechanism, he finally slammed the vehicle into drive and gave it gas with the thumb feed at the very same time that two shadows loomed in the doorway.

"Stop!" one of the men shouted.

The other fired his pistol into the air.

"Head down," Tyler told Hannah. He felt her bury her forehead against his shoulder blades. Swallowing back any hesitation, he opened the throttle and wished they had helmets.

The snowmobile shrieked and shot forward over the snow. The force surprised him. He chanced a quick glance behind him and saw Daycon's thugs running toward them in the darkness. They soon fell behind and it took all Tyler's concentration to navigate the slippery mountain slope.

Hannah's warm breath tickled the nape of his neck. "We're getting away," she said giddily, her euphoria contagious.

That's my girl.

Recalling how she had looked not so long ago in Marcus's basement—distraught, pale, anxious, Tyler couldn't help smiling. She had rebounded magnificently. Hannah was a fighter.

He zigzagged over the craggy terrain, dodging trees, maneuvering around rocks and underbrush. He thought of only one thing. Getting Hannah to safety. He was her warrior, her hero, her protector. He did not know where they were headed, he simply drove, his eyes trained straight ahead, but his heart, oh, his heart was on fire with longing for the future he did not dare believe in.

They could no longer see the lights of Marcus's house. It had disappeared into black sky and white snow. Their whole world was black and white. Cold and damp. Dead and scary. Except for one thing. The throbbing aliveness between them. They were a virtual maelstrom of masculine and feminine energies. Pulsing hot and quick. Spreading, growing, consuming their bodies. As Hannah hugged on to Tyler, they welded in a bizarre amalgamation the like of which he had never experienced.

Her touch filled him with a calm inner peace, and he felt with absolute certainty they could handle anything as long as they were together.

They drove for what seemed like hours, swooping over moguls and dodging around trees as they traversed their way around the mountain. One wrong move, one false turn and they could tumble heedlessly into an endless abyss. Tyler's bare fingers grew numb against the handlebars, his body stiff from constant alertness. The engine droned so loudly he feared he was going deaf.

Like a steady mainstay, Hannah's head lay against his back. Occasionally, he would reach down and pat her hands. She would squeeze his waist and on they would travel, each fortifying the other. When at last Tyler feared he did not have the energy to go one more yard he spotted a sprinkling of lights up ahead.

"Taos?" Hannah whispered, her voice grown hoarse from the cold night air.

"I don't think so. Not big enough. Taos should be farther south. I imagine this is a ski resort."

She pressed her lips lightly to the back of his neck, renewing his strength, pushing him onward toward the ski resort and their uncertain destiny.

By the time they reached the resort and parked the snowmobile outside the main chalet that housed two restaurants, the ski rental/lift-ticket shop and main office, dawn was breaking over the horizon. Skiers were already packing the restaurants, stoking up on a hearty breakfast before making their run on the slopes.

"Brrr." Hannah rubbed her reddened palms together.

"We've got to get you some gloves," Tyler said, draping his arm over her shoulder and pulling her against his shoulder. "And snow boots."

She nodded.

Tyler smiled inwardly. She no longer shrank from his touch the way she had when they'd first met. Feeling a bit macho after successfully eluding their pursuers again, Tyler put a spring in his step and guided her along the snow-covered sidewalk toward one of the bustling restaurants, pungent with the aroma of coffee and bacon.

They found a spot in a back booth and sat side by side instead of across from each other. Tyler took Hannah's hands and warmed them in his own while they waited for the waitress to bring their order. Neither of them spoke. They had no need for words and they were too worn-out to do much more than grunt.

Their food arrived. Belgian waffles, coffee, hash browns, Canadian bacon and egg-white omelets. Tyler fed Hannah a forkful of potatoes. She reciprocated by offering him a bite of bacon. They nuzzled like new lovers, delighting in their food and each other. Neither of them wanting to think about what they had just left behind nor what lay ahead.

After they had lingered for more than an hour, watching the crowd shift in and out, Tyler finally paid the bill with a platinum credit card and helped Hannah to her feet. "Let's go get a room," he suggested. "We could both use a few hours to sleep and regroup."

"This is the height of ski season," she said, pointing to the steady procession of vans, buses and sport utility vehicles making the trek up the only road stretching between Taos and the ski resort. "I hope they have a vacancy."

Hand in hand they walked to the rental office and inquired about booking a chalet.

"I'm sorry," the girl at the front desk told them with a shake of her head. "We're completely sold out."

Tyler groaned.

"Except," the girl ventured, "there is the honeymoon suite."

"We'll take that," Tyler said quickly.

"Are you aware, sir," the desk clerk said, "it rents for six hundred and seventy-five a night?"

He pulled out his credit card and tossed it on the desk. "Just charge it."

Hannah tugged at Tyler's sleeve. "That's much too expensive," she whispered.

Leaning over, he kissed her forehead lightly. "Don't worry about it. For six years I've had no one to spend my money on. Let me do this for you. We need a place to rest. I don't care how much it costs."

The desk clerk gave them a key and directions to their chalet. They stopped to shop at the only boutique open that early, buying overpriced gloves, heavy parkas and snow boots. Loaded with packages, but feeling lighter, freer than they had felt in days, they took the snowmobile over to their accommodations, passing near a frozen pond that served as an outdoor ice rink along the way.

The honeymoon suite was lavishly decorated and featured a fully stocked kitchen. Here, they would want for nothing. There were two adobe fireplaces, one in the bedroom and the other in the sitting area. The wood box overflowed with logs. The bedroom held not only a king-size bed, but a luxuriously huge Jacuzzi.

In the bathroom they found complimentary toothbrushes, razors and other toiletries. Even condoms. Which was a good thing, Tyler realized, because they had left all their personal effects in his car parked outside the front gate at Marcus's house.

"I've never seen anything like this place." Hannah marveled over the thirty-two-inch color satellite television, digital video player, surround-sound setup with a full accompaniment of movies in the side cabinet. "No wonder it costs so much."

"Will you stop worrying about the cost?" He shrugged out of his coat and tossed it across the bed.

"Hey, I'm a lowly scientist. You just shelled out what is equivalent to almost a week of my take-home salary for one night in the honeymoon suite, not to mention the clothes we bought, and we're not even on a real honeymoon."

"We could pretend." He smiled.

Hannah blushed and looked away.

"How are you feeling?" he asked, changing the subject so she wouldn't withdraw from him again. He had to watch himself with her. The slightest offhand remark could send her guard shooting up like a drawbridge.

"Physically, just fine. Mentally, I'm a little numb," Hannah confessed. "Things keep changing so quickly I can't keep up."

"Come." He kicked off his shoes and sat down on the bed. "Curl up and let's take a nap."

She piled in the middle of the bed beside him and only stiffened a little bit when he tucked her into the curve of his body and pulled the covers over them.

In a matter of seconds, Hannah was sound asleep, her gentle breathing music to his ears. He savored the weight of her head against his shoulder, the delightful scent of her in his nostrils. Tyler realized it had been a very long time since he had been happy.

To get a second chance at love was truly a gift, but to lose love a second time would be a living hell.

"Not if I can help it," he whispered, his chest swelling with the power of his emotions. "I refuse to let you go."

Unexpected tears crowded his eyes but he blinked them back. And then he knew for certain what he had suspected the very moment Hannah had shown up as Jane Doe in his emergency room.

He was falling in love.

It was midafternoon when Hannah awoke thirsty and disoriented. Tyler's hand was at her waist, his hip pressed tightly against hers. She lay in the circle of his arms, savoring the moment, enjoying the softness of the bed, the nearness of his hard body. Heavy draperies blunted the sunlight, but she could hear voices outside in the courtyard as people passed by, laughing, talking and joking.

She was jealous of their carefree casualness. They had no idea how lucky they were to be having fun with their friends. But Hannah knew just how fragile life could be. Closing her eyes, she wished that for one simple day they could be like any ordinary couple.

"You awake?" His deep voice rumbled near her ear.

"Uh-huh."

He hugged her. The clock on the nightstand ticked loudly. Dust motes circled in the slant of light sliding around the drapes. She noticed a palm-sized water stain on the ceiling.

"We need to get out of here," she said, anxiety zipping through her as she thought about Marcus and what might have become of him. "Daycon's men can't be far behind."

"Hush. Let's live in the moment, Hannah. Just for today. Let's pretend there's no elixir, no Daycon, no limit on our time together."

A lump formed in her throat. How she wished it could be so! But she knew better.

His dark eyes turned serious. "The present is all we have. Let's not waste it."

"We can't hide from reality."

"What is reality, other than our perception?"

It sounded so good. Chills chased up her spine. Her innermost feminine parts ached each time she gazed into Tyler's darkly handsome eyes. How she wanted him! To touch him, kiss him, make love all night long. But it wasn't possible, no matter how much she might wish things were different.

"How about a nice hot shower?" he asked, lightly running a hand along her ribs.

"Together?" she ventured.

"Is that an invitation?"

"Only if you want it to be," Hannah said, shocked by her boldness but secretly thrilled she had said it.

She had wanted him to make love to her since that interlude they had indulged in at the motel outside Abilene. Now, when she knew for sure she literally might not live to see tomorrow, she did not want to spend one more minute regretting not having made love with this wonderful, caring man who had come to mean so much to her in such a short time.

"What do *you* think?" he said gruffly.

She turned in his arms and they were facing each other, his dark eyes bright and hopeful.

"Are you sure?"

He took her hand, gently guiding it to the bulge in his blue jeans. "Does that answer your question?"

She touched his hardness straining against the seam of his pants. Wonderment filled her. She did this to him.

"Oh, Tyler," she breathed.

He slid to the floor, held out a hand to her. She accepted, willingly following him as he walked backward, leading her into the bathroom, his gaze never leaving her face.

I want this. More than I've ever wanted anything.

She caught a glimpse of their reflections in the mirror. Who was this bedraggled woman with this handsome man? Her eyes ringed with dark circles, her hair a mess. And still, he found her attractive. Unbelievable.

Tyler turned on the shower, adjusting the temperature and testing the water with the tender side of his forearm before turning his attention back to her. "You're so beautiful," he whispered.

Bashfully, she ducked her head.

"Come'ere." He pulled her to him and slowly began unbuttoning her flannel shirt.

One, two, three. Fascinated, she watched his long fingers work the buttons. The farther he went, the warmer she became until she feared she had melted into a puddle at his feet.

Unbidden, her own fingers rose and plied at the buttons on *his* shirt. Hannah wanted this to be a mutual seduction, to give as much as she received. A nest of black hairs curled at his chest, inviting further unveiling. Lower she went, picking up the tempo until at last his shirt lay open, as did hers.

Tyler growled his approval. When she raised her head, she saw he was smiling.

Steam from the shower filled the room, streaking the mirror with mist. She arched her back and he slipped the shirt from her shoulders and dropped it to the floor. Next came her camisole and in a twinkling she stood before him, bare to the waist, her breast rising and falling to match her rapid breathing.

Reaching out, she splayed a palm against his flat abdomen. Tyler hissed in his breath as if he had been burned by her touch and his eyes glowed like twin black coals.

Hannah loved the way he felt. He was firm and smooth, his skin thick in an unexpected way. She was giddy with joy, overwhelmed by the moment.

His shirt fell to the floor beside hers and he wrapped those muscled arms around her, pressed his hard chest flat against her soft breasts. He hooked an index finger under her chin and tilted her face up in order to kiss her.

Softly.

Just when she was ready to deepen the kiss, he removed his mouth from hers and reached for the snap on her blue jeans.

"Oh," she whispered.

He nudged down her zipper inch by excruciating inch.

Hannah wriggled her hips, anxious to be free of the restricting garment.

"Easy, sweetheart." He chuckled and the sound rumbled deep within his chest. "Relax. I'm not going anywhere."

Embarrassed, she rested her forehead against his shoulder. Did he find her too brazen? Too eager?

He hitched two fingers through the belt loops at her hips, lowered her jeans to her knees and helped her step out of them. She was left with only a pair of skimpy white cotton panties.

"You are gorgeous." He softly pressed his lips against her belly button.

Hannah giggled as pulses of hot pleasure shot throughout her entire body. He straightened and kissed her again.

She kept sneaking peeks at them in the mirror even though the image was blurred with steam. She was surprised at how sexy they looked, their bare flesh entwined. Her excitement grew.

"Voyeur," he teased, reaching over to clear a spot on the mirror with his palm. "If you want to watch, then watch."

For a second, before the steam clouded it over, she captured a glimpse of their faces. They looked blissfully happy.

Amazing. How was this possible? Their lives were in chaos and yet, in the midst of it all, they found the courage and the resilience to reach out to each other.

To give solace with their bodies.

"Time for a shower." He slipped a finger into the elastic of her flimsy panties and began to edge them down. When she was completely naked, he held out his hand and helped her into the shower.

Warm water closed over her like a welcoming embrace and her sighs of pleasure erupted deep and throaty. Hannah was facing forward, eyes closed, water slicing down her face so she heard and felt his presence rather than saw him when, a second later, Tyler edged open the etched-glass shower door and stepped in behind her.

He touched her back with a bar of scented soap, and she sucked in her breath at the sheer poetry of the moment.

She had never showered with another person. She found the notion erotic and intriguing.

His slippery hands went to work on her neck. Hannah purred and leaned forward, her wet hair falling across her face. Her skin tingled with delight every place that he touched.

His fingers explored gently, ascertaining which spots made her squirm with pleasure and which areas were sensitive to the slightest provocation. The heat inside her built, growing and growing and growing. She was wet and hot and needy.

Oh, so needy.

The soap dropped to the bottom of the shower stall. Neither noticed.

He took her by the shoulders and turned her around. They kissed under the shower spray, water sliding into their mouths along with their tongues.

Her nerve endings came alive with enjoyment. She relished every sensation, from the taste of his lips to the feel of his fingertips strumming her nipples.

He was so damned sensual. He knew exactly where to touch. She writhed in anticipation, desperate for more.

"That's it," he cooed and his seductive voice sent her blood racing through her loins.

He nudged her against the back of the shower stall, away from the water. The tile was cool against her blazing backside, his manly appendage throbbing at the apex of her womanhood. Here she was, neatly positioned between two very hard surfaces.

She reached for him, but he blocked her hand. "Patience."

Lowering his head he captured one nipple that stiffened to a pebble between his teeth. His hand trailed over her hip before entangling in the patch of hair between her legs.

Hannah groaned. Not a sweet, delicate feminine moan but a groan born of hungry need.

Like a match to gasoline, he inflamed her. Hannah could think of nothing but Tyler and this incredible wanting surging through the floor of her pelvis.

"Tyler," she murmured. "Tyler."

"I'm here. Always here." He nuzzled her throat with his lips while his magical, miracle fingers kept caressing and massaging, threatening to send her over the edge of sanity.

Using soft, rhythmic movements, he stroked between her legs until she moaned loudly.

Her climax came hard and sudden, taking her breath and leaving her weak-kneed. If he hadn't tucked her securely in the crook of his elbow, she would surely have fallen.

"There now," he whispered, after her shudders had subsided. "There now."

She clung to him, her hands around his neck, her head buried at the hollow of his throat. Tyler held her until the hot water grew too cold to tolerate any longer, then he gently lifted her from the shower stall and settled her onto the bath mat. Retrieving a towel from the towel rack, he began to dry her off, patting her hair, dabbing at her face, frisking her skin with the terry cloth.

"Arms up," he said.

Obedient as a child at bedtime, she raised her arms over her head while Tyler dried beneath her arms, then dropped to his knees in order to whisk off the rest of her body.

"What's going on?" she asked, still stunned from the exquisite pleasure he had just bestowed upon her. "Are we through?"

"Sweetheart—" he smiled up from his position at her feet, his tone lazy "—we're just getting started."

His words brought a thrill and she shivered again, but from excitement, not the cold.

He wrapped her in a fluffy white bathrobe provided by the ski resort and lifted her onto the bathroom counter. As lovingly as a mother, he found a blow dryer in a drawer and dried her hair, gently running a brush through her curls.

Thirstily, she soaked up his pampering. She studied his face, memorizing every dear sweet inch. All throughout his courtly caretaking, Tyler remained unclothed and unashamed of his nakedness. Hannah admired his composure, his self-acceptance and wished that she possessed such aplomb.

She also enjoyed sneaking quick, thrilling peeks at his exquisite figure. A week ago, if someone had told her she would be holed up in a ski chalet in the New Mexico Rockies with a handsome, desirable man, she would have laughed herself silly. Now, Hannah didn't know what had taken her so long to start living.

When her hair was dry and her body had returned to some semblance of normal, Tyler took her hand and led her to the bedroom.

"Come," he whispered.

Anxiety careened through her insides and she was breathing harder than a chain-smoker halfway up Mount Everest. Hannah didn't know what she was doing. She was no expert at lovemaking. Would she disappoint him in bed?

His superb, beautiful buttocks flexed as he walked across the room, Hannah trailing behind him like a kite. If he hadn't tethered her to the earth she feared she would fly through the roof, buoyed skyward by a heady mixture of joy and trepidation.

This is really happening to me, she marveled. *Me. Socially inept, sexually neutral, workaholic Hannah.* Except at this moment, she felt anything but sexually neutral.

One look, one touch from Tyler and all the libido she had stifled for thirty-two years came charging forth, more unstoppable than a rampaging buffalo herd.

He sat on the edge of the bed and reached for her, his warm hands gliding inside the terry cloth bathrobe to gently cup her breasts.

She was on fire, completely ablaze. His fingertips grazed her skin, raising goose bumps, heightening her desire.

How she wanted him! With a devotion and intensity that took her breath and made her long for things she had no business longing for. Like a home and a family.

"Lovely, lovely," Tyler murmured and buried his head against her chest.

When he took one of her nipples into his mouth, she arched her back, cried out with pleasure and helplessly tangled her fingers in his dark, silky hair.

Urgency swept over her. And need. Starving, insatiable need. More. She had to have more of him. All of him. Now.

"Hannah," he whispered. "I want you so much, but I want to savor our joining. I want to remember this forever."

"Please, don't deny me!"

"Shh, I'm not denying you." He smiled and tickled her lips with his fingers. "Simply enhancing the anticipation. Lay back. Relax."

She tried to do as he suggested but she was tense with yearning. She settled against the pillows but then a horrible thought occurred to her. "Wait," she said.

"What is it?"

"We can't make love."

"Why not? If it's birth control…" He held up a condom he'd had palmed in his hand. "Courtesy of the honeymoon suite."

"It's not pregnancy that worries me."

"Talk to me."

Hannah sighed and clutched a pillow to her naked breasts. How to explain her fear so that is didn't sound irrational. "It just occurred to me. What if I'm contagious?"

"Contagious?"

"You know." She waved her hands. "What if we make love and I pass this defect on to you? I'd never forgive myself."

"That doesn't sound very logical, Hannah."

"And developing the power to heal from exposure to radiation and a miracle drug is? Come on, Tyler. We're dealing with the supernatural here and there's no parameters for what we're up against."

"We've got a condom."

"Yes, and how many times have condoms broken? How many AIDS victims have infected their partners even though they were practicing 'safe sex'?"

"You're saying we can't make love." The disappointment on his face reflected the distress in her heart. How she wanted him inside her! But she simply couldn't take the risk.

Tyler flopped down on the bed beside her. "I'm willing to take my chances."

"I'm not."

"I think you're jumping to conclusions."

"Better safe than sorry."

"Wait a minute." Tyler snapped his fingers. "I've already been exposed to your blood."

"What do you mean?" She frowned.

He held up a thumb and opened his mouth to explain when a sound from outside the chalet garnered their attention.

A distant rumbling noise.

"What's that?" she asked.

He met her gaze. The rumbling grew from a rattle into a muffled roar, accompanied by screams and shouts of panic.

Hannah's eyes widened. "Something's wrong."

Tyler's face paled. "Avalanche."

Chapter 12

They scrambled for their clothes, pulling on sweaters, tugging on blue jeans, jamming their feet into their shoes.

The hinged windows and front door of the chalet blew open, spilling snow into the foyer. Hand in hand, Tyler and Hannah struggled to the entryway and peered outside.

What they saw stunned them into silence.

A shelf of snow approximately two hundred yards wide was quickly descending upon a group of half a dozen ice skaters struggling uselessly to scatter out of the way.

They watched helplessly as the snow covered the pond and its victims, mere yards on the other side of their chalet.

"Oh my God," Hannah cried. "Those poor people. They're buried alive!"

"We've got to help or they'll suffocate. Every second counts," Tyler exclaimed.

Together, they dashed outside but there was so much snow flying in the air they couldn't see more than five feet in front of them.

"This way," Tyler shouted, pulling her in the direction of where they had last seen the ice-skaters. "And don't let go of my hand!"

Inch by inch, they labored forward, taking many precious minutes to traverse a few meager yards.

Cold air filled Hannah's lungs making each breath as painful as inhaling icy fire. The tip of her nose was numb, her fingers stiff inside her mittens. Her throat ached with fear and her heart thundered in her chest.

There had been at least two children among the group of unfortunate skaters. She lunged through snow piling deep as her hips, all the while clinging to Tyler like a lifeline.

The swirling residue from the avalanche began to dissipate, sharpening their visual acuity somewhat, but fresh snow was falling in fast, giant flakes dropping from a gray cloudy sky, and a restless wind gusted against their backs.

They trudged forward, eyes on the ground, ears cocked for cries for help. Their clenched hands trembled. Powerful electrical currents flowed back and forth between them. They were connected, united by their mission and their burgeoning feelings for each other. She never wanted to let go of his hand.

People from neighboring chalets who had also seen the incident joined them.

"I think this might be the spot," Tyler said to Hannah and dropped to his knees in a heavy pile of snow. She sank down beside him and they began to dig with their hands.

Watching Tyler work, Hannah was thrilled. All his concentration was focused on the task at hand. Saving lives. His firm jaw was locked in determination, his shoulders rigid. He had dedicated his life to healing the sick. He helped anyone who needed him, just as he had taken her under his wing, given her shelter at his beachside home.

He was that kind of man.

Then a sudden thought hit her like a blow. Was she anything more to him than simply another life to save? Had he rescued her because it was so much a part of his personality that to *not* help was an impossibility? Was she nothing more than a charity case?

Her old insecurities nudged at her. *Men don't do anything*

without a motive, Hannah, her mother's discouraging voice rang in her ears. *Always remember that. Never lose your head to any charming cad and you'll never have a broken heart.*

"Are you all right?" Tyler's voice cracked her reverie.

"Huh?"

"You seemed dazed. And you're shivering. I think you should go back to the chalet." His brow was knit in sincere concern, his tone compassionate.

"No," she insisted, shaking off her self-doubt in the wake of his concern. "I want to stay."

"Are you cold?"

Cold? Sizzling hot was more like it. Hannah shook her head and stared down at the ice. Why was she so afraid of these feelings? Because she knew it couldn't last? Because both of them were going to end up getting hurt?

Because there was no such thing as happily-ever-after.

No. Her mother was wrong.

She raised her head, her gaze traveling from his broad chest encased in a thick down coat, up his neck to his jaw and beyond to face those immutable eyes again. Her longing for him increased tenfold. With a single glance, he demolished her control, chiseled past her armor.

And it wasn't bad. Not at all. In fact, there was an unexpected freedom in letting go of control. Of accepting whatever came. A sudden lightness of being unlike anything she'd ever felt before swept over her as she gazed into his dark, mesmerizing eyes. She knew then she could trust him. Utterly, completely without the slightest reservation.

"I'm fine," she murmured and gave him a slight, reassuring smile.

"All right. But, please, don't overdo it. If you find yourself getting weak, tell me."

Nodding, she began digging once more.

"I found something," she cried a few minutes later and unearthed a child's bright red ski mask. At the sight of the festive garment, her bottom lip quivered. That mask said so much. A family had come here for a fun vacation and they had met with a horrible accident. She sat staring at the small mask until Tyler gently removed it from her hand.

"Be strong," he said softly. "There's no time for emotions. Most avalanche victims die within the first thirty-five minutes and they've already used up at least ten. These people are counting on us to save their lives. Keep digging."

Bolstered by his encouragement, Hannah returned to her task with a vengeance.

Next, Tyler found an ice skate. Grimly, he dug faster. Soon, two dozen rescue workers had linked up with them and were frantically combing through the snow.

"The avalanche has blocked the main road," one young man, a ski resort employee, said. Worry wrinkles marred his forehead. He had ridden up on a snowmobile and was busy passing out shovels. "The crisis staff can't get up from Taos to help us and the snowfall is preventing helicopter flight out. We're completely on our own." The young man surveyed the area and shook his head. "I'm afraid lives will be lost. The resort doctor went down the mountain this morning to take an emergency appendectomy to the hospital. All we've got left are a nurse and three paramedics."

"I'm a doctor," Tyler said. He glanced at Hannah. "And so is my wife." He was telling the same lie he had told the motel owner in Texas. But it was an honest lie. When they found the victims no one would question Hannah's involvement.

She looked at her hands and thought about the ordeal that lay ahead of her. This would not be easy. If each healing sapped her own strength, how would she hold up with so many needing her attention?

"I heard something!" one of the other diggers exclaimed. "I think someone is crying for help."

Immediately, everyone converged on the area and in rapid succession, they had extracted four victims from the snow. All alive and breathing. Tyler examined each one of them.

"Is this everyone?" he asked, several minutes later.

"There was a lady and her little boy," a teenage girl who'd been caught in the avalanche, replied. "I'd just met them this morning at breakfast. She was teaching her son to skate. We saw the avalanche and we were trying to get out of the way before it hit." The girl's eyes misted with tears. "I saw the snow slam into them first and then it tumbled on top of me, too."

"Get her and the others to the resort clinic," Tyler commanded the paramedics. "We'll keep searching."

With grim resolve, he returned to the task of uncovering victims. Hannah dug beside him.

"Tyler," she said, a few minutes later. "I see a hand!"

In an instant he was by her side, dragging a woman from the snowy embankment.

The woman's jaw was slack, lips blue and her eyes rolled back in her head. She shook in convulsive shudders.

Tyler crouched beside her and a ski resort employee threw a blanket over her.

"Hannah," Tyler said and reached out to her.

She knew what he wanted her to do. Taking a deep fortifying breath, she kneit beside the woman, closed her eyes and ran her hand over her quaking body.

Instantly Hannah felt the now-familiar tingling warmth surge through her hands, circulating from her to the injured ice skater. She willed herself to perform a miracle, tried her best to direct the power over which she had no conscious control.

She experienced an odd popping sensation deep within her solar plexus as if a dam had broken. She had never felt it before, not when she had healed Margie Parks or Tyler or Angie Henry. It would have concerned her except a peaceful lightness overcame her, soothing her, calming her, keeping her mind fixed on the ailing woman and off her own health.

The woman's jerking stopped and she groaned.

Hannah continued to run her palms along the woman's face, touching her hair, caressing her cheeks. The woman's skin pinked. She opened her eyes and looked up at Hannah.

"You saved my life," she whispered. "I was going down a long dark tunnel. I could see a light at the end. I felt warm, fuzzy and weightless. You pulled me back."

Shocked by the woman's words, Hannah clenched her jaw. "Are you all right?"

"My little boy, Jake…" the woman said, then reached up to grasp the collar of Hannah's coat. Desperation rose to her eyes. "We were ice skating when the avalanche hit. I think the snow broke the ice and he fell into the pond. I lost my grip on his hand. Find him. Save him. Please. Oh, please. He's only five years old!"

Tyler didn't think. He simply acted. Barely noticing the sharp bite of winter through his damp clothes, he shoveled deeper into the snowbank, searching for the missing boy.

Two things occurred to him. One, over half an hour had passed since the avalanche, placing the boy in grave danger and, two, he could not allow Hannah over here. He had seen how pale she had become after touching the boy's mother, how her strength had visibly zapped from her slender frame. She would insist on helping with the child and in her state of compromised health, Tyler feared for her safety. He would allow her intervention only if there was no other way to save the boy's life.

He leaned forward, burrowing like a frenzied mole and tossing shovel after shovelful of snow over his shoulder. Snow drifted from the sky and packed down the collar of his coat. In a matter of minutes he had peeled back the thick layering to reveal the frozen pond underneath marred by a long crack and a jagged hole six feet in diameter.

The woman had gotten to her feet and staggered over. "Jake," she wailed, then clutched Tyler's sleeve. "Please, mister, save my baby."

"Keep her back," Tyler said, nodding at a male bystander.

"Let the doctor work," the man coaxed, reaching for the boy's mother and drawing her away. Sobbing helplessly, she turned into the man's embrace.

Tyler spared a moment to peer at Hannah over his shoulder. She was on her knees in the snow. Her eyes were closed and she had a beatific smile on her face. It took every ounce of resolve he possessed not to go to her. His heart pushed for him to stop what he was doing and take care of Hannah but his head told him the boy was in more immediate danger.

He forced his attention to the gaping cavity and the turgid dark water below. He stared hard, willing himself to detect the child's little body buried beneath the ice, but he saw nothing. His blood slurried through his veins and fear chilled his belly.

"Tyler."

Looking up, he saw Hannah swaying on her feet a short distance away. From the expression on her face, it was clear she knew he was going in. She swallowed hard. He saw the word *no* in her eyes. Instead, she surprised him by saying, "Find him."

He nodded, then took a deep breath, prepared himself for a shock and plunged into the icy water.

The sensation defied description. Every muscle in his body seemed to cramp in unison. He thought he screamed but it must have been only in his mind. His mouth was locked tight, his lungs frozen in stunned silence. His clothes weighted him like anchors, his world suddenly silent.

Prying open his eyes, he forced his legs to tread water. He felt as if he were moving through a nightmare, frigid and viscous. Desolate. Dead. Rendered insensate by the freezing liquid.

Nothing made sense any more. From the time Hannah Zachary had appeared in his emergency room, Tyler's whole life had changed in unimaginable ways. His comfortable world of granite reason and steely logic was eroding around him and he was powerless to halt the degeneration.

Mentally, Tyler shook himself. Get with the program. Hannah was depending on him, and so was the child and his mother.

Where was that boy?

He whipped his head first left, then right. His spirits rose when he caught a glimpse of red. Lunging through the water, he grabbed the parka, catching hold of the boy's wrist.

The child was unconscious. How long had it been? Tyler wondered, grateful for once that the water was so cold. Hypothermia gave him a fighting chance at survival. With the boy in tow, Tyler kicked toward the light that indicated the opening in the ice.

He buoyed to the surface, lungs ready to burst. He gasped and sputtered. A paramedic reached for the boy. Two more men pulled Tyler from the hole. He lay on the ice, gasping like a fish. He heard a multitude of voices but they sounded far away.

Talking noisily, people gathered around him. He could make out blue jeans and ski pants and woolen leggings, but overall his vision was blurred and he couldn't see more than a few feet in front of him.

His body jerked with shudders so severe they felt like grand mal seizures. His teeth slammed together. Someone threw a blanket over him. He tried to mutter, "Thanks," but no sound came out.

And then he felt soft hands on his face and he knew at once those hands belonged to Hannah.

Wherever she touched him, his skin heated instantly and he experienced a calming sense of tranquillity. Gradually, his convulsions subsided.

"The boy?" Somehow, he managed to push the short question past his stiff lips.

"They're giving him CPR."

Tyler winced, closed his eyes and prayed he had not been too late to save the child's life.

She had to remain composed. For Tyler's sake. Those few minutes he had been under the ice had been the longest minutes of her existence. She had ripped off her gloves and chewed her nails to the quick. When the boy's mother had asked if she was Tyler's wife, she had nodded, too frightened to bother with the truth. She couldn't have loved him more if she *had* been his wife.

If he dies, she had thought, *I'll surely die, too.* Because without Tyler, nothing was worth fighting for.

She could not have begrudged him for what he had done, jumping into the frozen water to save the boy's life. That's the kind of man he was. Brave, strong, idealistic. His actions defined his personality. His courage was one of the many reasons she loved him. Tyler would always place the needs of others ahead of his own. He had been the only person in a crowd of three dozen or more who had been willing to risk himself to rescue the child.

But when the paramedics had extracted his rigid, colorless body from the hole, Hannah had been certain he was dead. So certain she had burst into tears.

Then she realized she possessed the power to resurrect him.

I'm coming, my love.

She had pushed through the crowd to where the paramedics had laid him on the ice and covered him with blankets, but when she tried to get close enough to lay her hands on him, they stopped her.

"Step back, ma'am."

"But I'm his wife," she said, surprised at how easily the lie came to her lips.

They were magic words. The men stood aside and Hannah crouched beside Tyler.

The minute she touched him, all fear vanished. She literally felt him grow stronger beneath her fingers. She closed her eyes and concentrated, no longer awed by her power but interested in learning how to use it to capacity.

Her own energy drained until she was as light-headed as someone who had donated two pints of blood in one afternoon. You could have stirred her knees with a spoon.

Strange sensations were taking place in her body. Hannah didn't understand what was happening. Odd as it sounded, she felt as if her very cells were collapsing, sucked dry of vital fluids and nutrients. But what did it mean?

Can't waste time thinking. Must help Tyler.

She was functioning on pure epinephrine and nothing else. She tasted the "fight or flight" hormone in the back of her throat, a bitter flavor like rancid coffee.

"The boy?" Tyler said, his voice clear and firm. The color had returned to his cheeks and he was struggling to sit up.

Hannah looked over to where the paramedics were still working frenetically on the small body laid out on a yellow fiberglass backboard. He was not responding to CPR. Hannah's own heart fluttered in her chest like a dying butterfly.

"Not good," she answered.

Tyler's jaw clenched, anguish clearly etched across his handsome features. Love for him filled her, revived her. He was a very special man and she had been lucky to know him. But she could no longer cling to him. He could not save her. No one could save her. She knew that much. Her body was failing and in the short time she had left, Hannah was going to use her healing power to salvage that boy's life.

"You're all right now," she said. "I'm going to help them with the boy."

"Hannah, no." He grabbed her wrist. "You're fading fast, I can see it in your eyes. Let the paramedics do their job."

"It's not working."

"Please." His pleading almost broke her in two.

"I have no choice. Just as you had no choice when you jumped in the water after the child. You're a healer, that's what you do. And now, I'm one, too."

"Then do your best," he whispered.

"I will."

He let go her hand and she ran over to the paramedics. "I'm a doctor," she said, not bothering to explain that she was not a medical doctor. She knew basic life-support but that was not important. "May I relieve you?"

She looked at the young paramedic doing compressions. He was tiring; she could see it in his flagging form. Hannah could only pray that she herself had the strength to take over.

"Thank you," he said, and moved aside as Hannah knelt at the boy's chest, laid her palm against his sternum and turned her attention to the second paramedic positioned at the child's head. He was squeezing an ambu bag, forcing air into lifeless lungs. He stopped a moment, checked the boy's carotid pulse and shook his head.

"Continue CPR."

Hannah pressed down on the boy's frail chest about an inch with the heel of her hand and desperately willed the lifeless heart to start beating again.

Come on, come on.

Slowly, her palm heated and the customary tingling spread outward through her hand and fingers.

"One, one-thousand. Two, one-thousand. Three, one-thousand," she counted. On the count of five, the paramedic delivered air with the ambu bag.

Hannah watched the child's passive face. His tiny lips were blue, his wet hair plastered to his forehead. In the background she heard his mother helplessly sobbing.

Please, don't let this strange healing gift fail me now.

But the boy did not respond.

No. Impossible. She had healed that little girl, the boy's mother and Tyler, twice. She could do this.

Except she was exhausted. The tingling did not engulf her entire body as it usually did. She was wrung-out, empty. Her arm hung like loose string, lightweight and insubstantial. But she kept at it because there was nothing else she could do.

A minute passed. Two. Three.

Useless. The boy was dead.

The crowd held its collective breath. All eyes were trained upon Hannah, but she paid no attention to anyone.

She was a woman possessed. Her hair flew about her shoulders in wild disarray when she rocked forward, compressing the boy's chest with the heel of her hand. She could feel the color drain from her face, knew her skin was deathly pale, her cheeks hollow and that dark circles must be ringing her eyes. Fatigued to the core of her being, she felt as if a sharp wind could slice her into two pieces.

But undaunted, she kept working.

And then, miraculously, just when she was about to give up, Hannah felt a stirring beneath her palm.

A heart beat?

She peered at the child's face. His lashes fluttered.

"We got a pulse!" the paramedic crowed triumphantly.

A shout of joy went up from the crowd.

The boy coughed up water and then began to cry.

Trembling all over, Hannah rose to her feet.

And collapsed.

Trauma.

Tyler knew the details intimately. Blood loss. Cardiac arrest. Shock. Systemic shut down. Rescuing others came as second nature to him. Correcting the tragedies brought about by illness, disease and accidents were part of his identity. He was trained to handle whatever emergencies life might throw his way.

Except when it concerned those he loved.

His eyes were trained on Hannah, watching her as she labored over the boy. He was worried for the child, yes, but he was worried about Hannah even more. He knew what effects each healing had upon her. Knew all too well that each might be her last.

He lay shivering on the ground, barely able to breathe following his plunge into the icy water. Bystanders kept plying him with warm blankets and shoving mugs of hot coffee into his hands, but Tyler could not stop shaking.

Get up. Hannah needs you.

His mind prodded him to move, but his body refused to obey.

Until he saw Hannah stagger to her feet and then fall face-first into the snow.

In an instant, he was galvanized, leaping to his feet, tossing off the blankets, sprinting the few yards to where she lay surrounded by people. He shoved them aside.

"Hannah!" He bent down and scooped her into his arms.

She did not respond. Her head lolled back against his elbow. Her eyes were shuttered closed. Her deathly pallor and icy cold skin scared him. He needed to get her inside. Immediately.

Tyler swiveled his head to the young man in the paramedic uniform who had helped Hannah perform CPR on the boy. The paramedic was ministering to the child who sat in his mother's lap and cried against her shoulder.

"You saved my boy's life," the grateful woman said. "You and your wife."

"Quick," he said to the paramedic. "Where's your clinic?"

"I'll take you," said the ski resort worker who had passed out the shovels. His snowmobile was hitched to a cart parked nearby. He nodded at the contraption. "Get in."

Tyler climbed into the cart with Hannah still clutched securely in his arms while the mother and son got in beside them. He wanted to reassure the mother and tell her everything was going to be all right, but he was too preoccupied with Hannah. She hadn't moved a muscle since her knees had buckled and she'd fallen onto the ground. He fixed his gaze on her chest, making sure she was breathing through the short ride to the resort's small emergency clinic.

He had a lot of work ahead of him, between examining the other avalanche victims and taking care of Hannah.

Gently, he brushed her hair from her eyes and fought back the tears that stung his throat. *Hang in there, sweetheart. Don't leave me now.*

A nurse was waiting for them at the clinic. She ushered the mother and son to two cots set up in the corner while Tyler deposited Hannah on a third. The other four victims had already been brought in by rescue workers and were lying about the room on similar cots.

"This guy's a doctor," the resort employee told the nurse.

"Thank God," the nurse breathed. "With Dr. Malix in Taos I wasn't sure how we were going to handle all the casualties."

Tyler heard them speaking but his attention was concentrated on Hannah.

"Doctor." The nurse tapped him softly on the shoulder.

"Yes?" Distracted, he turned to peer at her. She wore a name tag that said, Trisha Martin RN, and was giving him a set of green cotton scrubs to wear.

"You're soaked to the skin. Go put on some dry clothes before you catch your death. "

The nurse was right but he hated to leave Hannah even for a single moment.

"Go on," she said, gently pushing him forward. "You can change in the men's room around the corner."

Tyler cast a backward glance over his shoulder at Hannah. "Do you have a centrifuge here?"

"Of course," the nurse answered.

"Spin a hematocrit on her, will you? She's too pale."

"Will do, Doctor. Now go change. You're going to need all your strength and concentration to get through this day."

Feeling dazed in a way he hadn't experienced since Yvette had finally told him about her cancer, Tyler shuffled to the men's room, his mind blank. Perfunctorily, he tugged off his wet clothes and slipped into dry comfortable scrubs.

Hannah can't be dying. Not now. Not yet. I never told her I love her.

Then right there in the men's room Tyler rested his forehead against the wall's cool porcelain tile and allowed himself to cry in a way he had been unable to cry for Yvette. His shoulders shook and his stomach tightened, his heart breaking into a thousand little pieces.

You can't indulge your sorrow. There are people out there who need you. Hannah needs you. Pull yourself together. Swallowing his bitter tears, he swiped at his eyes with the back of his hand, then squared his shoulders and strode purposefully into the clinic, slipping into the role of physician like a second skin.

"I've got the warming blanket on the boy," Trisha Martin told him. "And I'm spinning a crit on your wife. Her BP is eighty-three over sixty and she's bradycardic."

"Good job."

Tyler forced himself to examine the boy and his mother before allowing himself to check on Hannah. Once he ascertained that they were stable, he hurried over to Hannah's cot. Unbidden, the memory of that moment in Saint Madeline's E.R. when he had first laid eyes on her came flooding back. He wouldn't have given two cents for her recovery then. She looked worse now.

"Hang in there, sweetheart," he soothed. "Everything is going to be all right."

But was it?

"Are there any more victims?" Tyler asked the paramedic who had stayed behind to help them. It was the same young man who had done CPR on the boy.

"That's all," the paramedic said. "No more resort guests have been reported missing."

"Thank God for that," Tyler said.

"Doctor." Nurse Martin tugged at his sleeve. "This is the first chance I've had time to read your wife's hematocrit."

Tyler met the woman's eyes, and they were grave with concern. "Yes?"

"It's twenty."

His guess had been correct. Somehow, during the healings she had performed, she had depleted her own red blood supply. If her hematocrit dropped any lower, Hannah would be in serious danger.

Tyler dashed to her bedside and picked up her hand. Her breathing was shallow and she remained unconscious.

"Get another set of vital signs on her."

The nurse did as he requested, wrapping the blood pressure cuff around Hannah's limp arm and pumping it up with the bulb.

"BP seventy-nine over fifty," she whispered.

Her blood pressure was dropping. Tyler swallowed. Not good.

"Pulse fifty."

Leaning over, he kissed Hannah's forehead. "Come on, babe, wake up and smile at me. We need to get your blood pumping."

"Her heart rate accelerated when you kissed her," the nurse marveled, two fingers resting at Hannah's wrist. "It jumped up to seventy-two."

He raised Hannah's hand to his lips and kissed each knuckle one by one. "Come back to me, sweetheart."

There was no response.

Fear congealed in his stomach. Why wouldn't she wake up?

"Spin another crit," he told Trisha Martin grimly.

"Will do."

He waited anxiously while the nurse pricked Hannah's finger with a lancet and piped blood into the thin glass tube. She took the sample and disappeared into the anteroom where the supplies and equipment were stored.

Arms crossed over his chest, Tyler paced from one end of the room to the other, stopping to check on the other patients while he waited for the test results. They were all resting and doing fine despite the ordeal they had been through. If only he could say the same for Hannah.

He went back to her cot and pulled up a stool beside her. He held her hand, kneaded her knuckles with his fingertips.

"Doctor," the nurse said, alarm written across her face. "Your wife's hematocrit is only seven! She has to have blood right away."

Tyler blanched and sprang to his feet. "Are you sure?"

"Come read it for yourself. I ran it twice to be certain. I don't understand how it could drop so quickly when she's not bleeding. Did she suffer an internal injury during the avalanche?"

He shook his head and followed the woman into the anteroom. He peered at the calibrated wheel that allowed him to read the level of red blood cells in the slender glass tube.

Seven. He read both samples and they were identical. There was no mistake.

"What are we going to do? The avalanche has blocked the road and the helicopters can't get in because of the snowstorm."

"I know."

"Without a transfusion, she'll surely die."

"Dammit!" Tyler slammed the wall with his fist and didn't even wince at the pain that shot through his hand. He could not let her die. He was a doctor. He was supposed to save people.

Think! Think!

He stalked back to the main room, the nurse at his heels. The paramedic looked up from where he was making notes on the boy's record sheet. The boy's mother was watching him, too.

Why was Hannah's hematocrit so low? She hadn't been injured. There could be no internal bleeding. She had simply collapsed after healing the others. Had her heroic actions somehow depleted her own blood count? Was it due to continued side effects from exposure to *Virusall*? Did that account for her ongoing weakness and occasional dizziness? Even though he could not explain the etiology, he realized that had to be the case.

The room went utterly silent. He looked around at the faces. Everyone had already written Hannah off as a corpse. He saw reality in their eyes.

He shifted his gaze to Hannah. Still unconscious. Still as vulnerable and enchanting as Sleeping Beauty. Oh, if only a kiss from him would awaken her.

"There's nothing we can do, Doctor." The paramedic came over and draped an arm over Tyler's shoulder. "We have no way to get blood up here in time. I'm so sorry this had to happen to such a brave lady."

"I refuse to accept that." Tyler wrenched away from the young man. "You're wrong. We'll give her a transfusion. Right here. Right now."

"We're not equipped to administer transfusions," the nurse protested.

"You have IV tubing and large bore needles, don't you?"

The paramedic looked bewildered. "Yes, but do you even know her blood type?"

"She's AB negative," Tyler said, his jaw set in grim determination. He would not let Hannah go without putting up the fight of his life. "But I'm O negative. The universal donor. I can give blood to any other type."

The entire process was incredibly risky. He knew that. But there was simply no other option. Hannah needed a transfusion and she needed it quickly or she wasn't going to last another hour.

Fear grabbed him by the throat and refused to let go. What if he was making a huge mistake?

Tyler shook his head. Now was not the time to get indecisive.

"It's tricky." The paramedic shook his head. "Administering a patient to patient transfer without a type and crossmatch."

"Have you got a better idea?" Tyler snapped, stalking toward the white metal cabinet with glass doors that held a small supply of emergency equipment. "Get busy. Start an IV on her. Normal saline with an eighteen gauge. Do it quickly."

"She's your wife, sir. You're emotionally involved and I'm not sure you're thinking straight."

"If you won't help, then fine, get out of my way." He glared at her and the paramedic.

"Don't misunderstand," the nurse said. "We want to help. But what if she dies?"

"How is that going to be any different than the current situation?" Tyler started yanking needles, Betadine swabs and IV paraphernalia from the shelf and tossing them onto the cot beside Hannah. "She slipping away before our very eyes."

"Well." The nurse hesitated. "If she dies because of the transfusion, then *you* will have been the one to kill her."

Chapter 13

Precious moments ticked away.

Nurse Martin started the IV on Hannah while the paramedic initiated an identical one in Tyler's right forearm. Tyler lay on the cot staring up at the ceiling, listening to his pulse thundering in his ears.

Hurry. Hurry.

He clenched his hands, knotting them into hard fists. His head was turned toward Hannah and he never took his eyes from her sleeping face.

"Are you ready?" the nurse asked.

He nodded.

She released the three-way, stopcock valve on the blood line trailing from Tyler's arm to Hannah's and shut off the flow of normal saline. Slowly, his blood began to inch down the tubing toward Hannah.

If she was going to have a reaction to his blood it would most likely occur in the first few minutes of the transfusion.

The paramedic was stationed beside Hannah, constantly monitoring her vital signs, the crash cart within easy reach. To Tyler's relief, one of the vacationing skiers turned out to be a third-year medical student who had slept through the entire avalanche and subsequent rescue, but upon hearing of the disaster had immediately shown up at the clinic and offered his services. He and the other paramedics were taking care of the rest of the victims. Everyone seemed to be recovering.

Everyone that is, except for Hannah.

As he watched, his blood pushed the remaining saline from the end of the tubing into Hannah's veins.

Drip. Drip. Drip.

His blood flowed into her.

Taking a deep breath, he held it. And waited.

"How's her vitals?" he asked the paramedic and was surprised to hear his voice come out hoarse and thready. Anxiety constricted his throat. Fear froze his chest.

This was a drastic, last-ditch effort and he knew it.

Come on, Hannah. Don't give up.

Memories of Yvette flashed in his mind, stark and unrelenting. He remembered how she had looked after the chemotherapy. Bald, weak, pale. She hadn't wanted the chemo, but Tyler had insisted, even though in his heart he'd known it was too late. He had been wrong to make her suffer the indignities of chemotherapy when it would be ineffective, but he was a doctor and determined to use everything in his arsenal. He simply had been unable to let her go without a fight.

The same way he refused to relinquish Hannah.

Was he making a second mistake?

Briefly, Tyler closed his eyes. No. He could not believe that was the case. He felt certain Hannah would want any chance at life. She was not sweet, accepting Yvette. Hannah was a warrior. She stood up for what she believed in even if it meant placing herself in jeopardy.

"Vital signs are stable," the paramedic said.

Tyler opened his eyes, allowing himself to breath normally.

The transfusion continued until a pint of blood had been drained from him and infused into Hannah. It took over an hour but there were no signs of an adverse reaction.

Her color pinkened. Her respiration increased. Tyler experienced some lightheadedness when he sat up, but he ignored it. All that mattered was Hannah's welfare.

Nurse Martin removed the IV from his arm. Tyler got to his feet and gripped the bed railing to steady himself. He looked down into Hannah's sleeping face.

She was so incredibly beautiful. The sight of her clutched at his heart, produced an intense ache.

He would never allow her to heal anyone again. No matter what happened. He took her hand. "Hannah?"

No response.

"Pull another crit," he told the nurse, then gently massaged Hannah's shoulder. Leaning down, he whispered in her ear, "Wake up, darling. It's me, Tyler."

Still nothing.

He kissed her forehead, her nose, her lips. *What now?* He had assumed administering the transfusion would bring her around.

It hadn't.

His gut torqued.

"Her hematocrit is up to twelve," the nurse said. "But you know it takes a few hours to get a comprehensive reading."

He nodded. Hannah was out of danger. At least for the time being. "I'm going to take her back to our chalet."

"Are you sure?" Nurse Martin asked.

"Yes."

If Hannah was dying, then he wanted to be far away from the glare of the public eye. If she recovered, he wanted their reunion to be an intimate one. Either way, he could take care of her just as well at the chalet as he could here.

"I'll get the gurney," the paramedic offered. "And help you transport her."

"Thanks." Tyler turned his attention to the nurse. "If you need help with the other patients, come and get me."

"I'm sure the medical student can handle it." Nurse Martin waved in his direction. "You get some rest and take care of your wife."

"I will." He nodded, realizing just how much he had missed

hearing that word, *wife*. Hannah might not be his wife in the legal sense but he couldn't have felt more joined to her if they had had the world's biggest wedding.

If only he could save her. If only there was an antidote. If only they could share the rest of their lives together.

A miracle. That was what he needed.

But Tyler had stopped believing in miracles a long time ago.

Blackness. Heavy and oppressive.

Headache. Temples pounding. Leaden arms. Cement legs. Fight. Kick. See.

No strength. No energy. Syrup. Sucking me down. Where am I? What's going on? Why do I feel this way?

What happened?

Hannah searched her brain and came up empty. It was hard to think. Impossible to concentrate. She heard a distant voice. A far away buzz. But she could make out nothing for certain.

Danger.

Her pulse quickened at the realization although she could not say why. She simply knew she was in serious trouble.

She felt pressure on her hand. "Hannah?"

The voice was warped. Like a record played on slow speed. She frowned. Who was calling her name?

Come on, come on, wake up. You've got to get out of here. You've got to hurry.

Hurry? Why the rush? Anxiety weighted her chest.

There had been a catastrophe. She couldn't remember what kind. Had she been in a car accident?

That sounded familiar, but wrong somehow.

"Hannah, honey, it's me, Tyler. Can you hear me?"

The voice was sharper now. More in tune. *Yes. Tyler. Talk to him.* Her tongue lay like a lump of clay in her mouth.

Then there were lips on her forehead and tears on her cheeks. Tyler's lips. Tyler's tears. She inhaled deeply, breathed in his unique scent.

"Tyler," she whispered.

"My God, Hannah, you're alive."

She blinked and his dear face come into view. "Yes. I'm alive. Where are we?" She glanced around at the room decorated like a Swiss chalet. Lots of thick rich material, broad-beamed furniture, a Jacuzzi over by the window, a crackling fire in the adobe fireplace.

"We're at the ski chalet."

"Are we alone?"

"Yes. The avalanche buried the road. We won't be able to leave here until morning, if then. I'm worried about that. I want to get you to a hospital as soon as possible."

"Why?"

"We almost lost you."

"Lost me? How?"

He was sitting beside her bed, her right hand clutched in his. Tears dampened his eyes and he did not bother to wipe them away. He reminded her about the avalanche and how they had saved the lives of six people. He explained how she had collapsed after giving CPR to the small boy, how she had slipped into unconsciousness.

"You think it's from using my healing power?"

"I'm afraid so. You're hematocrit was extremely low. Apparently you've been effected on the most elemental cellular level." His tone grew cautious when he described transfusing her with his own blood. The transfusion that had saved her life.

"I was so frightened," he confessed. "Terrified that I was doing the wrong thing. That I was going to lose you no matter what."

"I'm too stubborn to die." She squeezed his hand.

"I'm beginning to believe it." He smiled gently.

"Your blood is inside me?" she marveled and held her hands to her face, examining them with newfound respect.

"Yes."

"You're part of me."

He nodded.

"We're one."

"In a manner of speaking."

"Oh, Tyler. Thank you."

His hand trembled. "May I kiss you?"

"You'd better. Before I find someone else to do it," she teased.

"We can't have that." Leaning over he brushed his lips lightly against hers.

"You call that a kiss?"

"I don't want to hurt you."

"I'm not a china doll. I won't break."

"You sure looked like it four hours ago."

"That was before I had your plump, juicy red blood cells pumping though me. Now give me a proper kiss this minute."

"That transfusion made you bossy."

"Guess I'm taking after you." She hooked a finger under his collar and tugged him toward her.

"Are you calling me overbearing?"

"If the shoe fits."

His mouth closed over hers and Hannah was washed away on a sea of happy emotions. And she was growing stronger. The more he kissed her, the more his blood mingled with hers and swished through her veins, the better she felt.

A tingling warmth surged through her until she was electrified. She had a sudden urge to jump and run and shout with joy. His kiss, her recovery.

One. He and I. We're the same.

For so long she had been all alone. Even when her parents were alive, she had basically been by herself. Few friends. No lovers. Work had been her only focus, her only goal.

She had been taught to live outside her emotions. To observe and analyze. To study and quantify. Emotionalism had been discouraged, feelings regarded as something to be suppressed. She had learned to keep herself above the fray of most human frailties. She had avoided vulnerability, but she had also avoided love.

It felt strange to let herself go. Strange but wonderful. Emotions surged through her, incredible and new.

Tyler tasted so good. A drink from heaven. His mouth warm and soft. Ah, such pleasure.

"Hannah," he whispered, pulling back and gazing deeply into her eyes. "I thought I'd lost you forever."

"No. Not yet. I'm here. I'm yours. I feel like Superwoman! I feel like making love to you."

"Hannah." He breathed.

"But I'm still afraid of passing my affliction on to you."

"I never got to tell you," Tyler said, kissing her fingertips and sending jolts of pure pleasure flying up her nerve endings. "I've already been exposed to your blood. If I was going to 'catch' something from you, I would have symptoms by now."

"But when? How?"

"That night you came into the emergency room, when I drew that second vial of blood from you. I accidentally stuck myself in the thumb at the lab."

"Oh no." She frowned.

"Don't worry. I'm fine. There's no reason to hold back any longer sweetheart. If you want to make love to me as badly as I want to make love to you, then say the word."

"Make love to me, Tyler." She raised a finger, stroked his cheek, and then tapped the left side of her chest. "In here. I feel it. Making love is the right thing to do. In fact, it's the only thing to do. Be with me, Tyler, in every since of the word."

"Sweetheart," he exclaimed and kissed her again. "Are you sure? Are you really sure?"

"I've never been more certain of anything in my life."

Blood flowed through her veins. His blood. She was fortified, renewed. All because of him and everything he had done for her.

"I don't want to hurt you."

"Don't you get it? Haven't you noticed? No matter how sick or weak I am, every time you kiss me or hold me, I get stronger. There's no logic to it, but somehow you're my medicine, Tyler Fresno."

"That's true," he marveled. "I hadn't realized it before. You do seem to get stronger after we kiss."

He angled his body beside her in the bed. His eyes intensely centered upon her. It seemed he was committing her to memory.

"I never want to forget the way you look at this moment."

She raised a hand to her mussed hair. "I must look a fright."

"You're radiant. In fact, I've never seen anything more beautiful than the light in your eyes."

"Are you sure you want to do this? I can't be part of your future, no matter how much we wish it so. Even though your transfusion revived me, we both know I am still dying. Is the present enough for you?" Her bottom lip trembled. She did not want to make him suffer or cause him pain.

"The present is all any of us has, Hannah—haven't you figured that out by now? I held on to Yvette too long. I used my grief like a shield, blocking out the world, keeping love at bay. But you changed all that. Made me see what was really important. Even if our time together is short, it will be great. Tulips only bloom for a few weeks in the spring. A few short weeks. Some gardeners might say tending them is not even worth the effort, their life span is so short. But for those short sweet, incredible weeks, they are breathtaking."

Tears formed at the corners of her eyes. "I love you so," she murmured and he responded in kind, whispering his love for her into her left ear.

She caught her breath as his hand slid down the buttons on her sweater, popping them open one by one. His knuckles trailed over her bare stomach. His head was so close to hers. His dark eyes shone coal black with desire. He dipped his head and with lips hotter than fire tickled the hollow of her neck, his hair brushing against her chin. The tickling caused her to shimmer from the inside out.

The sensation deepened into an ache of pure neediness that spread through her breasts, her belly, between her legs. Even her knees and elbows panged with wanting. He moved against her, all shirt and skin, man and heat, smelling of snow and sweat and Tyler.

Hannah squirmed as his lips explored her body. Then when she could stand it no longer, she hungrily reached for the snap on his blue jeans.

"Easy. Easy." He covered her wrist with his hand. "We've got all night. We can't go anywhere, nor can anyone come in here after us. The roads won't be open until morning. It's just you and me, darling."

"I want you so badly."

"You'll have me." He met her gaze, his lashes impossibly long, his eyes soft with amusement. "Over and over again. I promise."

But even as he talked, she was busy, unbuttoning his shirt, pulling it down his arms. Tyler laughed and slid free from the shirt. "You're good for a guy's ego, you know that?"

"You're good for a woman's soul."

Tyler hugged her to him, his laughter filling her ears. He was solid and confident and she wanted him so much she feared she might explode with the fierceness of it.

"Don't deny me any longer. Make love to me. This minute. And no cheating like before. I want us to climax together."

"Hannah." He groaned, and undid her blue jeans. "Do you have any idea what you do to me?"

She smirked. "If I make you half as hot as you make me it's a wonder you haven't melted into a big ole puddle."

"Oh, I'm melting all right."

She arched her back, allowed him to shuck off her restrictive garment. Once she was naked except for her pair of skimpy white panties, he fumbled with his belt.

Hannah wriggled with anticipation, unable to lie still. She half sat up and reached to help him, her hair swishing along her bare back. She freed the snap of his jeans and eased the zipper down over the expanding crotch seam. Her fingers tingled and her breath fled when she realized he was not wearing any underwear.

He kicked off his pants with comic awkwardness, one foot getting hung up in the leg, but Hannah didn't laugh. She was too busy enjoying the sights. Narrow hips, flat abdomen, the dark triangle of hair flaring above his flagrant arousal. "Okay, so coordination and balance aren't my long suits," he admitted with a wry grin as he returned to cover her with his body.

They were eye to eye, his breath warm against her skin. He propped his weight upon his forearms, his throbbing erection pressed against her soft belly. They lay pelvis to pelvis, skin to skin. The smoothness of her breasts flush against his hard chest. It was an exhilarating and erotic moment.

The length of her vibrated and quivered, filled her with a yearning so blind she could think of nothing but satisfying her needs.

He kissed her and so thirsty was she for his kisses that Hannah sucked his bottom lip to her mouth, trying desperately to pull him inside her any way she could.

"Now, now, now," she whimpered.

"Hold on, darling, hold on."

He leaned over the edge of the bed, retrieved his pants and extracted a condom from the pocket. Scrambling like an inexperienced high school boy, he struggled to open the packet and slide the thing on.

"Let me." She reached out, touched his hand, which was poised over his erection. She rolled the condom on, surprising herself by how easy and natural it felt to touch him there.

They were sitting up in the middle of the bed, gazing into each other's eyes, completely naked. Elbows flat against his sides, Tyler raised his palms. Tentatively, preparing herself for the jolt of incandescent combustion she knew awaited her, Hannah splayed her palms flush against his.

She hissed through her teeth, enervated by the riotous sensations generated by his touch.

Their skin seared together, instant heat spreading from him to her and her to him. She stared and stared and stared at him. Past the thickly lashed eyes, over the dark irises and into his pupils. She tumbled down, down, down into the abyss of Tyler's eyes and, amazingly, touched his soul.

At once she experienced a deep-seated peace, felt something inside her click into place.

Yes. This was what she had waited a lifetime for. This man. This moment. This love.

Her breath slipped through her parted teeth and she licked her lips with the tip of her tongue. Tyler dropped his palms and leaned forward to kiss her, edging her against the sheets, which were icy cold against her blazingly hot body.

He slipped his hand between her legs and caressed the inside of her thighs. She trembled and jerked her hips upward, begging, begging, begging for more. He pressed her into the mattress and she wrapped her legs around his waist as his mouth found her breast and he suckled her hard while he stroked her with his fingers.

She went wild. Raking her fingernails over his back, pulling him to her while angling her hips higher.

Tyler spread her thighs with his and she cried out at the electrical pleasure that shot through her body when he drove himself inside her. Cried and cried and cried at the sheer ecstasy.

"Baby, baby," he cooed. His hands cupped the sides of her head, his fingers entangled in her hair.

She looked up, met those heavenly eyes again. He stared back at her, his gaze serious and intense, all the while moving inside her.

"I love you, Hannah Zachary. Do you hear me?"

Her lip trembled as an emotion so profound she could not name it suffused her body and lifted her to a level of awareness she had not known existed.

And then she was crying. Great tears filled with love and happiness.

Tyler grew alarmed and drew back his head to examine her face. "Hannah, darling, what's wrong? Have I hurt you?"

"I never really believed this could happen to me," she sobbed. Finally, finally the dam had broken and she was free to experience every bright, stunning emotion flooding through her body. She lived!

He stopped moving but he was still inside her, full, warm and comforting. His own eyes misted. Softly, he pressed his lips to her eyelids and cheeks, kissing away the tears before taking her mouth with the sweetest kiss of all.

"Why not? You're smart and sexy and beautiful. Why didn't you believe it would be easy for any man to love you?"

She swallowed and thought of the man she'd had sex with in college. The one who had proclaimed her a cold, unfeeling fish. "I was afraid I wasn't capable of loving anyone."

He trailed a finger over her chin, stroked her gently. "Well, you were mistaken."

"I know. That's why I'm crying."

"Shh. Hush and just relax."

And then he was moving again with a slow and lulling rhythm.

She matched his tempo, her early desperate wildness replaced by a blissful serenity.

You're wrong, Mother. Wrong, wrong, wrong. There is such a thing as true love. Just because you and Father didn't have it, doesn't mean that it's a fairy tale.

For the first time in thirty-two years, Hannah realized she had finally found her home in Tyler's arms. The knowledge changed everything she had previously held dear. Hard work, study, science. It all seemed foreign now, and had no place in her present life.

"Stop thinking," he whispered, uncannily reading her mind. "And feel."

She did as he suggested, concentrating on the hot, fierce sensation splitting her midsection and bringing her alive in ways she never believed possible.

His stroking intensified, driving harder, faster, more urgent, carrying her with him as if his physical body was a magic carpet and he was flying her to the stars.

"Tyler," she moaned his name.

"Yes, sweetheart, yes. Let yourself go."

Gripping his shoulders with her hands, she pulled him into her, urged him on. The sounds of his pleasure filled her ears, heightening her own excitement.

A mighty rapture occupied her body. A feeling of completeness so true and real it took possession of her mind, heart and soul.

She and Tyler were one. His blood gushed through her veins. Hers through his.

Hot. Wet. Bright lights. Erotic noises. Sexy smells. Their entwined bodies moved in unison. Faster and faster. Higher and higher, they raced toward the ultimate release.

And found it at the same moment.

Tyler's back arched. Hannah cried out.

Then they collapsed into an exhausted heap.

Hannah woke sometime later. The room was dark and she was confused until she realized Tyler's naked body was wrapped snugly around hers.

Staring up at the ceiling, she smiled into the darkness. Smiled and smiled and smiled.

Splendor. It was pure splendor lying here in his loving arms. She felt rich and spoiled and oh, so happy!

"Tyler," she whispered his name aloud. Not to awaken him but simply to hear the sound of it upon her tongue. "Tyler, Tyler, Tyler."

He stirred. Mumbling in his sleep, he tightened his grip around her waist as if he never intended on letting her go.

Luxuriating in the pressure of his hand across her belly, Hannah closed her eyes and allowed herself a sacred dream. She pictured the two of them getting married, buying a house together. Having children.

And just when she was enjoying the most magnificent fantasy, reality bit into her.

The dream was not hers to possess. She had a strange healing power that was slowly destroying her blood cells. Two armed men were after her, maybe more. She was still wanted by the police for arson. Her friend Marcus, the only man who could actually help her, was missing, if not dead. How could she be thinking of herself at a time like this? How could she be dreaming of love when Daycon was plotting to put a drug capable of turning ordinary citizens into wild-eyed killers in the hands of zealous terrorists?

She had spent her life striving to be someone important, to create a drug that would cure the sick. She had been so devoted that she had never spent anytime on herself. She thought of her empty apartment back in Austin. An apartment she had never even furnished with personal items. She had told herself how altruistic she was, working hard for the good of mankind, trying her best to defeat the disease that had struck her parents down before their time.

But the truth was, deep inside, she was not superwoman with a holistic agenda to save the world. She was that six-year-old girl who desperately wanted to believe in Prince Charming and happily-ever-after. She wanted to be a wife and a mother. She wanted to attend PTA meetings and dance recitals. She wanted to fit in, have friends and a place in the community.

But most of all, she simply wanted to be loved.

Apparently, it was too much to ask.

Why had it taken a tragedy to make her see what was really important? Why had it taken this long for her to realize she had been living her parents' dreams and not her own? Why, now that she had finally found what she had secretly been searching for, was it going to be ripped away?

"Hannah?"

"Uh-huh." She couldn't say anything else. She didn't trust her voice not to give away her sadness. Whatever short time they had left together, she wanted it to be perfect and not clouded with fears of their very uncertain future together.

"You were impressive."

"I was? I was worried," she admitted. "I'm not very experienced and I was scared I wasn't doing things right."

"Shh." He laid a finger over her mouth. He smelled like sex. Their sex. "You were perfect. Beyond perfect."

She curled into him, reveling in the feel of his hard body spooned against hers.

"Are you hungry?" he asked.

"Starved."

"There're provisions in the kitchenette. Wanna go investigate?"

"Sure."

He wrapped a blanket around her, tied the top sheet around his own waist and drew her from the bed. She padded into the kitchen holding tightly to his hand, the blanket tucked over her breast.

"Come." He pulled out a bar stool and Hannah perched upon it. Without turning on a light, Tyler trailed to the refrigerator, almost tripping on his sheet that dragged on the ground behind him. He bent over to rummage through the shelves, his magnificent tush accentuated by the folds of the thin cotton sheet.

Hannah sucked in her breath at the lusty urges rattling around inside her. She quickly tore her gaze away, forcing herself to peer out the kitchen window at the deep snow beyond, backlit by cloudy gray skies. It looked cold and dreary and she was very happy to be inside safe and warm.

Safe.

For now.

But how long would it last? Sooner or later, Daycon's men would find them again.

"What time is it?" she asked.

Tyler consulted at his watch. "Five-thirty."

"Morning or evening?"

"Evening."

"I've gotten so turned around. All this staying up late, grabbing sleep when we can. I'm not sure if I'm coming or going."

"You just need food and more rest. And you'll get it. The avalanche closed the roads. For the next twelve hours we're going to eat, sleep and make love."

"Sounds like heaven."

"Yep, we'll be living large."

"And then?"

He turned to face her, his eyes serious. "We let 'and then' take care of itself."

Chapter 14

She's the most beautiful woman I've ever seen.

Tyler stared into Hannah's eyes. He felt something monumental inside himself shift and melt into something new and wonderful. He had thought he would never feel this happy again. He was delighted to discover he had not lost his capacity for sensual enjoyment.

They were sitting in the Jacuzzi, warm bubbles surrounding them, a glass of wine in their hands. They had just finished a sumptuous meal they had prepared together of broiled lamb chops, boiled new potatoes and tossed green salad. He felt fat and happy and satisfied.

Well, not totally satisfied. Resting in the soothing water, watching Hannah through half-lidded eyes, sent his thoughts back to the bed and whet his appetite for more of the same.

Water glistened on her smooth, bare skin. Her damp hair lay draped over her shoulders, framing the tops of her breasts. He grew hard. So hard he felt it straight to his brain.

Lord, she was incredible.

Steam rose up around them. He stretched his foot across the length of the tub and ran his big toe along the bottom of her foot.

"What are you doing way over there?"

He was light-headed. Giddy from giving blood, the wine and her intoxicating presence. Hannah smiled that sweet, self-depreciating smile of hers and ducked her head, denying him access to his favorite part of her, the window to her soul, the mirror of her heart, those stupendous ocean-blue eyes.

"Would you like for me to come closer?" she asked, coyly peering at him from lowered lashes.

"Oh, yeah." *In the worst way!*

Laughing lightly, she inched toward him, her wine glass raised to avoid the churning bubbles. Her laughter sent him into a full tilt. He loved that laugh. Wanted to hear it ringing in his head forever.

"How about here?" she asked. "Is this near enough?"

"Closer," he murmured, feeling very, very lusty.

She scooted again. "Here?"

"Closer."

"You sound dangerously like the Big Bad Wolf coaxing Little Red Riding Hood into bed." Her eyes twinkled, enjoying the game they were playing. He liked the game, too. Tyler hadn't felt this free, this lighthearted since he was a teenager.

He crooked a finger at her. "All the better to eat you with my dear."

She giggled and splayed a delicate hand across her mouth.

"I think you've had too much wine," he diagnosed.

"Only one glass." She smiled smugly and raised a finger.

"I have a feeling you're a cheap date. If one glass of wine could do you in."

"Not drunk," she proclaimed. "A little tipsy maybe, but definitely not drunk."

She suddenly had so much verve. So much energy. Amazing. Where had it come from? During the avalanche emergency, Hannah had worked herself to the point of collapse. He had feared for her health. But now, she seemed completely normal. Tyler was stupefied by the changes in her.

"You are unbelievable." How was it that he had found this marvelous woman? And why now? When their lives were so complicated by external forces they could not control?

"How so?" She arched an eyebrow.

"You're a dream come true."

"So are you." She hiccuped, then grinned and slapped a hand over her mouth. "Oops."

He leaned closer and pulled her into his arms. "I know a sure-fire cure for hiccups."

"You do?" Her eyes widened.

He slid his tongue past her lips. Her laughter dissipated.

God, she tasted so good! Like wine and honey and heat. He kissed her. Hard and long and thoroughly.

"Wow," she murmured, when he broke the kiss. "Wow."

"How's the hiccups?"

"They're gone," she marveled.

"Voilà."

"Magic cure."

"Just call me Dr. Love."

"Well, medicine man." She reached out for his hand and tucked it between her legs. Tyler's heart leapfrogged. "I've got this ache. Right here. Have you got a remedy?"

"Have I got a remedy!" He pulled her smack-dab onto his lap. Her thighs straddled his. "You tell me," his voice grew husky. "Do I have the cure for what ails you, sweetheart?"

"Oh my." Her fingers searched for his arousal, and wrapped around him.

"Uh." Tyler grunted at the intensity of the sensation. He cupped the soft curves of her bottom in both hands and tugged her closer.

Her breasts bobbed above the water, shimmering with wetness, her nipples sweetly puckered. Tyler lowered his head, placed his mouth over first one pink straining nipple and then the other. Her hands went to his shoulders, her fingernails digging lightly into his flesh as she moaned with pleasure.

She bumped against him with her pelvis. "My ache, Dr. Love, it's getting worse. You better do something. Quick."

"I'm a doctor who likes to take my time."

He watched a trail of perspiration trickle between her breasts. He licked it, savoring the saltiness of her heated skin. He lowered his hand, came up behind her bottom and slowly began to stroke her between her firm, supple thighs.

She made soft keening noises that told him she was winding up for something incredible.

"Make love to me, Tyler. Now. Right now," she pleaded.

Happy to oblige, he lifted her higher in the water and up onto his bludgeoning erection, sliding deep into her sweetness. She hissed in her breath. Tyler closed his eyes, relishing the glory of their joining, relishing Hannah.

"Kiss me," she commanded.

He roamed his mouth over hers, sucking, licking, reveling in her warm moistness. He slipped his tongue inside, feeling the rough edges of her teeth, tasting the wine's tart sweetness.

She moaned, and then leaned back, breaking their kiss. He held on to her with both hands wrapped securely around her waist. She moved over him, using her knees as a fulcrum to deepen his penetration.

They soared together on the wildest of roller-coaster rides, lurching steadily higher and higher, anticipating what was coming next, knowing there would be a frantic plunge, hurtling down into ecstasy as they climaxed together in one powerful shudder.

Tyler finally floated down from the upper reaches of passion, his breathing hard, his mind scrambled.

Hannah lay draped over him, her face buried against his neck, her wet hair sticking to her face. From the waist up they were drenched in sweat. From the waist down, they were drained.

Chagrined, he realized that they had forgotten about birth control. How could he have been so stupid? How could he have allowed himself to get so carried away? It wasn't that he minded the thought of a baby. In fact, a warm shimmering settled in his stomach at the idea. But Hannah's health was unstable. Her future uncertain. He didn't want to do anything that might jeopardize her.

Looking at the sweet face that had become so dear to him in such a short time, Tyler's heart wrenched.

"Hannah," he whispered, nudging her mildly.

"Huh?" She barely lifted her head and squinted at him.

"Come on, sweetheart, we've been in here far too long." He scooped up a palm full of warm water from the whirlpool and gently bathed her face with it.

"I'm paralyzed," she giggled. "My legs won't work."

"You've had too much wine."

"Not the wine." She grinned. "Too much Tyler. No, wait." She lifted a finger. "There's no such thing as too much Tyler."

Her levity was infectious. Was this the serious-minded scientist he had first given refuge to at his beach house? Hard to believe she had such a light, engagingly endearing aspect to her reserved personality. He could get very used to this.

He stepped from the Jacuzzi, tugging her after him. She giggled again and slumped against him. He looked at her, tenderness overwhelming him. He wished he could bottle these last few carefree hours and save them forever.

Because no matter how much he wanted to deny it, they had some very big issues to overcome. Insurmountable issues. Suddenly saddened, Tyler scooped her into his arms, carried her to the bed and made love to her all over again, trying his damnedest to block out the desperate ache dominating his every move.

Long after Tyler fell into a deep sleep, Hannah lay beside him battling the abiding pain in her heart. They'd had so much fun tonight. Too much fun. They had made love, bonded emotionally, and become as intimate as two people could become.

She loved this man more than she had ever loved anything or anyone. Leaving him was going to be the toughest thing she had ever done, but she had no choice. Even though she felt pretty good right now, Hannah had no doubt her dizziness, malaise and headaches would return. She would continue to get weaker and weaker, sicker and sicker. Wasting away before Tyler's eyes.

She didn't have much time left. Tyler's blood transfusion had bought her some time, yes, but it was not a panacea. Hannah recognized that fact and faced it with scientific fatalism. Even if by some miracle she did manage to stumble upon an antidote, it would most probably be too late to save her life.

But she had little choice. She would return to Marcus's lab alone and try to concoct a remedy. As it was, she refused to torment him by forcing him to witness her steady decline. He had already suffered so much, watching Yvette die, she wasn't about to put him through that agony all over again. Much kinder to slip out of his life unannounced.

She looked over at him, admired his sleeping form, his chiseled features. Leaving him was an agonizing choice. She hurt clean through her bones and could not have suffered more if a limb had been ruthlessly severed from her body.

Disassociate, disconnect, disengage.

She recited the chant her mother had taught her those many years ago as a way to repress her feelings. But this time, the familiar mantra did not work.

How could she disassociate herself from the man who was the other half of her soul?

Distressed, Hannah bit down on the back of her hand, seeking to assuage her emotional pain with a physical one.

It didn't work, either.

She had to find a way to separate herself from the gale-force emotions threatening to blow her into uncharted terrain.

Hannah lay still, listening to the slow steady rhythm of his breathing, unconsciously matching it. She drifted. Caught in a web of unending anguish. The longer she stayed, the harder it would be to leave. The time was now.

When she was absolutely certain that he would not awaken, she slipped from the bed, gathered up her clothes and slipped into the bathroom to get dressed. It was the most difficult thing she'd ever done, but she had to do it.

The avalanche had blocked the only road into Taos, but the perimeter of the snow slide was fairly narrow. She could take the snowmobile they'd confiscated at Marcus's place and maneuver around the snow slide. The thought of going out into the darkness alone was terrifying but she had no other option. She must go.

For Tyler's sake.

Tears misted her eyes as she tiptoed back through the bedroom again. She stopped at the foot of the bed and for the longest moment stood watching him sleep.

He was incredibly handsome. Any woman's fantasy mate. He'd helped her when no one else would have. Seeing him bare to the waist, one arm thrown across his forehead, she resisted the powerful urge to crawl up beside him and rest her weary head on his strong shoulders. Turning, she forced herself to walk out of the room.

And out of his life forever.

Before heading for the front door and the snowy weather beyond, Hannah detoured to the kitchen, stuffing a sack with provisions—bottled water, raisins, a loaf of bread, a jar of peanut butter. She acknowledged, with a forlorn pang, this food would most probably be her last. Tears trickled down her face, hot and fast. She swiped them away with the back of her hand, bolstered her courage by reminding herself she was doing this to spare Tyler the agony of watching her die.

With trembling hands, she sat down at the kitchen table to write him a note, but the words would not come. There was so much she wanted to say but had no idea where to start. Finally she simply wrote:

I'll never forget you.

Leaving the note propped up against the salt and pepper shakers, she pulled her parka from the closet, put it on and zipped it up. She slipped her gloves over her fingers, jammed her feet into snow boots, then shouldered the backpack. She hesitated in the doorway, glancing one last time toward the bedroom.

"I'll always love you," she whispered aloud even though he could not hear her. "Always."

She waded outside into the knee-deep drifts and closed the door tightly behind her. With her heart breaking into a thousand pieces, she took the key from her pocket, and climbed onto the snowmobile they had left parked under the chalet's eaves. She allowed the engine to idle for a while, then put the snowmobile into gear and drove away into the dark, lonely silence of the New Mexico Rockies, preparing to sacrifice her own life in order to bring down Lionel Daycon and his evil CIA counterpart.

* * *

"Hannah?" Tyler stumbled from the bedroom, rubbing his eyes, when he'd awakened to find her gone. "Hannah, where are you?"

He flicked on the light in the kitchenette and stood there blinking against the glare for a moment. Then he spied the note propped against the salt and pepper shakers.

Snatching up the note, he read the four short words. *I'll never forget you.* His heart ripped.

"Hannah," he bellowed. Crumpling the note, he tossed it to the floor and went rampaging back through the bedroom. He searched under the bed, peered in the closet, double-checked the bathroom, but he knew she was gone.

Dammit! She'd left him.

I'll never forget you.

What the hell was that supposed to mean? Why has she taken off? He thought that after all they'd shared she'd let down the last vestiges of her fears and had finally trusted him.

But no. He was alone.

Totally and completely alone.

He hadn't felt this lonely or this desolate since losing Yvette. Hannah had left him.

Well, he wasn't going to accept it. Tyler tugged on his blue jeans and a thick cable-knit sweater. He was going after her. They were a team, and one way or the other he was determined to make her see that.

A knock sounded at the door of the chalet. It was after midnight. Who could it be?

Hannah? His heart leapt with hope. Had she realized her mistake and come back? He hurried to the foyer just as the knock sounded again.

"Dr. Fresno, it's an emergency," came a male voice from the other side of the door.

He sighed. Not Hannah after all. It was probably the intern needing advice about one of the avalanche victims. "I'm coming."

A blast of arctic air hit him when he opened the door, but that wasn't all. One tall, thick-waisted man tackled him, knocking him to the floor. The next thing Tyler knew he was staring up into the barrel of a very nasty-looking handgun, clutched in the hammy fist of a second man who looked like Robert De Niro in *Raging Bull*—broken nose, cauliflower ear, crazy eyes.

"Don't move."

The first man was on his feet and lumbering toward the bedroom, dusting off his pants as he went and tracking slushy footprints in the carpet behind him.

A deathly cold calmness came over Tyler as he assessed his chances for overpowering the gunman. He was quick and he was strong, but the guy had some fifty pounds on him, not to mention some serious firepower. Hannah was out there alone somewhere. If he got killed, she would have no one. He could not afford to go off half-cocked. What he needed was an escape plan.

The first man trotted back into the main room. "She ain't in there, man."

"What do you mean, she ain't here?" Cauliflower Ear asked. "She's gotta be here."

The first guy shook his head. "I looked everywhere. Not in the bed, nor the bathroom, neither."

They both turned to look at the kitchen only a few feet in front of them. It was obvious no one was hiding there. The first guy did a walk around and came back with Hannah's crumpled note.

"Looks like he's telling the truth. It's a Dear John letter."

"Gimme that." The other thug tugged the paper from the first. "I'll never forget you," he read in a derisive voice. "That don't mean she left him. It could be a trick. Didja look in the closets?"

The first guy nodded.

Cauliflower Ear swore colorfully, then turned his attention to Tyler. "Where is she?"

"You read the note. You know as much as I do."

"Don't get cute with me, medicine man." He raised a threatening hand. "Where'd she go?"

Raw anger, pure in its intensity, shot through Tyler. He would not let these goons get their hands on Hannah. Acting on gut instinct, he cocked his knee and slammed his foot squarely in the man's groin.

Cauliflower Ear shrieked, dropped his gun and sank to the floor on his side, desperately trying to suck in a wheezy breath.

The other guy hurried over and kicked Tyler in the ribs before he could scramble to his feet and dive for the loose weapon.

"Uh." Air left his body in one painful explosion. The thug kicked him again. This time in the head. A multitude of stars burst inside his brain. Red, white, yellow, orange. Blindly, he got to his hands and knees and crawled for the open door.

"Not so fast, Doctor."

Another boot to the head.

Tyler grunted and his knees gave way. He found himself sprawled alongside Cauliflower Ear who was still writhing in pain.

"Come on now. Fess up. Where is she?" The first thug squatted beside him, arm draped over a broad thigh, gun held in his hand.

"I don't know who you're talking about."

"Let's try this again." The thug grabbed Tyler by the hair, raised his face up off the carpet and punched him hard in the right eye.

His teeth jarred together at the impact. Okay, maybe this was the guy who could pass for Jack LaMotta, not the one on the floor.

"Does that help your memory any? Or should I blacken the other eye?"

Knowing he was going to regret it, Tyler opened his mouth and told the goon exactly what sex act he could perform upon himself.

A hammy fist smashing into his left eye was the last thing Tyler remembered.

Without Tyler beside her, Marcus's desolate, destroyed home looked even worse than it had before. The garbage that had just begun to smell two days earlier had ripened into an overpowering stench that forced her to slap her hand over her nose and mouth while she picked her way over the debris on her way into Marcus's basement laboratory.

A spike of lonely devastation drove through her. Until this moment she hadn't realized how much comfort she had drawn from Tyler's calming presence. Not having him beside her forced Hannah to admit how much she had come to rely upon him in such a very short time.

"Tyler," she said aloud, "I wish you were here."

Dejected, Hannah descended to the freezing cold basement, then slumped into the worn leather chair parked behind a desk strewn with papers. What on earth had she been thinking? Slipping away in the darkness, leaving Tyler without a proper explanation for her behavior. Had he awakened and discovered her gone yet? It was almost dawn. Was he at this very moment reading her letter, agonizing over her departure? Was his heart, like hers, in shreds?

Or was he relieved to be free of her and the trouble she had put him through?

Don't be silly, Hannah, he loves you.

Yes, a thousand times, in a thousand different ways Tyler had proven his love for her. Idly, Hannah tapped on the desk with a pencil. Maybe that was the issue. Maybe she couldn't tolerate being loved. She had never had love and she didn't know how to deal with it.

There you go again. Putting up a wall, making excuses, running away from your feelings.

Love.

A truly wondrous emotion, but one that carried with it so many responsibilities. Her parents had been cold and unemotional. They had never shown her how to love. But she had learned that if you loved, then you had an obligation to share yourself. No secrets. No holding back. If she loved him then she had to give her all.

Was that the real reason she had left? Not, as she had told herself, to save him from pain. But rather, had she run away because she had no idea how to open up and tell him the things she felt deep inside? Because she still didn't really trust him to accept her unconditionally?

Hannah sank her head in her hands. Surely she wasn't that shallow, so afraid of getting hurt that she would abandon Tyler simply to keep from revealing her true self to him. A self he might find unpleasantly lacking in admirable qualities.

Conflicted, she curled her hands around the edges of Marcus's desk and frowned.

What was that?

Her fingertips skimmed along the underside of the wood. There was something carved into the desk. Numbers. Symbols. A mathematical formula.

Excitedly, she dropped to her knees and peered upward.

Could it be? Was it her formula for *Virusall?* She scarcely dared breath, her trembling fingers running over the notched wood, her mind racing.

Yes!

Quickly, she searched for a pencil and clean paper, pulling open drawers, pushing aside rubbish, digging deep.

Triumph filled her when she found a broken pencil stub and a small yellow notepad. She began to scribble, copying down the equations he had carved into the underbelly of his desk. Then just as quickly, her spirits plummeted. It was only a partial rendition.

Unfortunately her quirky, paranoid friend often carried his formulas in weird places but left them incomplete in case they were discovered by others.

Biting down on her bottom lip, she set to work trying to finish the chemical recipe, adding, subtracting and rearranging the elements. She prodded her memory, cast her mind back over seven long years of hard research, and slipped into a mental trance, zoning out in the mathematical equations, losing herself in the chase for her elusive elixir. Adrenaline lifted her spirits and she buzzed along, completely engrossed in her project.

When she finally raised her head to massage the kinks from her neck, she spied the clock on the wall. Six o'clock in the evening. She had worked all day without respite. The road into Taos might even be open by now. It had been over twelve hours since she had abandoned Tyler.

Just the mental mention of his name provoked a sharp ache inside her. She should call him. Explain her decision. Tell him about the formula she had found. Hannah rubbed her eyes with her fists and sighed. If she called him, he would insist on coming to her. And even though she did possess part of the formula, it wasn't enough. Half was almost as useless as none.

Who was she kidding? Discovering part of the formula wasn't going to help her solve anything. Not without Marcus himself to help her piece it together. She had no antidote and she still had no idea of her friend's whereabouts.

She couldn't go back to Tyler. Nothing had changed. She was still dying. She had made the right choice to leave.

If that were true, then why did it hurt so damned much?

Hannah fought the overwhelming temptation to cry and laid her head on Marcus's desk. Taking a deep breath, she struggled to calm her riotous emotions. *Stay centered,* she coached her sluggish mind. *Concentrate on the job at hand. You can mend your broken heart later.*

But she could not stop thinking about Tyler. Especially when she could still taste his unique flavor on her tongue, still smell his scent on her skin. She had whisker burn around her mouth and both of her nipples were a little sore. And the tenderness between her thighs was a bittersweet reminder of what they had shared not so long ago.

I will not cry. At least it has to be this way. I will die alone, here in Marcus's house. I will have succeeded in keeping the formula from Daycon.

Yes, she had achieved the goal she'd set for herself, but she had missed so much in the process. She had lost the love of her life and there was no way to redeem it.

And yet, she wanted nothing more than to call Tyler, to hear his wonderful, soothing voice one last time.

Except Marcus's phone was out of order.

The BMW was still parked at the front gate. She'd seen it when she had ridden in on the snowmobile. She could drive into Taos and call him at the resort.

"What about the keys?" she muttered.

Maybe he was one of those people who kept a spare set of keys hidden in a magnet key holder somewhere on the vehicle. It was worth a shot.

Don't call him, Hannah. If he begs you to come back, you won't have the strength to stay away.

Ignoring the plea from her rational brain and following her

heart, Hannah pushed back her chair. She put on her parka she'd peeled off sometime during her marathon work session and made her way back through the house, and outside into the gathering twilight.

It took several minutes but she made it to the BMW. She searched the car's belly and smiled at Tyler's predictable prudence when she found the key holder. She took it as a sign. Wrenching open the driver's side door she climbed in and started the engine.

Chapter 15

Hannah stood in a coffee shop in Taos, her mind a jumble. Part of the road to the ski resort had been cleared but the authorities were only allowing essential vehicles through. Turned away, Hannah had headed straight for the nearest pay phone and dialed Tyler's cell phone number.

It rang and rang and rang. Closing her eyes, Hannah could envision the empty rooms at the chalet. Fear, remorse and regret solidified into a cold, gelatinous substance at the base of her spine.

Where was Tyler?

Had he gone looking for her? Or had he gone back to the clinic to check on the avalanche victims? She had no idea, but one thing was for certain. She was going back to the ski resort, authorities or not.

"Hello." A man's voice finally answered. But it wasn't Tyler's. It was deep and raspy. "Is this Hannah?"

Hannah gave a small cry and dropped the receiver. It dangled from the black spiral cord, swinging ominously back and forth.

She stared at the receiver as if it were a poisonous snake, her pulse slowing to a miserable crawl.

Daycon.

On Tyler's cell phone. That could mean only one thing. Daycon had gotten to Tyler.

No. *No!*

Impossible.

"Dr. Zachary." The phone wheezed at her. "I've been searching a very long time for you."

She did not want to pick up the receiver. She would rather shove her hand in boiling oil.

"Hannah." A raspy singsong. "Come. To Austin. To my temporary new offices I'm renting from Perfidia Labs. Nasty of you to burn mine down, by the way."

Hand shaking so hard she feared it might disconnect from her body, she picked up the receiver and brought it to her ear. "Nasty of you to try to use my drug to create terrorist assassins."

"We're waiting for you," Daycon said, his voice mesmerizing as a snake charmer's. "Dr. Fresno and I."

"You let him go," she whispered.

"Come to me and he's free to leave."

"All right," she said. "I'll be there."

"That's a good girl," Daycon purred. "Catch the next flight out of Santa Fe." And then he hung up.

She was stunned. Ill. Sick to her stomach. Disoriented. Overturned. Severed from her roots and crushed into an abject state of mental misery, knowing that she had risked Tyler's life by involving him in her chaotic problems.

Legs churning, she fled out into the night, to Tyler's BMW parked outside the coffee shop. Time was running out.

She should never have accepted Tyler's offer of help and gotten him mixed up in this. Why, oh, why had she allowed herself to hope for something that could never be hers?

That night at Saint Madeleine's, she should have turned away from him. His kind face and winning ways had made it easy for her to give in to his persuasion when she'd known all along that she was bad news. She had allowed her lonely desperation to dictate her actions and now they both were paying the penalty.

Guilt and disgust mingled inside her.

Guiding the vehicle down the steep mountain road, headed for the airport in Santa Fe, she struggled against the rank terror that tasted like stale sweat socks in her mouth.

Time was running out.

She was dying. More quickly now, sped up by her emotions. The pain in her temples escalated to an unrelenting pulsation, but she could not give in to her discomfort. She drove like a demon, taking the icy mountain at a perilous pace in the omnipresent darkness. Only one thought dominated her mind.

Tyler.

Tyler was vaguely aware that he was lying on some unyielding surface. He smelled formaldehyde and sulfur, and heard the far off ticking of a clock. The kind of cheap, large-faced noisy clocks they put in school classrooms or hospitals. But he couldn't see anything. He opened his eyes and still his world was black.

What had happened to his vision?

His mouth was dry, his throat raw and he needed to go to the bathroom. His head and ribs throbbed relentlessly. He was sore all over, as if he had been thoroughly beaten. Disoriented, Tyler searched his memory for the precipitating event.

Had a psychotic patient attacked him? It had happened to him once before, years ago when a huge bear of a man—bushy red beard, dressed in leather and studs and high on PCP, had jumped him in the E.R. when he had attempted to suture a forearm gash the man had acquired in a barroom brawl.

Tyler had felt the same way then as he did now, battered, bruised and none too happy. But he did not remember treating such an out of control patient. In fact, he didn't even recall working at Saint Madeleine's.

Funny.

Then reality came back in a welcome rush. He hadn't been treating patients. He had been in a New Mexico ski chalet with Hannah. Two thugs had burst in looking for her and when they had found her missing, had taken their anger out on him. He tried to raise his head and realized then there was a blindfold over his eyes. That explained why he couldn't see.

Where was he? And why was he here?

More important, where was Hannah?

Greasy nausea slithered in his guts and he feared he might regurgitate. If those thugs had done anything to harm her, he would hunt them down and kill them with his bare hands.

Except he could not move his arms. Tyler acknowledged that there was a rope tied tight around his chest, above his elbows, fastening his upper arms against his body.

Damn. Damn. *Damn.*

His feet were tethered by some heavy object. Even around the edges of the blindfold, he could not make out any light. He tried to sit up but dizziness assailed him and intensified his nausea.

Hannah. Somehow, he had to get free. Had to find her before it was too late. Before she sacrificed something important in order to save him.

Tyler's heart wrenched. Daycon was using him to draw her back to Austin. He knew she would come.

Escape. Get to Hannah before she surrenders to Daycon.

Tyler made his move. Ignoring the pain in his wrists, he worked himself free from the ropes and ripped the blindfold off to discover in was in a lab and laid out on one of the tables. At that same moment Cauliflower Ear walked into the room eating a meatball hoagie, marinara sauce dripping over his hammy fists.

Startled, he stared at Tyler for a moment before realizing his hands were no longer tied and the blindfold was off.

Tyler took full advantage of the big man's hesitation and flung the rope bindings in his face.

Cauliflower Ear stumbled backward, stubbornly clutching his sandwich.

Hobbled by the sandbag anchoring his legs, Tyler lunged his torso off the table, going for the gun in Cauliflower Ear's waistband.

"Hey," Cauliflower Ear shouted. "Hey."

Triumphantly, Tyler snagged the gun, waved it in the thug's face and regained his precarious balance. "Don't move."

"Listen, man, you're in over your head. Daycon's gonna win. You might as well make it easy on yourself," Cauliflower Ear wheedled. He was on the ropes and he knew it.

"And," Tyler said, reaching down to untie his shackled ankles while still trying to keep the gun trained on Cauliflower Ear, "you can cooperate while I tie you up. See how you like it."

Daycon's goon sighed, wiping his hands along his pants legs. "Well, damn."

Tyler kicked off the ropes, hopped to his feet and then advanced on the man. "Lie down on the floor. Hands behind your back."

"Oh man, Daycon's gonna kill me," Cauliflower Ear whined, but complied by sinking to the floor on his stomach and extending his wrists behind him.

"Better you than me."

After Tyler had him firmly secured, he nudged him with the nose of the gun. "Roll over."

Cauliflower Ear squirmed onto his back and squinted up at Tyler. "Watcha gonna do?"

"For one thing, I'm going to take that blindfold you slapped over me and use it on you as a gag."

"Hell."

"I know, ain't life a bitch? But first, I want information."

"I don't know anything," Cauliflower Ear replied in a sullen tone. "They don't tell me anything."

Tyler traced a line down the side of the man's cheek with the gun. "Where's Hannah Zachary?"

"I told you, I don't know nothin'."

"That's a shame," Tyler drilled the gun against his temple.

"I'm not scared of you." Cauliflower Ear grimaced. "You're a doctor, you won't kill me."

"You willing to put me to the test?" Tyler narrowed his eyes. "Then you underestimate my love for that woman. I would do anything to keep her safe. I'm going to ask you one more time," Tyler said, "and if the answer isn't satisfactory, then too bad for you. Where is Hannah?"

"I don't know anything about her," Cauliflower Ear said, stubbornly clinging to his statement.

Was he telling the truth? Tyler cocked the hammer, calling his bluff. "Sorry about your luck, but maybe ignorance isn't bliss after all."

Instant sweat popped out on his face. "Wait!"

"Oh? You got something to tell me?"

"She's on her way to trade the formula for you. In fact, she might even be in Austin already."

Hannah was here? Joy was instantly replaced by fear and a cold sweat broke out across Tyler's body. If Daycon already had Hannah in his grasp, he had no more time to waste on Cauliflower Ear. Daycon was his quarry. Quickly, ignoring the heavy thud of his heart, Tyler gagged the hoodlum, turned out the lights and stepped cautiously into the vacant corridor filled with closed doors.

He had no idea where he was or even where to start his search. The corridor was dimly lit with faint florescent lights overhead. Clutching the gun firmly in his right hand, he tried first one door and then another. Specially coded security locks barred each. He was on the ground floor, Tyler decided, or maybe the basement. There were no windows, nor were there any signs directing the way, save for a red Exit sign at the very end of the corridor.

The way out.

Except he was not leaving.

Not without confronting Daycon.

His own breath roared loudly in his ears. Only the noise of his sneakers squeaking against the linoleum disrupted the silence. Daycon was probably hidden away upstairs somewhere, in his cushy office. What Tyler needed was an elevator.

Turning right down another long corridor, he kept his body pressed against the wall as he moved, the gun outstretched.

Hang on, Hannah, I'm coming. He mentally spoke to her, sending his thoughts into the ether and hoping she could pick up on his vibrations wherever she might be.

He trod a hundred feet. No elevator or stairwell here, either. What was this place? A dungeon? At the end of this second hallway, Tyler spotted a door where light bled between the cracks. Aha. Activity.

Quietly as possible, he crept forward. When he reached the

heavy metal door that was already open a crack, he paused to press his ear against it, listening.

He waited. Two minutes. Three. Four. Hearing nothing that indicated there were people beyond, he braced himself for whatever might lie ahead and nudged the door open with his foot.

It swung inward.

Daycon's other thug stood with his back to Tyler at a second door, fumbling with a security pass card and muttering curses under his breath.

Tyler hoisted the gun by the nose, took a deep breath and whacked him on the back of the head with all his strength.

The man crumpled without a whimper.

Two down. One to go.

Stepping over the man's prostate body, Tyler plucked the security card from his hand and hesitated only long enough to make sure the man was still breathing. He'd live.

Tyler swiped the security card through the lock and stepped inside a glassed-in area that lead to an isolation room.

A metal table and shelf housed barrier gowns, gas masks, sterile supplies and various other medical equipment.

Should he gown up and go beyond the safety of the glassed entrance?

Trepidation passed through him and he suppressed a strong urge to turn and run. It was instinct. He had seen many isolation rooms similar to this one in the army and what lay on the other side was never a pretty sight. He thought of some of the cases he had seen during the Gulf War, most of them victims of chemical warfare. Seizures, vomiting, diarrhea, body parts turning black and sloughing off. Men writhing in pain from headaches so severe it made them insane. He shuddered.

What if Hannah was on the other side, hurt or contaminated in some way? The thought caused him such much mental anguish he squelched it immediately.

He shut the door between him and the prostrate goon and moved through the anteroom. He set the gun on the counter, donned protective gear, covering himself from head to toe. He had no idea what waited for him but he was taking every precaution.

For Hannah's sake.

If he saw her again he did not want to be responsible for exposing her to yet another disease.

Not *if* you see her again, but *when*. No pessimism allowed. He would see her again. He was meant to be with her. He'd waited too long to lose her at this stage of the game.

Once he was completely gowned up, Tyler retrieved the gun, wrapped it in a red plastic biohazard garbage bag and stuck it under his arm. He wasn't leaving the weapon behind for Daycon or his men to find and use against him.

Marshaling his courage, Tyler tried the thick glass door with a heavy dark blind on the inside that kept him from seeing into the isolation room.

It was locked.

He felt a little disappointed. He stood there a moment, peering at the door and wondering what to do next, when he heard movement from beyond.

"Hello," Tyler said. "Is someone in there?"

More movement.

"Are you hurt? Can you open the door from inside? My name's Tyler Fresno. I'm a doctor. A surgeon. Can I help you?" His voice took on an urgency that matched the blood racing through his system.

More noises. Then suddenly the blinds blocking the glass door snapped up and Tyler found himself looking at a thin man about his own age in wire-framed glasses and baggy scrubs. He appeared exhausted beyond endurance. Sores crisscrossed his face and he sported a black eye.

They stared curiously at each other. The man was apparently surprised to see him.

"What's your name?" Tyler asked, his mind whirling with possibilities.

"I'm Marcus," the man said. "Marcus Halpren. And I'm being held against my will by Lionel Daycon."

Hannah fought nausea during the entire flight from New Mexico to Austin, Texas. Turbulence contributed to her misery but mostly, her battle against fluctuating stomach acid was due to worry over Tyler.

She would do anything to procure his release, even if it meant surrendering the formula to Daycon. It was 3:00 a.m. when the private plane touched down at a small airfield shrouded in a thick fog. A slight rain fell, griping the city in a damp, hazy fist. It took almost thirty minutes to get a cab. Hannah spent the entire time pacing the empty concourse and praying that Tyler was all right. Her heart ached unbearably.

Hurry, hurry.

She ignored the weakness in her bones, the exhaustion that claimed every cell and the pitiless pounding in her temples. Saving Tyler would most probably be the last act of her life.

Finally the cab arrived. She tumbled into the back seat and gave the driver directions to Perfidia Labs. The closer they got, the greater her apprehension grew.

The laboratory which was located just a few blocks from Daycon's burned-out labs loomed out of the darkness, a monolith eerie in its starkness. Most of the lights were out, but a few windows were lit up. The first floor lobby and two offices on the top floor. Were those the ones Daycon had rented?

The cab pulled to a stop. Hannah paid the driver with the last of the money Tyler had given her in Galveston and got out, her gaze fixed on the illuminated windows above.

Was Daycon up there? Was Tyler? Hannah's gut clenched into a hard knot.

Or, having successfully lured her back to Austin with the formula in her possession, had Daycon already eliminated Tyler?

No! Hannah slapped her hands over her ears, refusing to hear the fearful voice screaming inside her head. She would not, under any circumstances, accept that possibility. Tyler was still alive. He had to be.

Bolstered by that affirmation, she walked up the steps. Pressing her face against the tinted glass, she peered into the lobby.

The place was empty. But what had she expected?

Had Daycon left the door unlocked in anticipation of her return? Hannah swallowed hard and opened the front door.

Locked.

She would try the side entrance. Shoes scraping against the sidewalk, she forced herself around the side of the building to the Bowie Street access. Her legs felt heavy and uncooperative. She even stumbled and almost fell headlong onto the pavement.

Not much time left. Energy fading fast.

What she needed was a shot of Tyler's love. His kisses could revive her. They had before.

Too late.

She was drowsy, moving in slow motion, fighting her own body as it betrayed her.

Must get to Tyler.

Hannah stepped through the door and came face-to-face with the man she had run from over a week earlier.

Lionel Daycon.

With a very large gun in his hand.

Chapter 16

"Where's Tyler?" Hannah demanded, refusing to be intimidated by Daycon's weapon. So what if he decided to shoot her? She was dying anyway. Only one thing mattered to her: Tyler's safety. "What have you done with him?"

"All in good time, my dear. Come, move away from the door." He motioned with the pistol.

So much had changed in eight short days. She had changed in innumerable ways. Changed because she'd had the courage to act upon her beliefs. Changed because she had met Tyler. Changed because she had learned how to love. Lionel Daycon no longer possessed the power to frighten her as he once had.

Meeting her stare, he mustered a cool smile. "I'm glad you could join me, Dr. Zachary. I had a bit of trouble tracking you down. You're much more inventive than I anticipated."

He wore, of all things, a tuxedo with a dapper silk scarf draped around his neck, and clutched an ebony walking cane between in his hands. The song, "Putting on the Ritz," sprang to Hannah's mind. Except, in his obesity, he looked anything but ritzy.

"Forgive my lavish attire," Daycon said, narrowing his eyes. "But I haven't had time to change since the ball at the governor's mansion. Too bad you missed the affair. It's such a shame you didn't get to meet my compatriot from the CIA, Rudolph Cleveland."

Then with excruciating detail he outlined their devious plan for creating assassins. An elaborate plot so chilling it took her breath. With Cleveland's intimate knowledge of overseas terrorists and Daycon's ruthless skill at manipulation, he made the whole thing sound totally plausible.

"Thanks to your drug, I can create assassins at will. No need for lifelong indoctrination or brainwashing. One dose of *Virusall* and poof, anyone with type *O* blood becomes a killer. Now hand over the formula."

"Sorry, Daycon, but your plan has a fatal flaw. *Virusall* is no more. I destroyed the drug."

"Ah, but I have a friend of yours who has promised to help you recreate the formula right here in this lab."

"Marcus?" Hope rose inside her. Her pulse quickened. "You've got Marcus?"

Daycon nodded and licked his lips. "Yes, indeed. Marcus Halpren is here."

"He'll never help you," she said vehemently.

"That's not true. He has his weak spot. You. Just as Dr. Fresno is your weak spot. Funny. Halpren loves you, but you love Fresno. But I wonder—does Fresno love you in return?"

"Where is Tyler?" she demanded and crossed her arms over her chest. "I want to see him. Immediately."

"But of course," Daycon acquiesced, raising Hannah's suspicions. She had worked for the man for seven years and she knew that behind any agreement lay an ulterior motive.

"Right now."

"All right. Oh, and don't for a moment get any ideas about overpowering me. I still need you alive, but as your boyfriend found out the hard way, I have no compunction against causing a great deal of pain."

* * *

"If we can get into a lab, I can try to mix up an antidote for Hannah," Marcus Halpren told Tyler, then quickly explained his theory for reversing the side effects of *Virusall*.

Tyler kept a wary eye on the door, acutely aware the clock was ticking. Hannah's life was slipping away as they spoke.

"I interned here at Perfidia when I was in college," Marcus said. "They do a lot of work for government agencies. Including the FBI and CIA."

Tyler held up the security card he had stolen from the second thug. "Hopefully, this will do the trick."

Marcus grinned. "I knew I liked you."

They left the relative safety of the isolation anteroom and entered the quiet corridor. Marcus swiveled his head, studying the layout.

"Where are we?" Tyler asked.

"Ground level. Come on." He gestured over his shoulder. "We need to go to the basement."

"Where? I didn't see an elevator or a stairwell."

"This way."

Anxiety scaled Tyler's spine as he followed Marcus down the corridor. Would the scientist be able to come up with an antidote in time to save Hannah's life?

And even if he did, would they find her? Where was she now?

He'd never been so terrified. Not even when he'd given Hannah that blood transfusion.

She meant everything to him.

Their footsteps echoed in the empty corridor. Tyler's gut roiled. Marcus led him to a door tucked into a corner alcove that turned out to be a stairwell. Quickly, they descended to the basement. The hallway was dark and chilly, lighted only by a few florescent bulbs in the ceiling.

"Here," Marcus said stopping outside the second door on the left. "Lab sixteen. I used to work in this room. Try the security pass card."

Tyler swiped the card through the apparatus on the door. It clicked and swung open.

They looked at one another before stepping over the threshold into blackness.

The smell of formaldehyde was strong here, as was the odor of various and sundry other chemicals. The basement laboratory lay completely silent except for the rough sounds of their ragged breathing.

It felt eerily like a morgue.

Marcus switched on the overhead light.

Tyler squinted against the brightness, and then stared with openmouthed shock at what he saw.

"Gentlemen," Lionel Daycon said, his voice firm. Hannah, looking thin and frail, was clutched in the crook of Daycon's elbow, a pistol pressed firmly against her temple. "We've been expecting you."

Tyler!

His name leapt into her mind but no words came from her constricted throat. He looked tired, and haggard, his left hand bandaged with tape. His hair was disheveled, his eyes black and blue. Despite his junkyard dog appearance, Hannah had never seen a more beautiful sight.

He was a warrior. A hero. Her hero!

Their gazes locked.

A silent communication passed between them.

Are you all right? his dark eyes asked with concern.

Hannah nodded slightly, and cut her gaze at Daycon. *How are we going to get out of this?*

Tyler's expression was serious. He didn't know, either.

"Put down your weapon, Dr. Fresno, and slide it toward me," Daycon commanded.

Reluctantly, Tyler bent, laid the gun on the floor and pushed it over. Daycon kicked it behind him, well out of anyone's reach.

"See, he's perfectly fine," Daycon said to Hannah. "I kept my end of the bargain. Now, turn over the formula."

"I told you," Hannah said. "I destroyed it."

Daycon aimed the gun at Tyler and cocked the hammer.

"No!" Hannah screamed.

"Then stop lying to me," Daycon wheezed.

She noticed his hand trembled. What if she were to slam her body into him?

"Don't even think about trying to overpower me," Daycon said, reading her mind. "I'll kill him where he stands. You know I will."

"All right," she said hoarsely. "You win."

Daycon smiled. "At last, you've come to your senses."

"But first, you let Tyler and Marcus walk out of here." Stubbornly, she jutted her chin.

"I'm afraid that's impossible."

Tyler clenched his jaw and fisted his hand. *Do something, Fresno,* he commanded himself.

But what? Daycon held Hannah clutched tightly in his grip. And Cauliflower Ear's gun was now positioned halfway across the room. If he lunged forward for it, Daycon could easily get off a shot.

Marcus stood beside him, hands clenched at his sides, eyes staring straight ahead, seemingly hypnotized by the sight of the gun. Tyler scanned the room, desperate for either a weapon or a way to distract Daycon.

There was the usual array of laboratory equipment plus a glass cabinet filled with powders and potions. Then he saw the vial marked hydrochloric acid. Dare he use it as a defense against Daycon? With Hannah standing so close to him?

No. He couldn't risk it.

Tyler gritted his teeth.

Daycon followed Tyler's gaze. "Get that idea right out of your mind. It's not going to happen."

"I can't let you take her."

"You have no choice."

Tyler took a step toward him.

"Stop." Daycon pressed the gun against Hannah's temple once more. Her eyes widened and she whimpered. The sound was an arrow through his heart.

"Raise your hands over your head," Daycon commanded, waving the gun at them. "Both of you."

Marcus complied, splaying his palms against the back of his scalp, but Tyler resisted.

Save Hannah, save Hannah, save Hannah.

"Do it," Daycon shouted, twisting Hannah's arm. She cried out in pain.

To keep him from harming Hannah again, Tyler grudgingly did as he was told but his mind kept searching frantically for a plan.

"Now back away from the door," Daycon gestured with the gun. "Both of you."

Tyler and Marcus eased sideways a few feet.

Think! Think!

Dragging Hannah along with him, Daycon headed for the door. She tried to fight but she was exhausted. Tyler recognized the signs—skin pale, dark circles under her eyes, shallow breathing. He knew her pulse was slow, her blood pressure low.

She didn't have the physical energy to resist Daycon.

In that moment, Tyler made his decision and prayed his bluff would work. He lunged forward, grabbing the vial of hydrochloric acid.

Daycon fumbled with the gun, turning it from Hannah to Tyler. "Stop. Don't move."

Tyler held the vial aloft. "Take one more step and you get a face full of hydrochloric acid," he said, his fingers hovering over the lid, preparing to unscrew it.

Daycon stared first at the vial and then at Tyler, as if gauging his potential to carry out his threat. Then he swung Hannah in front of him, using her as a human shield. "Put down the acid."

Without warning, Marcus threw himself at Daycon.

The squat man spun, thrusting Hannah forward as he brought up the gun and shot Marcus point-blank in the chest.

Hannah screamed and stumbled against the counter.

Tyler wasted no time. He tossed the acid into a nearby sink and before Daycon could turn the weapon back on him or grab for Hannah again, he plowed his head into the large man's shoulder, tackling him to the ground.

The gun spun away under the desk.

Tyler and Daycon tussled.

"Hannah, the gun," he shouted.

She dropped to her knees, found the gun and handed it to him while Tyler sat on Daycon's chest.

Daycon blinked up at him.

"It's over," Tyler said. "And you're going to jail for a very long time."

"Marcus!" Hannah cried and ran to her friend.

He lay on his back staring sightlessly up at the ceiling, blood flowing from his body in an endless river. His breath came in gurgled gasps.

"How is he?" Tyler asked, unable to see Marcus from his vantage point on top of Daycon.

"He's dying." Tears streamed down her face.

"Hannah," Tyler said. She heard the fear in his voice. "You're not thinking about healing him."

She raised her head, peered around the corner of the table leg and met Tyler's eyes. He was begging her not to heal him.

"I have to do this," she whispered.

She could not allow her friend die. Not when he'd tried so valiantly to save her life. Not when she had the power in her fingertips to bring him back from the brink of death.

"Hannah, don't! You know how sick you are. One more healing, especially one as big as this will kill you."

"I know."

Her gaze never left his. "I love you," he said. "I don't want to lose you."

"I know that, too."

He swallowed hard.

"You would do the same thing in my position."

There were tears in his eyes. "I know."

Hannah pulled her gaze from his, turned her attention back to Marcus. "I love you, too, Tyler Fresno," she whispered, then sat down on the floor and slipped Marcus's head into her lap.

The familiar tingling began the minute she placed her fingers at his temples. The ensuing warmth engulfed her and the wondrous sense of peaceful calm settled over her. She felt as if she were floating on a vast sea, tossed by friendly waves.

In the distance, she heard Tyler talking to Daycon and tying him up, but they seemed so far away and not related to what was going on in her world. Her arms and legs became fluid. She closed her eyes, took a deep breath.

Heal.

She opened her eyes and stared down at her friend. He had stopped breathing altogether. His color was ashen. She felt for a pulse at his neck and found nothing.

Panic washed over her. Had she lost her ability to heal? Would Marcus die because of her? Trembling, she reached out and touched his chest. Her fingers came away sodden with dark sticky blood. The hole in his chest was huge, the smell of gunpowder hung in the air.

"No!" Hannah sobbed. "I will not let you die!"

She placed her palm over the gaping wound, squeezed her eyes shut tightly and concentrated on repairing the damage Daycon's gun had wrought. Tyler came up behind her, his aura pressing into hers. He was there for her. His breath was warm on the nape of her neck. His presence gave her the strength to continue.

"I love you," he whispered. "Never forget that."

Suddenly, a jolt passed through her and she jerked at the impact. Hannah gasped. It seemed as if everything inside her was coming loose and unraveling at the seams. Her pulse slowed to a crawl. She could scarcely get her breath.

She opened her eyes to see what was happening, but her vision clouded instantly, and the room turned to pure darkness. But beneath her fingers, she felt movement.

Marcus's heartbeat.

A heaviness unlike anything she had even known swallowed her whole. *Jonah and the whale,* she thought as she felt herself being pulled down, down, down by an unknown force.

She heard Tyler cry her name, felt his arms go around her, his lips against her cheek. Hannah sighed deeply and then she knew no more.

* * *

No! *No!*

He refused to accept this. He refused to let her go.

Tyler tugged Hannah's lifeless body away from Marcus, who was now sitting up and staring down at his pristine chest in utter disbelief.

"Wh…what happened?" he stammered, running a bloody hand along his rib cage.

But Tyler had no time to explain. Watching Hannah's chest for respiration, his fingers flew to palpate her carotid artery. No breathing, no pulse.

Start CPR.

Automatically, Tyler slipped into physician mode, performing the procedure with flawless execution. First, he pressed his mouth against Hannah's blue-tinged lips and gave her two quick breaths of air. Then he moved down her body to compress his interlaced hands against her sternum.

Live. Live!

She did not respond.

If only he had drugs and a medical team. But he had neither.

"I know CPR," Marcus said, staggering over. "Let me help."

"Are you sure you're up to it?"

"Hell, yes."

Tyler looked at the other man, a mix of emotions playing through him. He was grateful that Marcus had taken a bullet for Hannah. A heroic action that had given Tyler the opportunity to overpower Daycon, but he also experienced an overwhelming resentment. If Hannah hadn't saved Marcus's life, she would be alive. For Hannah's sake, he swallowed back his rancor. She had done what she had to do.

They worked for ten minutes without stopping, neither meeting the other's eye. "It's no use," Marcus said at last. "We can't keep this up."

"Go call 911," Tyler said. He knew Marcus was right. That Hannah was dead. But he would not stop trying.

"Tyler…" Marcus shook his head.

"Just do it!"

"I loved her, too, but she's gone."

"No!" Tyler shouted. "Don't you understand? She's my heart, my soul, my everything." He'd lost one love. He could not bear to lose another.

Marcus put a hand on Tyler's shoulder. "It's over."

"Go call 911," Tyler barked. "Now."

"Okay." Marcus held up his palms, got to his feet. "What about him?" Marcus jerked his head at Daycon who lay on the floor where Tyler had trussed him.

"To hell with him."

"I'll be right back." Marcus disappeared, leaving Tyler alone with Hannah.

He continued CPR even though he was splintering into a thousand pieces.

We never got to do normal, simple things, you and I, he mentally whispered to her. *No dinner dates, no walks in the park, no movies, no dancing. I would give up everything I own to have you back, Hannah. Everything.*

Memories of Yvette's death rose in his mind. He had loved her once, yes. And losing her had hurt, but not with this blinding, appallingly painful intensity.

Tears gushing down his face, Tyler stopped CPR and scooped Hannah into his arms. He sat rocking her, cooing a lullaby and crying.

He kissed her forehead and thought of the wonderful moments they'd shared. Making love in the chalet Jacuzzi, snuggling close in the big king-sized bed, showering together.

Gone. All gone before they'd had a chance to really explore their newfound love.

Tyler closed his eyes and prayed like he'd never prayed in his life. Cradling her to his chest, he rested his head against hers.

Please, let her recover, God. Please. Please.

He had prayed!

The awareness of what he had done hit Tyler with the force of a hurricane. Six years ago he had forsaken God, renouncing his belief in a supreme being when the one nearest and dearest to him had been taken away without rhyme or reason. Now, here he was actually uttering a prayer of desperation.

Lifting his head beseechingly toward the heavens, Tyler clutched her tighter to his chest. "Please." He said the single word aloud.

A strange tingling heat began in his fingertips and spread up his arms. Surprise rippled through him. Tyler frowned. What was this sensation? He'd felt it before. When Hannah had healed his cut hand.

The tingling intensified, overtaking his whole body until he was a humming, vibrating mass, alive with electricity.

What was happening to him?

His heart seemed to unfold like a rosebud opening to the sun. He felt filled with love and...

Peace. So very peaceful.

Why? Trepidation clutched his chest.

There's nothing to fear. The words leapt into his mind. Words spoken in Hannah's soft voice.

He opened his eyes.

Looked down at Hannah. And she was looking up at him with those wide blue eyes and smiling brightly.

Tyler stared. Could it be?

"How?" he croaked, praying he wasn't having a hallucination. Praying this was true, that Hannah was indeed alive.

"You healed me," she whispered.

He shook his head. "But you're the one with the healing power."

"And now," she said lightly, "so are you."

"I don't understand."

"You remember when I was afraid to make love to you, because I was worried I could pass my 'affliction' on to you?"

"Yes."

"And you told me you'd already been exposed to my blood through a needle stick?"

"Uh-huh."

"Well." She smiled shyly. "I did."

"Did what?" Puzzled, he frowned.

"Pass it on to you."

He shook his head.

"Don't you get it, Tyler? *You* healed *me*."

The tears he cried were now tears of joy. He'd wished and hoped and prayed. He'd wanted to keep her so desperately and now, by a miracle, he had.

"I left you," she said. "I died."

"We tried to save you," Tyler said, still disoriented and confused by what was occurring, but overjoyed to have her talking to him. "Marcus and me."

"I know. I saw you. I was floating above the ceiling watching you."

He brushed a lock of blond hair from her smooth forehead, desperate to touch her in every way he could and make sure this was real.

"It's true," she mused. "What they say about the tunnel and the light. I went there. It was the most serene and tranquil sensation. I can't even describe it adequately. But death is nothing to fear, Tyler. It's just another stage. Another evolution of our souls."

"I didn't fear death, Hannah. I feared spending the rest of my life lonely and miserable without you." His fingers trembled as he played them over her face. She was alive!

"It's okay. I'm here." She reached up to trace a finger over his cheek.

"Oh, my darling Hannah." He crushed her to him, holding her tightly, never wanting to let her go. "You've come home to me."

"Yes." Hannah sat up. They were on the ground, sitting crosslegged, gazing into each other's eyes just like they had on the night they'd first made love. He remembered that night and how their beautiful lovemaking had moved them both to tears.

"You trust me at last," he said.

She smiled that shy smile he loved so much. "How could I not? You've chased away all the shadows from my life. You've proven to me I'm worthy of being loved."

"And you've helped me let go of the past. I'm ready to move ahead into the future. With you."

"What are you saying, Tyler?" She audibly caught her breath. He held her gaze, clearly transmitting his feelings to her.

"I'm saying I want to marry you." Tyler lost himself in the stunning beauty of her sapphire eyes.

"Oh, Tyler." She exhaled the words. "Are you sure?"

"I've never been more sure of anything in my life."

"Wow," she whispered. "Wow."

"So is that a yes?" He lifted a tentative eyebrow.

"Yes, yes, yes."

Then Tyler kissed her again as the ghost of old memories and self-doubt lifted. And he knew that the adsventure stretching out before them was going to be the happiest one of their lives.

Epilogue

Time was running out.

But Dr. Hannah Fresno wasn't afraid.

Each time a contraction hit, her husband would reach over, lay his hand on her swollen belly, caress her with a swirling motion and the pain would miraculously lessen.

Hannah smiled to herself. Her mental clock ticked off the passing seconds. Soon. Very soon now, they would have a baby.

A girl, according to the sonogram. Conceived on the night they'd made love in the Jacuzzi at the ski resort chalet.

Jokingly, Tyler had suggested they call her Taos.

Hannah had quickly vetoed that idea.

The baby's first name would be Eden. Because paradise was what they had found in each other's arms. And when Hannah had told Tyler she wanted their daughter's middle name to be Yvette, his eyes had filled with tears, letting her know it was the right thing to do.

"You're the most spectacular woman in the world, do you know that?"

"Aw shucks, doc, don't go syrupy on me at a time like this."

"I love you so," he whispered and pressed his lips to her cheek. "For bringing me back to life."

"Excuse me," she said. "But if memory serves, you were the one who resurrected me."

"We saved each other," he said and squeezed her hand tightly.

She smiled at her husband and her heart filled with joy. In the nine months since that awful night Daycon had shot Marcus, so many things had happened. First, Daycon and the rogue CIA agent Rudolph Cleveland had been found guilty of treason and they were both serving extended sentences in federal prison. Marcus Halpren had created an antidote for *Virusall* and administered it to the unfortunate test subjects, all of whom had made a complete recovery. Tyler and Hannah had also taken the antidote and while it had cured them of their blood disorders, it had also taken away their healing powers.

Hannah had not mourned the loss of her supernatural abilities. Instead, she'd started taking courses toward her medical degree. There was nothing wrong with medicine practiced the old-fashioned way, using hands-on TLC. And Marcus was busily at work on *Virusall II,* attempting to replicate the original drug's healing potential but without the harmful side effects.

The most miraculous changes had taken place in Hannah's personal life. Tyler had opened his own clinic in Galveston and Hannah worked for him part-time. And their abiding love for each other expanded more every day.

The woman who'd once hated to be touched, the woman dubbed a cold unfeeling fish, the woman who'd never believed she'd find her Prince Charming had finally learned how to trust. She'd filled the missing void in her life with love.

And in a few minutes there would be another precious Fresno to embrace into the fold.

"I love you," Tyler told her once more and kissed her tenderly. "More than you will ever know."

"And I love you."

"You've finally gotten over being afraid of your feelings?"

She nodded.

"All those old demons are gone?"

"Uh-huh."

"That's good," he said fiercely. "Very good. Couldn't have you slipping out of my bed and running off in the middle of the night."

"Never again," she promised.

The expression on his dear face took her breath. "I'd die without you, Hannah. You came into my life and made me whole again. You and little Eden."

"It's time," she whispered, feeling the baby's head crowning between her legs.

Tyler called for the nurses and in a flurry of activity, they took Hannah into the delivery room.

Eden Yvette Fresno was born seven minutes later.

"Look, Mom," Tyler rested the crying, red-faced baby on her belly. Hands trembling with wonder, Hannah reached out to stroke her daughter's cheek.

Instantly, the baby stopped crying and wrapped her little fist round her mother's index finger.

Hannah looked down into Eden's face and felt the familiar hum like a high-voltage wire vibrating with raw energy.

"There's no denying it, you've got the touch." Tyler whispered.

Lying there, with her beloved husband beside her and their newborn daughter in her arms, Hannah's heart filled with a love so bright and true she knew that she would never be lonely again.

* * * * *

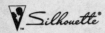

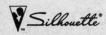

COMING NEXT MONTH

INTIMATE MOMENTS